ENJOY

Jerry Ralph

One After Another

by

Jerry Radford

authorHOUSE®

AuthorHouse™
1663 Liberty Drive, Suite 200
Bloomington, IN 47403
www.authorhouse.com
Phone: 1-800-839-8640

First published by AuthorHouse 7/18/2008

ISBN: 978-1-4389-0124-4 (sc)

*Printed in the United States of America
Bloomington, Indiana*

This book is printed on acid-free paper.

A racehorse can often fool you.
So can a person.

1

Two shots were fired. Sudden explosive sounds raging through the air interrupting the peace and quiet of a warm sunny Monday morning at the north end of Canandaigua Lake in upstate New York.

The tallest of the two bank robbers went down on the second shot, his body propelling forward as though he'd been slammed in the back of the head. He crawled, struggling mightily to get back on his feet. The other robber stopped in his tracks, grabbed his partner by the arm and tugged him up. Neither looked back, the fallen one dragging his left leg, holding onto his thigh with his left hand, desperately trying to run, his partner urging him forward.

The security guard took aim again, and fired.

He missed, or thought he missed. He wasn't sure. Just as he had pulled the trigger, the robbers disappeared around the rear corner of the Metro Bank branch office. With his gun held high above his head, both hands firmly attached, he hustled toward the corner of the building. From ten feet away, he dropped into a duck walk. When he reached the corner, he paused and tuned in the surroundings before easing his head past the edge of the brick, just enough to take a quick peek. His eyes darted beyond the bank parking lot to a grouping of pines that were part of the landscaping, and then beyond the trees to the adjoining strip mall. People were walking to and from vehicles, none looking his way. He spotted no one who resembled the robbers.

He stood, blew out a long breath, holstered his gun then swept the sweat off his forehead with the back of his right hand. His hand was shaking. In fact, his entire body had the quivers. Suddenly, the pancakes and bacon he'd downed for breakfast sought an exit that didn't require a restroom. While chucking the last of his morning meal onto the drive-in lane, he spotted a small pool of blood a few feet to his right. When he was again upright, three police cars poured into the lot, sirens blasting, tires screeching to a halt, officers hurrying out the doors.

He waved them over and pointed to the blood.

William Rollins saw it all happen. He'd seen it happen over and over again. He rewound the tape. One more time, he thought. He'd look at it one more damn time. He hit play, his focus never wavering until the tape went blank.

He slowly shook his head then stood and walked to the window of his third floor corner office. Daylight was no more than thirty minutes away. Perhaps the sun would provide the light to awaken some cells in his brain and help him recognize a clue. So far, he hadn't gained an inch since arriving at FBI headquarters two hours earlier. Below, street vendors were setting up shop at the corner of 9th and E. Streets, the acronym of the Federal Bureau of Investigation a big hit with tourists. You name it and they had it, a whole damn wardrobe if the old pocketbook came up with the loot. FBI this, FBI that.

Still with a little shake in his head, William turned from the window and paced his office. He had plenty of room to do so. A conference table occupied an area in front of a wall displaying a huge map of the United States. Edging around the table, he stopped and stood nose to nose with the map, beckoning some answers. The map couldn't explain why it was the home of seventeen pins. He shrugged, walked over to his black leather chair, sat and took a few turns with his head laid against its high back as though the chair might spin out a thought or two.

Finally he stopped with the spinning and glanced at J. Edgar who looked down upon him from a prominent spot on the far wall. William said to the black and white photo, "I'm trying, damn it."

He hadn't turned on the overhead lights. Instead, a small desk lamp provided illumination for the seventeen folders occupying space on his desk. Each folder contained details of an unsolved bank robbery. And each matched a pin stuck in the map.

William was the man in charge, the guy responsible for the bank robbery division of the FBI. He'd held the position for seven years and, up until this latest string of robberies, had maintained an outstanding record of closing cases. The job was big. He wasn't. At five eight and one-seventy-five, his stature wasn't imposing but everyone around him knew he could be one tough-ass-son-of-a-bitch, the kind of guy who took on all comers with a vengeance. He was a regular in the FBI weight room. Bunch of guys and gals with short haircuts—William's was dark brown—working the abs, strengthening the biceps, triceps, and quads. Nobody messed with William. And nobody called him Bill or Will. He liked his given name. In his college football days at Randolph-Macon in Ashland, Virginia, he had gained Little All-American status as a defensive back with a rep for sending offensive backs and receivers to la-la land. He liked competition and that's the approach he took to solving bank robberies but right now the opposition was up by seventeen and it flat out pissed him off.

He thumbed through the folder of the first robbery in Phoenix, Arizona, glanced at the map and spotted the green-headed pin dangling a white tag naming the bank, street address and funds looted. His eyes took in the other sixteen pins, each a different color. If there was an indication of a connection between any of the robberies, the pin colors would have matched. There were no matches. Damn map resembled one of those giant boxes of crayons, no two colors alike.

So far, he and his task force had uncovered zilch. It ate at him, took little bites at his insides making an ulcer trivial by comparison. He'd toss and turn at night, finally give in and head to the office at some ungodly hour such as four a.m., today, a Sunday. It was still pre-dawn. If he could come up with just one little clue, he'd make himself go home and head to Mama Johnson's Café and he and his wife would dive into the brunch of all brunches: Grits and hash browns, two-inch high buttermilk biscuits, coffee with chicory . . . all fresh, none of that pre-packaged mess. It didn't bother him that he and Kaylan would be the only white folks who showed up nor did it bother Mama Johnson. She was always happy to see them, a big hug required. William had been instrumental in her son receiving an academic scholarship to Randolph-Macon, his eyes set on a career with the FBI.

He reached into a drawer and pulled out a yellow legal pad then grabbed one of the twenty or so pens housed in an oversized coffee mug. This was part of his everyday ritual. Always ignoring whatever he'd written the day before, he'd start from scratch and search for a miracle. Seventeen unsolved robberies existed, each committed by two males, one slightly over six feet tall, the other in the five-seven to five-nine range. With each robbery, the taller of the two passed a note to a teller that stated that he or she had four minutes to stuff bills into a briefcase. Meanwhile the smaller guy stood at the entrance with gun in hand, instructing everyone else to hit the floor, face first. These facts were the same in each robbery but, and this was a huge but, each bank was held up by a different twosome. The security cameras, inside and outside, verified this fact. William had watched each robbery take place on tape repeatedly. The twosome would waltz out the bank doors and disappear in seconds. With the Canandaigua robbery, the security guard had managed to quickly follow the robbers and had fired and hit the taller of the two.

That was the reason William had again watched the tape from that robbery over and over again. It puzzled him. Agents had interviewed personnel at every medical facility within one hundred miles and come up with another big zero. Samples of the blood found on the pavement had been bagged as DNA evidence. Of course, William knew that a defense lawyer would have a field day with that one. But, it was something. Exterior cameras had captured the shooting. Clearly, the taller of the two went down when the shots were fired. But, he managed to get up and the twosome escaped into the shopping center parking lot and ducked behind a car. From that point forward they were no longer picked up by the cameras.

William leaned back and cupped his hands behind his head, sucked in a deep breath, eased it out then leaned forward and added more facts to the pad. The fingerprint situation baffled him to no end. In fact, it amazed him. Doors had been touched. Counters had been touched. In several instances, a desk was touched. Gobs of prints but no match was found in the FBI data base. Something was amiss. Didn't make sense.

He listed the locations in order. He knew by memory each location, the date and day of the robbery, and the time each took place.

Phoenix, Arizona
Spokane, Washington
Columbus, Ohio
Boise, Idaho
Shreveport, Louisiana
Harrisburg, Pennsylvania

Denver, Colorado
San Diego, California
Tampa, Florida
Chicago, Illinois
Canandaigua, New York
St. Louis, Missouri
Santa Fe, New Mexico
Newark, New Jersey
Omaha, Nebraska
Boston, Massachusetts
Miami, Florida

Each robbery had taken place on either a Monday or Tuesday, just after the lobbies had opened. He could see no rhyme or reason to when they took place or where they took place. In his mind, he drew a line from location to location, creating one of those connect-the-dots puzzles like a Shoney's placemat for kids. A pattern did not exist. He was looking at thirty-four males, seventeen in the six foot range and seventeen a little shorter. Twelve of the taller men were white. One was Asian. And four were Hispanic. Eight of the white males had dark brown hair, three were blonde, and one was red. One of the Hispanics had blonde hair and the others looked to be dark brown or black including the Asian. Of the shorter robbers, three were Asian, five were Hispanic and nine were white. The Asians and Hispanics all had dark hair but of the whites, three were blonde, two were redheads, two were medium brown, one was black and one was bald. He had photos enlarged from the videos along with descriptions from bank personnel. He had dollar amounts from each robbery. All bills were unmarked but he figured the robbers didn't know that. He had a few hints on getaway cars as well as accents and facial hair, but the bottom line was that nothing totaled up.

Headache City was what it was. What he needed was a break that had nothing to do with the robberies.

Ninety minutes later he was stuffing grits into his mouth, butter oozing down his chin. Kaylan was sitting across from him trying to understand the mumbles rambling from his mouth between forkfuls. She knew he was rolling around the robberies, talking to himself, acting like deep dark secrets were his and his alone. She had watched him do this for years. Sometimes she understood all that he said but most of the time she'd just pick up a tidbit or a couple of crumbs. She was a five-five redhead who would garner maybe a seven or eight from the guys but had blue eyes that were off the chart. They sparkled like gulfstream waters. And behind those eyes was one smart lady who was extremely observant and intuitive. She was a good listener and somewhere along the way she was prone to make a suggestion or two that was usually right on target. She'd nod at his mumbling as though she was right there with him, cuffs in hand. Very few bank robbers got by him but she knew that he was struggling with these seventeen robberies more than any he'd ever faced.

2

Mario Bozzela followed her for the third consecutive day.

About a month ago he noticed her standing alongside the rail at mid-stretch, arms resting on the fence with a racing program firmly gripped in her right hand and a pen in her left, obviously making notes on today's entries. Her head bounced around constantly, up and down, side-to-side, like a bobble-head doll. It took a few minutes of observation for him to discover tiny earphones hiding behind her hair. The portable CD player attached to her jeans should have given him a hint but he was too busy ogling a face that reminded him of Meg Ryan. Her short thick blonde hair sealed the resemblance. His heart danced the boogie-woogie before finding a new rhythm.

During the week she showed up around three. On weekends she was trackside about an hour before the first race. She was always alone and never talked to, or acknowledged, anyone. Before each race she visited the paddock, rain or shine. He watched her observe the horses, admiring her focus.

Problem was she had become a distraction.

Never, ever get distracted.

The first day he saw her, he lost money.

Yesterday, he lost money. Not a good sign.

Mario was an investor in horses. He bet, but he didn't gamble. His Uncle Geno taught him well, beginning at age eight. Tutored him on the principles of negative analysis, *what didn't happen*. The lessons applied to training as well as racing strategy and jockey decisions. At thirty-five, Mario had given up seventy-thou a year as a bean counter to become a track regular. Along the way, his girlfriend of ten years decided to seek a boyfriend with a little more stability. She could no longer handle the ups and downs of mutuel tickets. What she didn't realize was that Mario had a lot more ups than downs. Most excluded the IRS.

So here he was, distracted again, standing four people behind her in line to place a bet at the fifty-dollar window. He leaned and stretched his neck, trying to decipher what horse she was playing. She didn't bet every race, a sure sign she wasn't at the track for entertainment.

As she walked away she shot him a knowing glance. He offered up his best smile. It didn't take. She turned and hurried to the elevator. He followed at a distance. She made another bet, then hustled from the grandstand to the clubhouse side and made two more bets, at different windows. He had seen this happen daily and it nagged at his brain. She headed toward the grandstand again to the beat of her music as he hid behind a pole and stooped to tie his penny loafers. He didn't notice but she had caught sight of his blunder, and chuckled. He hustled to the fifty-dollar window and asked the seller which horse she had bet. The guy shot him a quizzical look before saying she had bet several tickets on the seven to show. He glanced at the board, 6-5. Probably pay the minimum, $2.10. Okay, he figured she had bet two hundred and would get a five percent return of ten dollars, if the horse came in first, second or third. He didn't bet. Not at those odds.

The seven easily won by three lengths and paid $2.10 to show just as he had predicted.

This is when the situation became more interesting. She cashed her tickets at four different windows. Not the same windows where she had placed her bets.

Same thing happened two more times that day and it had happened every day. Drove his ass crazy.

He couldn't decide if his interest in her was a result of her looks or her eccentric form of placing and cashing bets.

He slammed his hand against his temple and called himself a few descriptive names not listed in Webster's. How could he be so stupid as to allow a female to distract him from his job?

He decided to follow her home.

Luckily she had parked in another state. Happens when you come late. He never missed the Star Spangled Banner, so he always latched onto a spot just a few feet from the clubhouse entrance to Laurel Park.

He kept her in his sights as she made her way to her car which turned out to be a one of those new Volkswagen Bugs in royal blue.

At the second light he lost her when she whipped a sharp left from the right hand lane, turning onto Route 197 from 198. He was boxed-in by a black Cadillac. Guy driving was chewing on something long and red. Mario rolled down his window and blew his horn at Gimpy McFadden, a track regular he'd met when he was a kid. Gimpy acknowledged, extracted the long red thing from his mouth and used it as a pointer while shouting at Mario. "Hey, did you hit the six-horse in the seventh race?"

Mario answered, "No, did you?"

"Fucking aye, my man. 10-1 shot." He nodded, stuck the long red thing back in his mouth.

"Cherry or strawberry?" Mario hollered.

"Cherry."

Mario couldn't remember when he had seen Gimpy without a Twizzler.

The light changed. They raced to the next light.

Gimpy took a left and Mario a right onto Route 1 north.

So far, she had broken his concentration, cost him money and now had him driving in the opposite direction of his residence. But he was headed toward Baltimore, and that was good because Uncle Geno lived in Baltimore.

3

Geno Bozzela was a second father to Mario.

Mario's dad had died at the young age of twenty-nine, the victim of a drive-by shooting while standing in line at the Baltimore Arena to buy tickets for a basketball game. Mario had hold of his dad's hand when it happened. If he hadn't been so short, he would probably be dead, too. The two six foot guys standing in front of them were. A lady, two steps behind, was also hit but she made it, minus her left ear. Mario was seven at the time, observant, and smart. He spotted the license number and told his Uncle Geno.

Last year the shooter was killed, by the State of Maryland.

The driver became a favorite sex toy of inmates at the state penitentiary. Would be for life.

Certain images remain imbedded in one's mind. Just as Mario approached the beltway on his way to downtown Baltimore, the shooting flashed in front of his eyes like an old black and white newsreel. He could feel his father's hand leave his. He fingered the corner of his eye and wiped away a trickle of moisture.

His thoughts turned to his mom who routinely placed flowers on her husband's grave every Saturday morning, fifty-two weeks a year. Postal workers had nothing on her. Through rain, sleet, snow, floods, hurricanes, it didn't matter. She showed up at the cemetery. She still lived in the old row house around the corner from Memorial Stadium. Mario visited with her every Monday evening after spending the earlier part of the day with Geno. He always brought her chocolates. It used to be Whitman's Sampler, now it was Godiva's. Mom's taste buds had risen to a new level as had Mario's chocolate budget.

Monday was Mario's day of rest. He figured God would understand the switch from Sunday since the Almighty had created thoroughbreds in the first place. The track was open on Sundays, dark on Mondays. Made sense to Mario but just in case, he attended mass every Monday morning before making his visits.

Traffic was a monster, bumper to bumper heading into the Inner Harbor area. His eyes took a gander at the new home of the Baltimore Ravens. It was a terrific facility but he was nostalgic about Memorial Stadium for football. He liked it better. Camden Yards was another story, though. He loved going to games at Camden. Unlike Memorial, Camden was a true baseball park, majestic and noble. Made him want to run onto the field, scoop up some grounders or head for the outfield and wallow in the thickest, greenest grass ever planted. He was there the night Cal broke the record, still had half the ticket tucked away in a drawer, a keepsake he would give to a son someday, if he could ever find someone who would marry him, and the track.

As he weaved his way through traffic on Pratt Street, he wondered how Geno was going to react to his Friday evening visit.

Geno was famous in Baltimore. His restaurant, Geno's, served up the best marinara this side of Venice; at least, that's what Geno had told everyone for fifty years. It must have been true because hundreds stood in line every Friday and Saturday night to savor the sauce.

Geno missed greeting his customers. Two years ago, he suffered a stroke and almost died. His son, Geno, Junior, was now in charge and doing a commendable job, according to his dad.

There were enough cars parked in the lot to make Detroit happy, but Mario had no problem finding a spot. He had one with his name on it in big black letters. Geno made the arrangements years ago with one of his buddies who owned the lot that was a block's walk from the restaurant. If Mario wasn't there, the spot stood empty.

Geno's buddy was one of four guys who, with Geno, had a standing reservation in the dining room at Pimlico every Sunday during the meet. It was the closest table to the finish line, a great spot. The other guys owned restaurants with Italian names. They never allowed anyone other than Mario to sit in Geno's spot since the stroke. Mario, on occasion, would join them and learn the inside scoop on antipasto, cannoli, and sauce.

He parked and strolled up High Street. He passed an Italian restaurant then two row houses then another Italian restaurant then one row house then another Italian restaurant. On the front stoop of every row house, guys were sipping beer, listening to the O's broadcast on portable radios, originating from the home of the Green Monster at Fenway in Boston. Most were sporting the neighborhood uniform of baggy pants and a white sleeveless undershirt, Fruit of the Loom, no less. They had tan lines unfamiliar to golfers. Every radio was tuned to the game. Any car that came down the street bellowing rap music was subject to immediate death of its occupants. Could happen, according to Geno. It was a neighborhood rule.

Mario knew most of these guys. Everyone spoke and offered up a beer. He didn't know if it was actually legal to drink on the front stoop but it was a ritual. Mario loved the ethnicity. Suburbanites didn't know what they were missing. He'd live here himself except it was too far from Laurel Park.

He ducked into a small alleyway leading to stairs. Geno lived above the restaurant and had since it opened. His aunt greeted him at the door with a hug that would squeeze the air from a blimp. "Well, what are you doing here on a Friday night?"

"Just stopped by to say hello."

She leaned back and wiggled her finger from side to side, a smile attached. "Losing, huh?"

"Something like that."

Maria was her name. She was the salt of the earth. Their son, Geno Junior, was married to a Maria. Junior's son, who had just turned eight, was named Geno the Third. Odds were that he would marry a girl named Maria. Could happen. Mario always smiled when he was in a room with the whole crew. When he mentioned a name, more than one head turned.

She glanced over her shoulder and hollered, "Hey, Geno, Mario's here."

"Oh, yeah . . . must be losing." Mario shook his head, kissed Maria on the cheek and headed down the hall to the back room, Geno's Parlor, as he called it.

Geno waved him to the bed, patted an area to sit before sticking out his left hand for a shake. Mario grabbed his hand, squeezed it tightly then gave his uncle a love tap on the noggin. "How you doing, old man?"

"Probably better than you. I just hit the pick-three at Hollywood."

Mario acknowledged with a head bob. "So, you like my little gift?"

"It's a gift from God, but it makes me break all my rules."

After all the specialists had voiced their opinions, after all the tests had been run and all the rehab was completed, the bottom line was Geno was going to be confined to a bed for the rest of his life, paralyzed on his right side. The news had broken Mario's heart when he first heard, but Geno had become the strong one. He told everyone he planned on being around until they came up with something to get him walking again. Meanwhile, he would find a way to play the ponies, maybe write a cookbook, give away some of his secrets.

Mario found a way for Geno to play the ponies. A guy showed up one day carrying a dish in a box. Not something from the restaurant but a satellite dish that would allow Geno to watch programming from around the globe. A new channel had been established called TVG. Mario assumed the G stood for gambling but he wasn't sure. Somehow the TVG people had figured a way around wagering laws that would allow betting the ponies at tracks throughout the world with the push of a button. That Geno could do. He had been right-handed all his life but quickly adjusted to operating the remote with his left. He could speak and he could comprehend. In other words, he was good to go. Mario paid for the service. The day it was installed, he and Geno watched races for six hours from Florida to New York to California, even one from France. That's when Geno named the room Geno's Parlor, as in betting parlor.

Mario thought he should change the name to Geno's Photo Gallery and Betting Parlor. It fit more with the décor. The walls were covered with black-and-white photographs of baseball players, football players, jockeys, basketball players, coaches, movie stars, presidents, vice-presidents and heads of state. Most were autographed by the sauce lovers. Previously, the photos graced the walls downstairs but Maria insisted Geno's favorites be moved to the Parlor.

Mario took a quick glance around as he always did. Babe Ruth had Geno in a headlock. Brooks Robinson was standing beside Geno at some golf outing, attacking an ear of corn from left to right, butter spots splattered down the front of his pants. Tom Clancy had scribbled something on his headshot about the sum of all sauces. Johnny Unitas was handing off to Geno, Geno heading for a TD. Chris McCarron and Geno jointly held a trophy above their heads for a race named *The Sauce*. Larry Bird handed Geno an autographed ball from the world champion Celtics. Ted Williams demonstrated his swing. And then there was Secretariat, standing in the winning circle after winning the Preakness Stakes. An adjoining photo showed Penny Tweedy, Lucien Lauren and Ron Turcotte enjoying the sauce at a table with Geno the week of the historic race… reviewing strategy, no doubt.

He nudged Geno as he waved his hand around the room. "So, which is your favorite?"

Geno pointed to a photo sitting on the night table beside the bed. "This one. Maria just found it yesterday under the counter downstairs."

Mario's eyes followed the finger as it pointed to an old photo of his dad, Geno and him at Bowie Race Course. It was the first day they had taken him to the track. Mario was holding up cash, lots of cash. He smiled at the memory.

"Yeah, I like that one, too."

"Okay, kid. Let's get down to it. What's wrong at the track?"

"I don't know. I'm just not clicking."

"Are you following Geno's rules?"

"Uh, yes."

"Did I detect a little hesitation in your voice?"

"I know the rules by heart, but . . ."

"No buts, never a *but*." Mario knew what was coming, and he needed to hear it.

"Are you betting birthdays?"

"Never."

"Are you betting on horses' names?"

"Never."

"Are you betting favorite colors?"

"Never."

"Are you listening to touts at the track?"

"No."

"You're not betting astrology signs are you?"

"Of course not."

"Are you betting your license plate numbers?"

"No, and when did you come up with that one?"

"Just thought I'd throw it in to see if you're paying attention." Geno glared at Mario, "Are you betting every race?"

"No."

"Are you betting horses you haven't seen work?"

"Nope."

"Are you using negative analysis the way I taught you?"

"Always." It had taken some serious thought to grasp this concept but Geno had constantly stressed to him that it was the most important element in betting. Negative analysis was the study of what trainers didn't do, what jockeys didn't do, what owners didn't do, what the track super didn't do, what the starter didn't do. You don't have to be crooked or break the rules to fix a race. Many years ago he told Mario that he had to be at the track every morning and watch the workouts, take meticulous notes and observe with a cunning eye. Opportunities would present themselves as a result.

Geno recognized the puppy dog look. "What's her name?"

"What do you mean?"

"You know exactly what I mean. What's her name?" Geno winked. "You can't fool me, you know better."

"Okay, okay. I don't know her name."

"Come again. You don't know her name?"

"Nope."

Mario shrugged, then confessed to being distracted, even told him that was how he had landed in Baltimore tonight. Geno kept nodding and saying "Uh, huh" as he listened.

"And you haven't introduced yourself?"

"She keeps to herself."

"Damn, Mario. It's a racetrack. Everybody talks to everybody at a racetrack. It's the one place on this earth where everyone is after the same result. Surely you can start up a conversation with her."

"Okay, I will."

"But, I don't advise it."

"You don't advise it? You just suggested it."

"Nope. Didn't suggest it. Simply brought it up. If you want to win at the track you can't have any distractions. You know that. I know that. *And especially from a female.*"

"Yeah, I know. I know."

"Bottom line is you have two heads on your body and you are following the wrong one."

Mario laughed. "I hear you."

"You want some sauce?"

Mario hadn't thought about food but now that Geno had mentioned it, he realized the rumblings in his stomach were sending a message. "Yeah, I'd love some sauce."

"Hey, Maria," yelled Geno. "Call downstairs, get Geno to send up some linguini with clams." He looked at Mario. "You want red or white?"

"Red."

To Maria, he yelled again, "Two orders, red. Three if you want some. And get extra bread."

Mario took a deep breath before speaking. "Eternal Light is in tomorrow."

"That's the horse you told me about last week, trained by DuBose, right?"

"Yeah, he's prepping him now. Didn't get him ready for his last two, got beat twenty-one lengths last out."

"He's been pulling this crap for years. Backs off a horse, takes away his bottom, takes away his speed then decides it's time to cash a big check. It's his pattern, never deviates. Only those around the barn are in the know."

"And us."

Geno grinned, nodded, "Yeah, and us."

"Fifth race tomorrow. He dropped him in for a tag, twenty-five grand. Probably go off forty, fifty to one."

"You sure he's ready?"

"He worked him three days ago in the dark. I was there. So was the owner and that's a sure sign they're getting ready to win. Went four furlongs in forty-six and change. Clocker hadn't shown up yet."

"What's his last workout look like in the form?"

"Three furlongs in thirty-nine and two."

"Competition?"

"Two decent runners, enough to keep the odds up."

"Easy winner?"

"Sure thing."

"There are no sure things at the track . . . unless you use old Geno's negative analysis as a handicapping tool."

"You going to bet from here or do you want me to put something down for you at the track?"

"I'll bet from here but you need to do something for me. And it's important."

"Anything. You know that."

"It's time for Little Geno to get indoctrinated. I'll give him a fifty. That's the only race he can bet on."

"He'll beg me to let him bet every race."

"I know, but he can't. He needs to win and win big on his first day at the track." He pointed to the photo on the night table again. "Just like when your dad and I took you."

"How about Junior, is he going?"

Geno shook his head. "He needs to tend to business on a Saturday."

Mario thought about that for a moment, wished Junior could go. It would mean something to Little Geno later in life.

"What if the horse loses?"

"You have doubts?"

"Nope."

"Then make Little Geno a horse lover."

The food arrived. Maria had ordered for three. She joined them for a few minutes of silence. No one can talk with a mouth full of all that goodness.

After sopping up the last bit of sauce with the Italian bread, Geno used his good hand to grab Mario by the arm. "You want some tiramisu?"

"I'd love some but I'm going to have to loosen my belt to get out of here now."

"How about some biscotti to take home?" He didn't wait for Mario to answer. "Maria, call downstairs and tell Geno to box up a couple dozen for Mario.

"A couple of dozen?"

Maria made the call using the bedside phone.

"Pass them out at the track tomorrow. Maybe offer a couple to your new girlfriend."

"She's not my girlfriend."

Maria hadn't heard. "You have a girlfriend now? Bring her by, I want to meet her, warn her about the racetrack," she said with a wink.

"No, I don't have a girlfriend. It's just someone I've been watching at the track."

Geno said to Maria, "He follows her around all day. That's why he can't win any money. That's why he showed up tonight."

Maria cut her eyes at Mario. "You follow her around?"

"Not really. Well, maybe sort of."

"What's her name?"

"I don't know."

Maria looked at Geno, "What's up with his, I don't know?"

Geno grinned. "I think he's just horny."

"Geno!"

Mario didn't leave until ten.

On the drive home he started to think about Enternal Light, Little Geno, and what's-her-name.

Little Geno scooted behind the front seat and buckled himself into the rear before saying, "Let's boogie."

"Okay, let's boogie," Mario said. He glanced over his shoulder just to make sure the little guy had properly buckled his belt. He had.

"Hey, Mario, you going to give me some betting money, too? Papa Geno gave me a fifty." It was the first time Geno had called Mario by his first name. He smiled, liked it. *Buddies for the day.*

"No can do, Geno. Your grandfather gave me specific instructions to place one bet for you using the fifty."

"Yeah, my dad told me. But if you give me some more money, I won't tell."

Mario cut his eyes to the rearview mirror, saw a big grin shoot across Geno's face. The little guy was playing him. Using some charm.

"We'll see."

"And he told me about the chick. Does she have big *gaboomas?*"

"Gaboomas? Where did you pick that up?"

26

"Gee whiz, Mario. I thought you knew some stuff. Gaboomas. You know . . . boobies."

The mirror reflected Geno with his hands protruding from his chest, a big grin on his face. Mario laughed at the lesson in female anatomy. "Yeah, I know boobies." He shook his head. Must have missed out when he was eight.

"How much am I going to win today?"

"A lot, if the horse wins."

"How much is a lot?"

"Depends on the odds."

"Enough to buy a car?"

"A car? You got seven or eight years to go before you can drive a car much less buy one."

"I was going to buy it for you."

Mario glanced over his shoulder toward Geno. "Why would you want to buy me a car?"

"Cause you need a new one. This one's old."

Mario started to explain inheriting a thirty-year old Pinto with only 2700 miles on it from his dad, but he decided to save that story for another day. "I don't think you'll come close to winning enough to buy me a car but I appreciate the thought."

"How about if I bet some exactas and the triple and the superfecta?"

"Nope. The fifty is for a win ticket only. Besides, where did you learn all this stuff?"

"Papa Geno. I watch the races with him. I like it. We went over the *Form* early this morning. I like Eternal Light over the six, three and seven."

"Are you sure you're just eight?"

"Yep."

"Well no matter what you saw in the *Form*, no other bets."

"I brought twenty of my own."

At this point, Mario decided he'd never call him Little Geno again. Kid was something else, eight going on thirty.

As he paid the parking attendant two dollars he scanned the lot to the right and spotted what's-her-name's Volkswagen. A young guy about the size of most jockeys directed him to a spot beside her car. He parked and they hustled to the clubhouse gate.

Mario purchased a program.

"Where's mine?" Geno asked.

"We'll share."

Geno shot him an inquisitive look. "How am I going to learn if I don't have my own program?"

Mario plopped three more dollars in the attendant's hand, grabbed another program off the stack and handed it to Geno. "You know how to read it?"

"I can read the *Form*."

"Good enough."

Despite paying the freight for the clubhouse, Mario preferred to watch the races from the grandstand apron, close to the fence where he could get a solid look at the stretch run.

Four guys waved coffee cups as he and Geno approached the bench that the quartet had captured at the sixteenth pole. Geno missed the waves. His face was buried in past performances and he was talking to himself as he walked.

"Who's the little handicapper?" Gimpy asked.

"Name is Geno. It's his first trip to the track although he's been spending a lot of time watching TVG with his grandfather."

"Oh, yeah. Got any tips for me kid?"

"Two horse in the first. Who do you guys like?"

Gimpy answered, "We were just talking about the two. How old are you?"

"Eight."

Gimpy reached into his front left pocket and pulled out three flavors of Twizzlers. "So what flavor do you like?" He was chewing on strawberry as he spoke.

"Green apple." Gimpy handed him two and Geno thanked him.

"How 'bout you Mario?"

"I'll pass."

Mario introduced Geno to Tote Board Tommy, a five-foot-nothing forty-year-old who never bought a program or a *Form*. Watched the odds. When the odds dropped drastically on a horse near post time, he bet on that horse to win.

Then Geno shook hands with Longshot Louie, a heavy set guy over six feet who played nothing but longshots in exactas and triples. Sometimes he'd go a week without winning but when he won, he won big. He always celebrated by buying the group breakfast the next morning at the Waffle House.

Geno got a high-five from Railbird Ronnie, who had a keen eye. He watched the morning workouts every day and carefully picked his spots. Didn't play by Geno's rules but he sure did understand the concept. He and Mario often bet the same horse.

Geno had already met Gimpy, sort of. He wondered about the guy's name and without hesitation asked, "Why do they call you Gimpy?"

"That's my name?"

"Your momma named you Gimpy?"

"Yep, after my grandfather and my father. I'm Gimpy the Third."

Geno smiled. He knew how that worked.

As the flag was raised in the infield, the Star Spangled Banner boomed from the speakers. Geno stuck his right hand to his eyebrow and stood at attention. Mario stood at attention but his eyes roved, spotting what's-her-name occupying her usual spot.

One hour before post time. Like clockwork.

Mario couldn't take his eyes off her. Luckily he didn't have a distraction problem today. One bet, Eternal Light in the fifth, a no-brainer.

Geno tugged on his pants. "Is that her?" He was pointing at what's-her-name.

Mario rolled his eyes, played dumb. "What?" Geno threw him a stare. "Yeah, that's her."

Geno nodded then returned to his program.

"You want something to eat before the races start?" Mario asked.

With his head buried in past performances Geno said, "Pizza, with sausage . . . and a Pepsi."

"You stay right here with the guys and I'll go get it. Be back in a few."

"Can I make a bet on the two?"

"No bets until the fifth. You know the rules."

Geno asked Gimpy some questions about reading the board. The two was 8-1. Then he handed over his twenty and asked him to get two dollars to win on the two. Gimpy took the money and headed for the windows, not knowing that Geno wasn't supposed to bet.

Mario returned with the pizza and drink but Geno was not with the guys. His eyes quickly swept the area. With a touch of panic in his voice, he said, "Where's Geno?"

Three fingers pointed in the same direction, at what's-her-name.

"Oh, shit," Mario said, under his breath. He could see the two of them talking.

Longshot spoke, "The kid asked us if you liked the girl. We told him we didn't know anything about you and the girl other than you saying she reminded you of Meg Ryan and you thought Meg Ryan was hot."

"You said that to him?"

Longshot smiled.

Toteboard and Railbird nodded.

5

What's-her-name felt a gentle tug on her jeans. She looked down at a little boy sporting a grin from ear to ear. Geno said, "You sure do look beautiful today."

She tried to hold in a smile, but it escaped. "And you are?" She pulled her left earphone from her ear, just enough to hear his response.

He stuck out his hand. "Geno."

"Well, Geno, who taught you to greet a girl in such a charming manner?"

"My grandfather."

"And where is he?" She glanced around expecting to see an older gentleman searching for his grandson.

"Baltimore."

"Must be a ladies' man?"

"Yep. He's married to my grandmother."

After another smile, she said, "So, you like the horses?"

"This is my first time. Mario brought me."

"Mario? Is that your dad?"

"Cousin." He turned and pointed. "He's over there, the one with the green shirt."

She glanced, jerked her head back and stared straight ahead at the tote board in the infield. She recognized Geno's cousin as the guy who had been following her, possibly stalking her.

Geno tugged at her jeans again. "I think he loves you."

"Why would you say that?"

"He loves Meg Ryan and he thinks you look like Meg Ryan."

She shot another glance at Mario. Six two or so, dark wavy hair like the kid's, trim, maybe thirty-five, maybe younger. Nice looking, without a doubt. He was staring at her. Or maybe he was staring at the kid.

"So, Geno, do you think I look like Meg Ryan?"

"She used to live in Baltimore? She flew across the country to meet Tom Hanks. He had a little boy."

"But, do you think I look like her?"

Geno hesitated, picked a pebble off the ground, tossed it onto the track. "You have bigger gaboomas."

"Bigger what?"

"Gaboomas." Geno demonstrated with his hands.

She bit her bottom lip, closed her eyes, wanting to tell him that more than a mouthful was a waste. "How old are you?"

"I'm eight. Why does everyone always ask me that?"

Her peripheral vision caught sight of Mario who was quickly making his way in their direction.

"Is the kid bothering you?" he asked, from a distance of ten feet.

33

With the touch of a finger, she turned off the CD player. "Not any more than you following me around for the past few weeks." She allowed a moment for the red in his face to develop to its fullest. "Did you ever get those loafers tied?"

He thought he had been cool while following her, but obviously she had been fully aware.

"Took a while," he said, while holding back a grin.

"I bet."

Geno interrupted. "Hey Mario, the horses are coming." He stuck his feet and hands into the chain fence and climbed to the top for a clear view, wanting to get a good look at the two in the post parade. An outrider on a lead pony accompanied each of the nine horses for the six-furlong sprint. Geno watched with inquisitive eyes, and listened with great interest to the banter between outriders and jockeys.

Mario and what's-her-name joined him at the fence.

The few seconds gave Mario a chance to gather his thoughts, maybe redeem himself.

From the top of the fence Geno turned his head to what's-her-name. "I bet on the two to win. Who you got?"

Mario shook his head, wondering how in the hell had Geno placed a bet. He glanced at the board. The two's odds had risen to 10-1.

"I didn't bet this race. I'm very selective."

And disciplined and extremely conservative, thought Mario. He still wondered about her habit of placing bets at different windows for the same race.

"Me, too, I'm betting fifty to win on Eternal Light in the fifth."

She glanced at Mario. He didn't say a word. She flipped pages in her program to the fifth, her eyes sweeping the past performances of Eternal Light. She quickly figured the horse for a sixty-to-one shot, or higher.

"You like the name Eternal Light?"

"I bet horses, not names. Right, Mario?"

"Right."

She nudged Mario with her elbow. "He know something the rest of us don't know?"

Mario thought for a moment but couldn't decide if he should tell her or not.

She nodded at the lack of an answer. "So, he or maybe it's you, do know something that's not showing up on paper."

"Bet him," said Mario. "But don't do it until just before post time."

"Maybe I'll put down a couple of dollars just to placate you guys."

"Put down a couple of hundred, or more." He stared into her eyes. "But not to show."

The fact that he knew how she had been betting sent a chill through her body. She didn't need that kind of attention and didn't want it.

The call to post diverted their attention to the starting gate across the far side of the infield.

At the sound of the bell, the gates opened and the two came out fourth then settled in behind the nine, three, and five around the far turn. When the frontrunners hit the top of the stretch the two made his move and at the eighth pole was now one length behind the nine, but closing rapidly.

That's when Geno went into action. His feet were now firmly entrenched in the fence for balance. His arms were in sync, pounding space as he screamed, "Come on with the two, come on with the two. You got him. You got him!" As the two crossed the finish line on top, he jumped off the fence, displayed a huge grin, pulled a two-dollar win ticket from his pocket and proudly exclaimed, "YES!" He turned and ran toward Gimpy, waving his ticket high in the air for all to see.

Now, Mario knew how Geno had placed the bet. He shot a look at the board. Two paid $20.80. He glanced back. Gimby was patting Geno on the back as they headed to collect.

"Cute kid," said what's-her-name.

"Yeah, a real handful."

"The horse in the fifth. What's the scoop?"

"No scoop. I do my homework. Pick my spots. That's all."

Her eyes bored into his. "Why have you been following me?" She didn't blink as she awaited an answer.

His brain was stuck in neutral, couldn't get in gear.

"It's a pretty simple question," she added, determined to get a response.

"You want to go out for dinner some time?"

"Unbelievable. You can't explain why you're following me, but you can ask for a date. I don't think so. You don't want to get involved with me."

"Okay, I'll answer your question."

The planet took a breather and quit spinning on its axis. "I'm waiting."

"You remind me of Meg Ryan."

She smiled. "Yeah, I know."

"Geno?"

"Yeah."

"It's not a fixation or anything. I just happen to think she's . . ."

"Hot."

He dropped his head, shook it then looked back at her. "Yeah, what can I say?"

She shrugged. "You seem to be a nice guy but I'm just not interested in a relationship at this time. Sorry."

"Well if not a date and not a relationship, you could at least tell me your name."

She kicked a couple of losing tickets while her brain calculated the situation. Then she said, "Yeah, you're right. I'm April Ryan, Meg's sister."

"Well, damn, no wonder you look like her." The excitement in his voice was more than she expected.

"I'm kidding. My name is Cassie Crawford."

It was now six minutes to post time for the second race. Geno was chatting with the guys. It seemed they had accepted him in as a regular, after just one race. Mario suspected they had come up with a nickname.

She touched him on the arm. "Look, I need to hurry and make a bet."

"You going to four different windows?"

"Yes, and it's none of your business why. It's my way. I have my reasons."

"Okay, maybe I'll catch you later."

She took a couple steps toward the windows. Then she stopped, turned and said, "I'm very focused and I never listen to other people at the track but you got my attention with the horse in the fifth. I haven't *followed* you but I have noticed you don't bet often. That tells me something."

Before she could say anything else, he said, "Just bet him."

"Maybe I will."

"If he comes in, will you go out to dinner with me?" One more try.

"We'll see."

He nodded then headed toward the guys. The door wasn't open, but it *was* cracked.

"Hey Mario, I won over twenty dollars," Geno said, with excitement.

Mario cut his eyes at Gimpy. "I know."

Geno said to Mario, "She listens to Sinatra."

"How in the hell would you know that?"

"She has a CD player, I heard it."

"And, how would you know about Sinatra?"

"Aw, come on Mario, my dad runs an Italian restaurant."

Gimpy took a grape Twizzler out of his mouth long enough to ask Mario a question, "Did you get a name?"

"Yeah."

"Get a date?"

"Nope." He picked up Geno, held him over his head and played helicopter. "But I'm working on it."

Propped up on Mario's shoulders, Geno could now see the horses in the paddock.

Tugging at Mario's hair, he said, "He looks good."

"How about the rest of the field?"

"The six, three and seven look good, too. They're my other picks."

"One bet. You get one bet."

"I know. Fifty to win on Eternal Light, but I'm up twenty dollars and eighty cents."

Mario's curiosity got the best of him. "Okay, the six is second favorite at 4-1, the three is 8-1 but the seven . . . he's 50-1. Why do you like the seven?"

"Negative analysis. Take a look at his last two."

When he reached to pull his program from his back pocket, Geno's heels dug into his ribs. "Hey, watch the feet," Mario exclaimed.

Geno laughed while digging a little harder, his heels hard at work.

Mario said, "Got beat fourteen lengths. Got beat twenty-three lengths."

"And."

"And what?"

"In his second back, he got knocked down at the break. Last race, he got sandwiched on the turn."

"Yeah, but that won't move him up double-digit lengths."

"How about the addition of blinkers and first time lasix?"

"And you're eight, right?

"I'll be nine soon."

"You and your granddad have been spending too much time together."

"Hey guys." Mario and Geno twisted toward the sound of Cassie's voice. Mario knew she'd show up at the paddock, as always.

"I'm going to win the tri, maybe the superfecta," Geno said to her from his perch.

She squeezed in beside Mario, glanced up at Geno. "How's the weather up there?"

He giggled at an expression he'd never heard before.

For the next three minutes she didn't say a word, just watched the horses being walked by their grooms around a circle. She made notes on her program as she focused on ankles, knees and dapples. She was well aware that the appearance of dapples on hindquarters was a sure sign of a horse's good health. When she'd first heard the term she had no idea that those circular spots on a horse's rear end were called dapples but the term did fit the image. From experience, she knew better than to bet on a horse without them.

Eternal Light stopped in front of where they stood, eyeballed the three of them, took a huge dump then completed his walk to the number five stall where the jockey and his valet awaited him along with the trainer. His owner was busy chatting with other owners in the center of the paddock, playing big-time.

Geno tugged at Mario's hair. He wanted down.

As soon as his feet hit the ground, Geno broke into a run. Mario yelled at him. "Where are you going?"

Geno never turned his head but answered, "To find Gimpy."

"I'm going to kill Gimpy," said Mario to no one.

Cassie stuck her pen in a front pocket and rolled up her program in her hand before speaking. "I need to bet him, right?"

"Right."

"And you expect him to win?"

"Easily."

She glanced at the board. "He's 45-1."

"Stand at the window, bet him as they're entering the gate."

"And you?"

"Let's go together."

"Okay."

Damn, he thought. At least he had a date for the next couple of minutes.

He bet first, $2,000 to win.

She bet $500 to win.

"No show bet?" he said, smiling.

She didn't answer.

"Let's hustle."

They made it to the fence just in time. Geno had his feet stuck in the fence again, ready to cheer. The guys were hanging together. Mario shot Gimpy a look. Gimpy shrugged.

Cassie headed for her spot.

Mario hung back and slid beside Geno. "Did Gimpy get your fifty down for you?"

Patting his jean pocket, Geno said, "Got the ticket right here."

"Anything else in there?"

"Yep, two exactas, one tri and one super. I kept the rest along with the twenty I brought." He grinned and said, "For tomorrow."

"Where are you going tomorrow?"

"You're bringing me back here."

"Says who?"

"Well, if I'm going to buy you a new car, you ought to at least let me ride in it. Tomorrow would be a good time. You can bring me back here. I like this place. It's neat and I can win some more money."

Mario smiled at the kid's confidence.

The bell sounded. They were off and running. The race was a flat mile, out of the chute. Very quickly it turned into a one horse race. Eternal Light broke on top and maintained his position by eight lengths on the far turn, well in hand. He increased his lead to twelve at the top of the stretch. Geno hadn't evoked so much as a word until Eternal Light rolled by, fifteen on top. But when the next flight rumbled down the stretch, he was bloody screaming. Five horses hit the finish at the same time, a photo for second, third and fourth. Three were Geno's picks. He jumped from the fence and ran to Gimpy, who had a better view of the finish. Excitingly, he tugged on Gimpy's pants. "Who was second?"

"Think it was either the three or six."

"I got both."

"I know."

"How about the seven?"

"Not sure, but he's in the photo."

Mario glanced down the rail toward Cassie. She was looking his way and lifted a thumb in the air. Eternal Light's odds had dropped to 30-1 at post time, a result of insider information. But the payoff would still be generous. Her $500 bet would return something over $15,000. His would exceed $62,000. And Geno's return would be well over $1500. The kid would go bonkers when they flashed the payoffs.

It took fifteen minutes for the stewards to sort out the photo finish. All eyes were on the tote board in the middle of the infield.

In rapid order, the numbers flashed for second, third and fourth.

Six.

Three.

Seven.

Winner, number two, paid $62.20.

For picking the first and second place horse in order, the two-six exacta paid $397.80.

For picking the first three in order, the two-six-three triple paid $1973.20.

For picking the two-six-three-seven in order, the superfecta paid $43,768.60. The seven had closed at 80-1. Only one winning ticket existed.

Oh, my God, thought Mario as he focused on the numbers.

By this time Geno was right beside him, jumping like he was about to pee in his pants. "How much did I win? How much did I win?"

"Let me see your tickets," Mario said as calmly as he could, which wasn't calm at all.

Geno handed him six. Mario discarded two.

Gimpy hollered at Mario. "You might need to borrow a truck."

"How much?" Geno asked, for the third time.

"Let's see." Mario took out his pen. "You had the two to win for fifty, a two dollar exacta on the two-six, a two dollar triple on the two-six-three and a two-dollar super of two-six-three-seven. Total comes to . . ." He looked at Gimpy and shook his head. "Total comes to $47,694.60."

"Is that enough to buy a car?"

"Yeah, but Uncle Sam gets part of it."

"I don't have an Uncle Sam."

"Yes, you do. And you're not going to like him." Mario crouched into a Yogi Berra stance, face to face with Geno. As best he could, he explained the tax situation. At that moment he realized collecting could be a major league problem. Geno was not old enough to bet; therefore, he was not old enough to cash a ticket.

The guys came over and circled the two of them. Each had hit the exacta. Geno wasn't supposed to tell anyone else about Eternal Light. However, Gimpy had placed Geno's bets and rationalized that Mario knew something. He informed Longshot, Toteboard and Railbird. Each had bet exactas with Eternal Light over every horse in the field.

Gimpy volunteered to solve the tax problem. He would cash the super, provide his social security number if the others would walk around the track and pick up all the losing superfecta tickets they could find. He knew that the track would take out a bunch for withholding tax. He'd use whatever losing tickets his buddy's could gather from the ground, trash cans, and table tops to offset the payoff and maybe get some of his withholding back the following April. Mario thanked him and told him to keep whatever was returned.

Meanwhile, Geno had slipped from the circle to find what's-her-name. As of yet, he hadn't learned her name. She spotted him first. "Congratulations, Geno, your horse won."

He ran up to her and said, "I'm pretty good at this handicapping."

"Yes you are. And I appreciate the tip on Eternal Light. I won, too."

"Did you hit the exact?"

"No. Didn't bet it."

"How about the tri?"

"Didn't bet a tri either."

"Did you bet the super?"

"Nope."

"I hit 'em all."

She smiled, turned and looked at the board. Her smile turned into a serious stare at Geno. "You hit the superfecta?"

"Yep, but my Uncle Sam's going to get some of the money and I don't even know him."

She chuckled, looked at the board once again while blowing out a long breath.

Gimpy hollered, "Hey, Geno. Come on, let's go collect some money." Geno came running. There was nothing shy about this kid. Gimpy instructed him to not say a word. On the way to the window, he bought him an ice cream cone, figuring some soft serve would keep his mouth busy for a few minutes.

Mario walked to where Cassie was standing, leaned and captured a handful of tickets. She smiled, knowing what was about to happen. He fiddled with the tickets, discarding a few. "So, you think Meg Ryan would go to dinner with me now?"

"I can't speak for Meg Ryan but Cassie Crawford might."

"Might?"

"If you know a good Italian restaurant."

"Best sauce this side of Venice."

"Okay, but I want you to understand that we're talking dinner only. I'm not looking for a relationship."

"Tonight?"

"Kind of short notice, don't you think?"

"You betting on any other races?"

"Not today."

"Then I'll pick you up at seven."

She glared at him for a moment. "I'll meet you somewhere. How about the 7-Eleven down the street? The one just before the parkway."

He wasn't sure what to make of meeting at the 7-Eleven but he had a date and that was good enough for now. "Okay. Seven."

"Are you going to have any trouble getting a reservation?"

"I don't think so."

7

"Am I a millionaire?" questioned Geno from the backseat. Cuddled next to him was an extra large gym bag loaded with his winnings. An identical bag was riding in the passenger seat up front, bulging with Mario's take. Mario had left Geno, and the money, in the care of Gimpy while he scooted off to Wal-Mart in search of something that would handle all the loot. After returning to the track and filling both bags, Gimpy escorted the two big winners to Mario's car where he made fun of the vehicle before loading Geno's front pocket with a selection of Twizzlers.

"Not quite," said Mario, carefully eyeballing the kid while maneuvering through traffic on the parkway.

"I do have enough to buy you a new car, right?"

"Yes, but--"

"Let's stop and get one."

"Geno, you can't buy me a car. That's your money. You won it fair and square."

"Gimpy said you were taking her on a date tonight."

"Gimpy talks too much."

"We'd better stop and get you a new car. This one stinks. And it's hot back here. You don't even have air conditioning. She's going to hate it."

"How about we talk about a new car tomorrow?"

"Can you get one before you pick me up?"

Mario chuckled. "I'll think about it."

"You want me to give you the money now?"

"I won more than you did? I have plenty of money to buy a new car."

"Did you have to give some of your winnings to that Uncle Sam guy?"

"Not today. I didn't hit the super." Mario figured that was the best answer he could give the little guy. He probably wouldn't understand the 300-1 odds or better deal, requiring withholding. On the other hand, the kid was smart. Incredible statements were part of his everyday vocabulary.

Geno giggled before he said, "Hey, Mario, are you going to have sex tonight?" Geno was obviously a whiz with a remote. Who knew what the hell the little guy watched on the tube.

"How old are you?"

"I'm eight, and you've already asked me that a zillion times today."

Mario flipped open his cell, called ahead and made arrangements to drop Geno at the front door of the restaurant. Maria said she would be waiting and asked how Geno liked the track. Mario pondered the question and possible answers before telling her that Geno wanted to go back tomorrow. He also mentioned that he'd be glad to take him. Then he requested his favorite table for tonight, saying he had a date. Maria was happy for him since he usually arrived all by his lonesome.

Forty minutes later he parked at the curb in front of the restaurant. Maria was waving as he came to a stop. She tugged on the passenger door, finally yanking it open. Geno crawled out the back seat sporting a huge grin. He encountered trouble handling the weight of the bag so Mario came around and helped lift it out of the car.

Maria glanced at the bulging bag, slid her eyes back to Mario and said, "Don't tell me what I think is in that bag is in that bag."

"He hit the superfecta, and the triple and the exacta in addition to his win bet."

"How much?"

"Forty seven thousand, six hundred ninety-four dollars and sixty cents. He wants to buy me a new car."

She gulped before she laughed. "Yeah, he thinks your car sucks."

"The little guy feels the same way about Uncle Sam."

She nodded her head and smiled.

Geno tugged at his mom's dress, "Mom, can I take my money up and show Papa Geno how good a handicapper I am?"

"Just a sec, honey. I'll help you carry the bag."

"I got to run," said Mario. "But I'll be back."

Geno jumped into Mario's arms, wrapped his legs around his waist, squeezed off a giant hug, which was much better than a thousand words of thanks.

A warm glow spread across Maria's face.

Mario popped back into his car then eased from the curb. Twin waves reflected in his rearview mirror.

8

Damn, Mario thought, he might as well open a shuttle service between Little Italy and Laurel. He'd already made the trip twice, now he was going for three. But three's a charm. He smiled as he pulled into the parking lot of the 7-Eleven, early by twenty minutes for his date.

He found a parking spot near the phone booth. Actually, it was a phone attached to a pole, no booth about it. Hip-hop greeted him as he opened his door. The source was a boom box about the size of a small house. Booms could be heard across the Parkway at Fort Meade, probably causing some soldiers to grab a shovel and dig a foxhole. Two black dudes around fourteen or fifteen and a white kid about the same age were making sure they'd be candidates for hearing aids before hitting thirty. Each donned baseball caps. One black kid had the brim tilted to the right while the white kid had his going left. The other black kid had reversed his cap as though Nolan Ryan was in the house and about to let loose with one of his fastballs. They were straddling a brick wall, showing off shorts longer than most of his pants. The one holding the box on his shoulder pointed to Mario's car and made the same disparaging remark he'd heard earlier from Little Geno. The other two pointed at the car and laughed.

Mario shot all three a smirk before entering the store.

Inside, he browsed the magazine rack, flipping through a few, first checking out the babes then checking out the cars. He scanned the candy shelf while jingling the coins in his right front pocket. Despite experience and age, first date jitters were hanging tough. His stomach rumbled strange noises. Dampness had made an appearance on his lower back. Every few seconds, his eyes darted toward the parking lot.

By five after seven he thought it was stand-up city, but two minutes later the blue bug whipped into the lot. He was out the door and opening hers before she cut the engine. Cary Grant would be proud. His old black and white movies had taught Mario a thing or two about chivalry. Or perhaps it had been David Niven, or 007.

When she stepped from the car, Mario's eyes danced like a ballerina. Meg Ryan never looked this good. Ever. For someone not looking to get involved, she sure did dress to impress. Forget the jeans. Her legs were in full display tonight. A slit up the side of a black sheath-style dress drew his immediate attention. But, as he would tell you, sometimes he didn't have a long attention span. He stepped back, took in the whole package. Green eyes so vivid he figured they'd glow in the dark. Her skin was as smooth as the finest silk in the world. She possessed a body clothes loved. He wondered what was inside.

He stood there, speechless.

"Close your mouth, you're beginning to drool," Cassie said. She knew she had knocked him off his feet, the dazzle meter at its highest point. She had intended to mess with his brain a little, have some fun. And she had succeeded.

He swept a hand across his mouth and licked his lips, not wanting to expose any excess drool. "I'm a little embarrassed," he said glancing down at his olive golf shirt, khaki pants and loafers, thankful that he was wearing socks. "Maybe I should stop by my place and change."

"Okay. I'll wait here. How long will it take?" she said, still applying the fun, having absolutely no intention of visiting his residence.

He started to say twenty minutes but caught the twinkle in her eye. He reached deep inside and came up with some fun of his own. "Two days. I'd have to go shopping."

A smile graced her face. His body released its tenseness and relaxed a little.

She glanced around, looked at him, glanced around again, "Where's your car?"

Good thing the boom box and its friends had moved down the street.

He whipped a nod toward the Pinto.

She stared at the vehicle then smiled at Mario. "You're kidding?"

"Nope, that's it."

"What the hell is it?"

"Pinto."

"Pinto? Heard of a pinto pony, never heard of a Pinto car. What's it run on, hay?" She grinned, waiting for his response.

"I'm thinking about getting a new car first thing tomorrow."

"Really?"

"Yeah, really." He had said it, not knowing if he meant it.

"Is that the one Geno's buying you?"

The little shit, thought Mario. She already knew about the car. He dropped his chin, did a little tooth job on his lower lip, lifted his eyes and broke into a smile.

She wrapped her arm in his, escorted him the few steps to the Pinto. "Okay, let's see what this babe machine will do zero to sixty."

Well, he thought, at least she's a lot looser than she was at the track. Maybe the evening will go better than expected.

"What about your car? You can't just leave it here."

"Sure I can. I laid a twenty on the guy inside, earlier."

Earlier? When did that happen? She was so far ahead of him he wasn't sure he could catch up. *No date. Maybe. Okay. No involvement.* Now she's toying with him, showing signs of interest.

Go figure.

Matte brown. That was the exterior color. Dull and boring. The Pinto had an interior to match, a little lighter in tone. Mario went over the features: straight stick on the steering column, 1,000 watt AM radio with single speaker, floor mats uglier than dirt, an eighty horsepower engine, and interior lights that worked manually. He didn't point out the advantage of the bench seat. She could slide over . . . snuggle up . . . mess with his leg or something.

"No CD player, huh?" she said, tongue digging a hole in her cheek.

"Nope. Didn't want to clutter the dash."

He popped the clutch and off they went. The Pinto was so quick off the block he almost ran into a monster truck that was so high off the ground Cassie had to bend to see above the wheels. The cab was smaller than the tires. It probably required a hook and ladder from the local firehouse to climb to the door.

With the nimbleness of a cat, the Pinto scooted around the truck and circled onto the parkway.

"So, where's this Italian restaurant?"

"Little Italy." He wanted to look her way as he spoke but he was busy trying to find third gear.

"You're heading toward BWI. Are we going to park the pony and catch a plane, maybe visit with the Pope before dinner?"

He smiled. Oh yeah, she's coming around, throwing out the cuteness, warming up. He said, "Baltimore. Little Italy is in Baltimore."

She laughed. "I know. Been there, ate at Chiapparelli's. What a great salad."

"We're going to Geno's." Now that he was in third gear, he glanced over, curious about her response.

"Geno's? The little one's grandfather?"

"That would be it, but the little one's father runs the restaurant these days. His grandfather lives upstairs. He had a stroke a couple of years ago."

"What's his dad's name?"

He grinned. "Geno."

"Good food, huh?"

"Better than good. You'll see."

She nodded toward the dash. "How about pushing that button, check out the world of AM radio."

"You have to turn the knob. Pintos don't know anything about buttons." As soon as he turned the knob, a deep voice bellowed from the speaker. Talk radio. Some guy bitching and complaining about the lack of a closer on the O's staff. She decided to turn the knob to see if she could round up some music. She found Elvis and quickly shot a glance at Mario.

"I ain't nothing but a hound dog," he said.

"Don't be cruel."

Personality queen she was. Miss personality. He liked her playfulness.

She turned the knob another notch and found some static but kept searching until Johnny Cash was singing about some railroad.

"Good stuff, huh?" he said while nodding, using the opportunity to get in a little teasing before reaching down and killing the music.

After dodging tourists on Pratt Street, the Pinto made it to the garden spot. She went into shock when seeing the sign. "You have your own parking space?"

"Yep. One of Geno's buddies owns the lot."

"Which Geno?"

He laughed. "The one teaching the kid how to handicap."

"Thought you said he had a stroke."

"He did, but his mind's still a hundred percent. Geno loves him to death." He paused, sucked in a breath. "And so do I."

He opened his door and started to walk around to open hers but she was already standing on the asphalt.

He pointed and said, "This way." She slipped up beside him and they headed down the street. Mario knew what was coming. He nodded, waved at all the guys wondering just how far an eye could pop out of a head.

A guy bigger than Boog Powell whose name was Luigi commented, "Hey Mario, you find her in Hollywood or something? Think I've seen her in some movies."

Mario answered with a wink, questioning Luigi's bright orange suspenders over his white sleeveless undershirt, hoping he didn't show up at Camden dressed like that. He probably did, though.

When Mario opened the door to Geno's for Cassie, her five senses competed for the first spot in line. Smell was an easy winner. The aroma of garlic, olive oil, tomatoes, oregano, and basil brought on hunger pains. Touch came in second when Maria greeted her with a hug. Then Maria hugged Mario and spoke a few words in Italian, telling him that what's-her-name looked just like Meg Ryan. Mario introduced Cassie to Maria, explaining that Maria was Geno's mom, Geno's wife, and Geno's daughter-in-law.

She escorted the twosome to a table in the back, very private and very big. Numerous people spoke to Mario as they made their way. Cassie's eyes swept the interior, her sense of sight trying to gain its rightful spot. Pictures filled the walls. She recognized tons of people in the photos. The room itself personified the old country. Bottles of olive oil in every conceivable shape served as sculpture on shelves separating tables. Peppers swung from the ceiling. Bottles of Marsala topped a refrigerated case displaying an array of provolone, Parmigiano Reggiano, mozzarella and mascarpone. Loaves of freshly baked rustic bread filled the air with an aroma to die for. Red and white checkered tablecloths were a given.

Mario pulled out a chair for Cassie. She thanked him. He sat beside her, facing out. Without question, Mario had arranged for the best seat in the house.

Maria opened a menu and handed it to Cassie. He didn't need one. She scanned the offerings, repeatedly saying "ummm" as her eyes danced from pasta dishes to veal to shrimp. Mario grinned and said, "Can't decide, huh?"

"I don't know what to order, it all looks so good."

"How about I order us some small plates."

"Small plates?"

"Yes, a little of this, a little of that."

"Okay, I'm game, but we don't have a waiter."

"Sure we do." He motioned for a tall, distinguished-looking elderly gentleman to approach. The gentleman was decked out in a black tux, his thinning gray hair neatly combed straight back. "Hi Frank," Mario said. "I'd like for you to meet Cassie. Cassie, this is Frank, my personal waiter. Right, Frank?"

Frank reached for Cassie's hand and applied a kiss. "Nice to meet you. Mario's a nice boy. Hope he's treating you okay. I was here the day they brought him home from the hospital. His dad was so proud. But he gambles too much, likes those horses just like his uncle." Cassie smiled. "Nobody else is allowed to wait on him. He's kind of special around here." Turning to Mario, he asked, "What will it be tonight?"

Mario motioned towards Cassie. "She needs to experience the best of Geno's."

"Coming up." Frank nodded then turned and walked away.

She elbowed him. "The best of Geno's? What does that mean?"

"You'll see."

Frank returned with Bruschetta con Pomodoro e Basilico (grilled garlic bread with fresh tomato and basil), a bottle of Chianti and a pitcher of iced tea. He placed a small plate in front of each of them, suggesting that they enjoy, which they did.

A few minutes later, good old Frank placed a platter about the size of Rhode Island on the table. Every good Italian restaurant offers antipasti, but Geno's exceeded the realms of sensible intake.

Cassie didn't know where to start. The basics were there—salami, provolone, prosciutto, pimiento, anchovies and roasted red peppers. She looked to Mario for help on the other items.

Sometimes being polite by normal standards didn't count. He pointed as he explained. "This is marinated herring, this is fried ravioli, this is calamari, this is hot peppers with tuna, this is stuffed chicken rolls and this is creamed salt cod."

She glanced at him. "Do I need to leave room for dessert?"

"And soup, pasta and an entrée."

She hesitated. He didn't. He instructed her to open wide as he offered up some roasted red pepper on the end of his fork. Romantic devil that he was, he continued to feed her like momma bird. She loved every minute of it, her eyes meeting his with each forkful.

Frank arrived again, this time with cups of minestrone.

Salad followed. It was the best olive oil and vinegar dressing she had ever tasted.

Pasta time. Frank placed four bowls of pasta on the table: angel hair with *the sauce*, linguini with clams, fettuccine with pesto and cream, sweet potato ravioli with sage. Mario suggested she sample the angel hair first.

She twisted the angel hair pasta onto her fork and looked Mario's way. "Don't stare."

He smiled as she immediately went for another forkful. The sauce never met anyone it didn't like. Before twisting pasta for the third time she had to ask, "I have never in my life eaten anything so wonderful other than possibly swiss chocolate and right now the chocolate's in second place. What's the secret?"

He shook his head, "Can't give up the secret. Geno would kill me."

"Anything I could do to convince you?" She placed her hand on his thigh and blew him a little kiss.

"Sorry."

She cut her eyes at him as she continued eating the pasta. "You positive?"

"Nope."

He sampled each of the pasta dishes but spent most of his time with the clam sauce.

She sampled one forkful of each of the other dishes but constantly revisited the angel hair.

Suddenly, she stopped eating, using her empty fork to point to where music was pouring from a corner speaker. "That's my grandfather."

"Frank Sinatra is your grandfather?"

"No. My grandfather is the sax player. Listen." She closed her eyes and gently swayed her head. "The purest sound to ever flow out of a horn."

Frank was crooning "This Love of Mine." Mario knew the music well. It was an old cut, Sinatra fronting the Tommy Dorsey Orchestra. He waited until the song ended before speaking. "All these years I've been listening to your grandfather's sax right here in this restaurant. That's amazing."

"My father followed in his footsteps. He didn't have the opportunity to play with Dorsey but did join Buddy Morrow who carried on the tradition conducting the Tommy Dorsey Orchestra all around the country playing the old arrangements. Good stuff."

Mario nodded.

"You like it?"

"Love it." He hesitated for a moment. "Guess that explains what Geno told me."

Her quizzical glance told him she didn't understand.

"Geno said you were listening to Sinatra on your portable CD player at the track."

"How old is he?"

"Eight. But don't ask him."

"Picked up on Sinatra, did he. He's way too sharp for his age. Yeah, I listen when I'm at the track. I've collected just about everything re-issued on disc. My grandfather was just terrific working with singers. Knew when to stay in the background, when to step forward. My dad told me Dorsey allowed Granddad to do his own thing. You should hear him backing the Pied Pipers. He'd make tears come to your eyes, so melodic, so much emotion. But he could swing, too. Put a Sy Oliver chart in front of him and off he went. You know, I think Boney James, Kenny G, Grover Washington and Kirk Whalam, spent some time listening to my grandfather. Before anyone knew what it was, my grandfather put the smooth in smooth jazz." A head nod stuck an exclamation point on the statement.

"So, that's all you listen to?"

"No. I listen to my dad, too. Found a few Buddy Morrow re-issues."

"He still plays?"

She swallowed hard and blew out a breath. "He died when I was seventeen. I was traveling around the country with him at the time. He had a heart attack walking off a stage in Myrtle Beach."

"And your mom?"

"Never really knew my mom. Dad said she bolted when I was born, couldn't handle the responsibility of a child and all that travel. Dad raised me by himself."

Mario could sense she was about to spill some tears. Frank saved the day, showed up toting a platter of veal scaloppini with lemon and mushrooms and a platter of Geno's crab cakes.

She gathered herself, said thanks to Frank, turned to Mario. "I'm not sure I can eat another bite."

"Oh, but you must. Baltimore is famous for crab cakes, none more famous than Geno's. His homemade Italian breadcrumbs make the difference. Just sample a little."

"I thought Geno was upstairs."

"He is. But his son is the chef and he's in the kitchen. I'll go get him and introduce you."

A few seconds later, Mario returned with Geno who sat and listened to Cassie rave about *the sauce* for two minutes.

In the test of the five senses, taste won. No contest. Not even close.

They passed on dessert but Maria handed Cassie a small white paper bag after a goodbye hug. She told Cassie that it was a house rule that she couldn't leave without cannoli.

As they strolled toward the Pinto, silence prevailed. Mario wondered what she was thinking. He wanted to jump inside her head and find out what made her tick. This time his brain ruled his heart, allowing the silence to spook the clouds, not him.

As he opened her door, he noticed moisture in her eyes.

Just as he was about to start the car, she gently touched him on the arm. "I understand why you drive this car." Nodding, letting him know it was okay.

He turned the key and let the engine idle for a moment, then spoke, "Low mileage, I can't let it just sit and get all rusty."

"Oh, I think it has lots of mileage."

He found reverse, backed out, pulled the gearshift down into first and headed for the street. At the corner he caught a red light, drummed a tune on the steering wheel with his fingers while gathering some thoughts. He glanced at her but she was looking out the window gathering thoughts of her own. The light turned green. He eased off, drove two blocks in silence until the next red light.

She turned her head to him. "The kid told me about your dad leaving you the car."

"That Geno, Mister Informative."

"Good mileage?"

"Great mileage."

"I have my CDs, you have your car."

"Geno says I need to buy a new one . . . before I pick him up tomorrow."

"You two are quite a pair. He loves you. You do know that, don't you?"

He nodded. "Yeah, it goes both ways."

"Can I make a suggestion?"

"Suggestions are welcome, sure."

"Buy a new car."

Mario laughed. "What?"

"Buy a new car, but keep this one. Don't ever give it up. Park it and look into its soul. Savor the memories. When you feel the urge, take it out for a spin and have a conversation with your dad."

Her insight into his being shook him a little, made him conjure up some thoughts on life, on family and on death.

Miles later, Cassie caught sight of the sign indicating the turnoff was just ahead. She knew the next few minutes would be tough. She had tried hard not to like Mario. But she did like him . . . a lot. What an evening. Great food, the best she had ever put in her mouth . . . and great company. Mario was charming, and at the top of the gorgeous list, but involvement with him would cause major problems, problems he wouldn't want to face. And problems she couldn't face.

"I see that the bug is still occupying its twenty dollar parking spot," said Mario as he pulled the Pinto into the lot.

She bit her bottom lip, moved over and kissed him on the cheek before he could say anything else. "Please don't ask. Not tonight. I had a wonderful time, probably too wonderful. But I just can't get involved."

He smiled, knew she liked him, felt like there were issues, maybe some baggage attached to this beautiful creature but given time, she'd come around. "You mean I can't ask you if you'll be at the track tomorrow?"

"I'll be at the track tomorrow." She opened her door.

He dangled the little white bag, "Don't forget these. I'm required to report back on how well you like them."

She grabbed the bag, opened it, pulled out a cannoli and sampled. She ran her tongue around her lips, not wanting to miss any crumbs.

Of course, that action made Mario's pants dance. But he took a deep breath and worked through it.

"You can report back to Maria that the cannoli is right up there with the sauce," she said before stepping toward her car, little white bag in hand.

Mario leaned over, rolled down the passenger side window. "Cassie."

He paused, allowing her enough time to dip her head and peer through the opening. "I have every record ever made by the Tommy Dorsey Orchestra."

"Seriously?"

"Seriously." Smiling to himself, he slipped into reverse, backed out, waved and took off, leaving her standing beside the bug with something to think about, perhaps an invitation to listen to some music.

9

Mario handed the guy thirty-seven thousand, six hundred and twenty dollars receiving back three dollars and seventy-five cents in change, and a set of keys.

Not a bad deal, he thought.

The smile on the salesman's face mirrored his.

One of the great things about living in the Washington-Baltimore corridor is that a person can find just about anything the heart desires, even in the middle of the night.

At quarter after one, Mario found first gear and whipped out of the lot sporting a brand new silver Infiniti G35 coupe. He found second, third, fourth, fifth and sixth gear before he arrived home.

The Pinto remained at the dealership to be driven and parked in Mario's driveway by the salesman sometime Sunday morning. Another salesman would follow and give the Pinto driver a ride back to the dealership. The guy had offered to take the pony in trade but no way was Mario going to part with his dad's car. In fact, he had decided that the Pinto would remain as his means of transportation to the track to watch early morning workouts. In the afternoons, he'd show off his new wheels.

After leaving the 7-Eleven earlier without as much as a solid good-night kiss, he had driven home, flopped into a chair with the newspaper, read several dealership ads flaunting twenty-four-hour sales, thought about what Little Geno and Cassie had said, then headed out and bought the car.

He hadn't hit the sack until the big hand was on the twelve and the little hand was on the two. But he slept well.

Little Geno had spent the night at Papa Geno's, something he did often. Mom and Dad owned a two-story on three acres in Hunt Valley, about three miles north of Timonium Race Track in an area known as horse country. There was no need to make Mario drive that far to pick up the little guy. Maria loved having him over so she had extra clothes stuck aside in a drawer for such occasions.

Grandfather and grandson spent Sunday morning with the *Form*, trying to develop some betting strategy for the day. They decided that the nine-horse in the second race was the best bet. Papa Geno advised that it was the only bet to make, a predicted 6-1 or 7-1 shot. He told Little Geno to ask Mario what he knew about the horse's workouts. If Mario agreed that the horse was ready to fire, then bet him to win.

Of course, Little Geno had his own ideas and his own money.

Maria escorted Geno down the steps and out to the front of the restaurant at eleven-twenty, knowing Mario had a tendency to be early. Pick up time had been set for eleven-thirty. At eleven-twenty five, Mario arrived at the curb in his new wheels. Little Geno bolted toward the car to peek in the window while Maria was busy giving Mario a warm hug. She said, "So, you got the middle-aged crazies a little early, huh?"

Mario turned and admired his new purchase for about the hundredth time. "I still own the Pinto, couldn't give it up."

"I hope not."

Little Geno had slipped into the deep leather graphite color passenger seat, his eyes taking in the slick silver console that displayed a 6.5" color monitor. The unit contained a DVD-Rom database, *AAA on wheels*.

Mario fastened his seat belt and told Little Geno to hop in the back and fasten his. He did then raised two thumbs and said, "Cool."

"You think so?"

"Yep."

"Want to hear the sound system?"

"Yep."

Mario started the engine and pulled away from the curb. When he hit the on button for the audio system, six Bose speakers came to life filling the car with Bobby Caldwell belting out a song about Jamaica. Geno's grin was about as wide as a landing strip. Mario explained that they were listening to satellite radio, not a local station. He started to tell him about the bass boosting woofer and the two hundred watts but decided not to burden him with details.

"Can you get J.Lo on that radio?"

"J.Lo?"

"Ah, come on Mario. You know, Jennifer Lopez."

"Let's see." Mario pushed the seek button until he came up with some R & B. "Maybe they'll play her latest song."

"Cool."

Mario glanced around and found the button for the sunroof. As it slid into the rear portion of the roof, Geno's eyes followed, his nose now pointing toward the sky. He shouted, "Sweet!"

"What happened to cool?"

"It's cool, too, but that's," he pointed, "sweet."

Becoming adept at shifting the gears was going to take some time but Mario was working on it as he cruised toward Laurel, taking advantage of the two hundred and fifty horses under the hood. He was having fun, heading to the track with Geno. The siren caught him by surprise. Glancing back at the blue lights in the rearview mirror, he uttered a couple of four-letter words under his breath.

He slowed down and eased the car onto the grass. The officer remained in his car for a few minutes.

"Why did you stop?" said Geno. "We got to get to the track."

Mario turned and pointed to the police car. Geno said, "We're not going to jail are we?"

Mario laughed, easing Geno's tension somewhat. "Nah, just a speeding ticket."

"How fast were you going?"

"I don't' know. It didn't seem fast, smooth as silk."

Mario caught sight of the officer in his side view mirror, walking toward the car. He lowered the window before cutting off the engine.

"License and registration, sir," the cop said. It was a demand, and not real friendly.

"What's the problem officer?"

"License and registration." He stuck out his hand. "Eighty in a fifty-five."

Geno crawled forward between the seats and peeked at the officer. "He didn't know he was going fast. He just got this car and he's not used to it yet."

The officer tried to hold back a grin but failed. "He just got it, huh?"

"Yep, last night."

Mario let the little guy talk as he searched the glove compartment for the temporary registration.

The officer took a few steps toward the back of the car, checked out the temporary tags and made some notes on his pad.

Mario found the registration and handed it and his license to the officer. The officer spent a few seconds reviewing both before commenting. "Sir, you were going twenty-five miles per hour over the limit. That qualifies as careless and reckless."

He started to write up the ticket but Geno intervened. "He had a Pinto, it didn't go very fast."

"A what?" The officer looked to be about twenty-six or twenty-seven years old. Maybe he had seen a Pinto in his life, maybe not.

Mario answered, "A Ford Pinto that belonged to my dad."

The look on the officer's face softened. He backed up a step, took in the sleek lines of the G35 while scratching his head.

"I made him buy a new car, he's trying to get a new girl friend," Geno said.

"How old are you, son?"

Geno shrugged, didn't answer.

"He's eight, officer . . . going on thirty or something," Mario said, eyebrows heading north.

"Okay, here's what I'm going to do. I'm going to let you off on the careless and reckless."

"Thanks, thanks a lot."

"But, I'm writing you up for seventy." He wrote on his pad, handed it through the window. "Sign on the bottom line."

Mario signed, thankful as hell.

As the officer headed back to his car, Geno whispered, "You need to slow down."

The costs of driving a new car had just gone up.

After arriving at the track and parking beside Cassie's blue bug, they headed to the gate. Mario glanced at Geno before purchasing a program. Geno held up two fingers.

As they made their way past the clubhouse, Geno opened his program to the second race. He pointed at the nine. "Nine in the second race. What do you think?"

Mario took a quick glance, "Yep, been watching him work, like him a lot. Also like the two in the fifth. They're my bets for the day."

"Papa Geno told me to only bet one horse, the two in the second, if you liked him, so I'm going to bet the daily double, take all the horses in the first with the two in the second and hope a long shot wins the first."

"I don't think he meant for you to place that bet."

"What do you mean? I'm betting the two."

"I'm sure he meant for you to bet him to win."

"I am."

Mario patted him on the back. "Who am I to tell an expert how to bet?"

Geno smiled. "Yeah, I'm pretty good, huh?"

Out of the corner of his eye Mario caught sight of Cassie walking from the grandstand door toting a bottle of water and a pretzel, heading for her usual spot by the fence. He told Geno to run ahead and say hello to Gimpy who was huddled up near the fence with Longshot, Toteboard and Railbird

When she spotted him walking toward her, she turned off her CD player.

"Wouldn't be listening to a big band, would you?" he said as he approached.

"How'd you guess?"

"Just lucky."

For a second or two they stood and stared at each other, dead air filling the moment.

"Thanks for dinner last night," she said. "It was wonderful."

"You're welcome. Thanks for going."

She motioned toward Geno. "I see you brought the handicapper with you again. Who does he like today?"

"Nine horse in the second."

"And you?"

"Nine horse in the second and I may put something down on the two in the fifth."

She opened her program, studied the second race for a couple of minutes then turned to the fifth. She felt a tug on her jeans. "Mario bought a new car."

Glancing down at Geno and back up at Mario, she said, "He did, did he?"

Mario nodded.

"And he got a speeding ticket already!"

She laughed as she spoke to Mario. "And how fast *were* you going?"

"Eighty."

"It's a sports car," said Geno rapidly. "Silver, and it's got a roof that opens and all kinds of speakers and a television that has maps on it and a satellite dish. It is really cool."

She glanced at Mario. "A satellite dish?"

"Satellite radio."

"You bought a car this morning?"

"Last night, a little after one."

"You need to ride in it," Geno said.

She flashed her eyes at Mario. "Maybe I will, if I get an invitation."

"Anytime."

She glanced away then at Geno. "Enough about cars. Tell me about this horse you like in the second race."

"The nine. He's going to win."

An hour and a half later, she found out that Geno was on target. The nine won the second in a photo finish with the three. Paid $12.80 to win, having gone off 5-1. Daily double of 1-9 paid $63.40. Geno was up $50.20. He showed off his tickets and strutted his stuff.

Mario also won with the nine in the second. So did Cassie, neither saying how much.

After the race, Mario bumped into Lemon Drop Larry who had earned his nickname after cashing a big ticket on Lemon Drop Kid when the colt won the Belmont in 1999, the year Charismatic broke down in the stretch. Since that day, Larry carried a bag of lemon drops in his pocket at all times and passed them out to anyone in search of a pucker or two. He said it brought him luck. Mario took a couple and shoved them into his pocket for later.

For the balance of the afternoon, holding Geno back was impossible. Mario tried to convince him not to bet every race but he did, somehow. The little guy walked out of the track with empty pockets and a sad face.

Mario tried to console him during the ride home to Baltimore. Geno wasn't in the mood. Didn't say much until Mario pulled up in front of his house in Hunt Valley. Walking to the door, Geno said, "Guess you and Papa Geno are right. Can't bet every race and win."

"It's a tough lesson, but if you want to win money at the track you must be disciplined enough to pick your spots."

"I did with the first and second races. I should have quit after that."

"Yep." Mario patted him on the head.

"But it was fun anyway, even if I did lose."

"The races can be fun and you can bet on every race if you go for entertainment. It's no different than buying a concert ticket or going to Busch Gardens."

Geno nodded. "Next time, I'm going to pick my spots."

"Good idea."

Maria, his mom, met them at the door, immediately taking notice of the look on Geno's face. "No bag of money today?" she said.

"Nope, I didn't pick my spots." He glanced at Mario who shot him the confirmation look.

Good old mom gave her son a good old mom hug and thanked Mario for taking him.

"Got a date tonight?" she asked.

"Yeah, with a book."

Mario found a jazz station on satellite radio and cranked up the sound. He now had his own boom box. Boney, Luther and Grover accompanied him home. The car rolled along as smoothly as the music, now that he had perfected his six-speed stick moves.

The day had been interesting. He won the bet in the second and had cashed a ticket on the two in the fifth, ending up the day fifteen hundred ahead. Despite the losing, Geno had hopefully learned an important lesson. Cassie was friendly but he wanted more than friendly. He still found her to be a bit mysterious. She had bet the two to show in the fifth. He spotted her placing bets at different windows again, collecting the same way as usual. He wondered why, and it drove his ass crazy.

At three in the morning he crawled out of bed. Might as well, his eyes had been open since he crawled in at eleven. He opened a cabinet door below bookshelves in his great room, pulled out his Tommy Dorsey records and read all the album notes, running his finger down the list of band members on each and every album. He never saw the name Crawford.

10

Two males, both black, had robbed a bank in Newark, Delaware ten minutes ago.

The info stuck in William Rollins' throat like a fish bone that just wanted to hang around and choke him to death.

He took a quick gander at the map, picked up a purple-headed pin, added a white tag with the bank name and address and firmly stuck it in its proper spot. Once a dollar amount was determined, the figure would be added.

Local police and agents from the Wilmington office were already on the scene, searching for the suspects, dusting for prints, interviewing bank personnel and customers who witnessed the crime. He decided to join them. Five minutes later he was riding shotgun in a copter.

While in the air, Field Agent Hector Valdez called. Rollins covered one ear with an index finger and listened with the other. "Hector, speak up. Shout if you have to," he said. "I can't hear you over the blades."

Valdez screamed from the other end, scaring the crap out of some bank employees. "One of the robbers was standing near the entrance and picked up a bank pen, a giveaway item in a clear plastic wrapper. It's on the tape. The guy bit the plastic and took out the pen then dropped it on the floor. We dusted it. No prints. There were no prints."

"Was the perp wearing gloves?"

"No."

"Unbelievable."

"But we do have a witness who wasn't in the bank. She was parking in the lot when she saw two black males run out of the bank and speed off in a red Corvette. She wrote down the plate number."

"Got anything yet?"

"Owned by a surgeon over at the hospital."

"Stolen?"

"Oh, yeah, but he doesn't know it yet. Doc's been in surgery for the past two hours. A nurse said she walked right by the car parked in his reserved spot an hour and a half ago."

"Damn. Two white guys stole a doctor's car from a hospital lot and used it in the robbery up in Harrisburg last year."

"I remember."

"What?"

He spoke louder, again trying to overcome the roar of the blades. "I remember."

"Could be a coincidence."

"Could be a copy cat."

"Yeah, one of many."

Rollins leaned toward the pilot and asked where they would land. The pilot pointed to the football stadium parking lot at the University of Delaware, just ahead to his right.

"Hector, we're about to put this baby down. Pick me up at the Blue Hens' stadium."

"Will do."

Minutes later, Rollins ducked his head under the spinning blades and hustled to Valdez's black Ford Taurus. As they sped away, Valdez said, "You are not going to believe this but we found the car."

"Where?"

He laughed before answering. "In its parking spot at the hospital."

"That took balls."

"We're dusting and checking for DNA as we speak."

"Good. Maybe we'll get lucky."

"And we're interviewing anybody and everybody at the hospital. Maybe someone saw something."

"You'd think so."

Rollins liked Valdez, a five-eleven, two-hundred-pound, died-in-the-wool Mets' fan who grew up in Brooklyn just two blocks from old Ebbets Field. His whole family still hated the Dodgers for leaving. He played college baseball at St. John's. Married his college sweetheart and now has two children, a boy of twelve and a girl who is nine. Rollins loved Valdez's accent. The two of them understood each other when they talked, but no one else knew how.

After they arrived at the scene, Rollins gathered as much information as he could. The situation looked and sounded like the other seventeen unsolved robberies. One guy passing a note to a teller while the other stood guard at the door. Customers and other bank personnel were told to hit the floor. Robbery took about five minutes. Consensus said that the thief at the teller window was six foot, maybe six-one although one customer, a sixty-nine year old woman, described him as being seven foot three. The guy at the door was pegged at five eight or nine. The sixty-nine year old woman said he was tiny. Both robbers were described as light-skinned blacks. Bank security tapes verified what he had heard.

Rollins walked around . . . around the inside of the bank, the outside of the bank, the neighborhood, through the woods behind the bank, inside the adjoining two-story office building. He didn't take a single note, just observed, still trying to swallow the damn fish bone in his throat.

If they didn't catch these guys in the next few days, the eighteenth pin would remain on the map and eat at his brain.

The loudness of the blades didn't interfere with his thinking on the return trip to Washington. Problem was his thoughts were now galloping in eighteen different directions . . . none heading for a solution.

11

Just a pinch of light allowed Mario to make it to the bathroom without stubbing a toe, walking into a door or tripping over his bedside chair.

He was still young enough that he pissed from an awkward position every morning. His head and feet were equal distances from the target but his rear end was trying desperately to reach the back wall. His right hand attempted to control the direction of the outflow while his left provided balance. As usual, he hoped he didn't get any on his toes or the rug or the seat. As usual, lacking a NASA guidance system, he splattered all three spots. The morning erection is a thing to behold. Starts at about twelve years old and continues for years.

He had bolted from bed to the sudden sounds of Santana blasting from his clock radio. Yesterday the station brightened his morning with Sade, the day before it was Diane Krall, but Santana at five? Who in the hell was in charge of programming? He should call and complain, but what the hell, it wouldn't do any good. He was awake, wide awake. He had to be at the track in a few minutes. The station had done its job. Now it was time for him to do his.

His pal, the Pinto, provided the transportation. Talk radio provided entertainment, but he didn't hear a word. Not finding the name Crawford two nights ago had scrambled his brain.

Buster Jones handled the unscrambling.

Good old Buster was from Arkansas. He had worked for Wal-Mart for forty years, loading and unloading roll-back specials at headquarters for a modest salary. He spent every Saturday visiting the two-dollar window at Oaklawn Park. Three years ago he appeared on the scene at Laurel Park as a horse owner. It was a hell of a transition but Buster had taken advantage of every stock option offered by the company. He became a millionaire when he cashed in. The day after, he purchased a thoroughbred race horse. Not just any horse, a two-year-old stakes winner by the name of Cannonball. Cannonball happened to now be stabled in Chuck Coleman's barn at Laurel. He moved to Maryland to be close to his new pride and joy. His wife, Salle Mae, said they moved to be close to their two grandchildren, daughter and son-in-law who lived in a big two-story over in Columbia. Son-in-law Carl was a district manager for Wal-Mart who, following in the footsteps of Buster, capitalized on every stock option.

Mario and Buster had developed a friendship during countless hours of watching morning workouts. They could always be found hanging over the rail at sunrise or earlier. Mario had him by five or six inches but Buster had

Mario by a good fifty pounds, and thirty years. Both were astute when it came to the ponies.

Buster removed the toothpick from his mouth before greeting Mario. "You come over to watch my horse work or just to spend some quality time with an old man?"

"Both."

"Want some coffee?"

"That would be good." Forget Starbucks. Buster always showed up with a thermos full of his own brew, a blend of French roast and mocha java. Mario always showed up with a mug and sugar packets, part of his arsenal that included files on individual horses and trainers. He quickly whipped the mug from his backpack and stuck it forward.

Buster poured and steam filled the air. "You get that backpack from Wal-Mart?"

"K-Mart."

Buster shot him a glare.

Mario smiled. "Just kidding. Actually, I got it by being one of the first thousand patrons to enter Pimlico on opening day five years ago."

"And the mug?"

"A freebee." Mario held up the mug and turned it so that Buster could see Secretariat in full stride. He had more mugs than a coffee shop, each displaying the photo of a horse, jockey or track logo.

"Hell, you were hardly born when Secretariat ran."

"My uncle gave it to me. He bought it the day Big Red won the Belmont."

Between sips, Mario grabbed a pen and pad.

Cannonball was on the track galloping, getting ready to break off at the half-mile pole, breezing four furlongs. Buster's eyes were glued to the horse, his right thumb ready to click his stopwatch.

Mario had his own watch.

The five-year-old went handily and finished with a strong kick. Buster got him in forty-eight flat. Mario caught him in forty-seven and four. Same distance. Same horse. Different watches, different thumbs.

The gleam in Buster's eye said it all.

"You entering him in the stakes Saturday?"

"Shooting for it, yeah."

"Probably go off second favorite, if Shooting Star runs."

"Probably." Old Buster was chewing hard on his toothpick, working it around his smile. "But we might get him this time." Shooting Star had beaten Cannonball twice by a head. In each race, Cannonball closed hard but came up short. "I got a friend shipping a horse in from Oaklawn, a real speedball. Should put lots of pressure on Shooting Star up front and soften him up."

"But can you beat the speedball?"

"Yeah, he can't get the mile and an eighth."

"Why is he running?"

"Doing me a favor."

"He getting part of the pot if you win?"

Old Buster slipped out a sly grin punctuated by a wink. "Could happen."

Mario scribbled some notes.

Buster excused himself. He wanted to go over to the barn, talk to his horse and build his confidence.

For the next two hours Mario was his old self, totally focused on horses, trainers, jockeys, times, and track conditions. He totally ignored the chitchat spilling out of the mouths of owners now lining the fence in front of the clubhouse.

He loved the time of day and surroundings. Not because Laurel was the most gorgeous of tracks, far from it. It didn't compare to the serenity of Saratoga and it wasn't overlooking the Pacific Ocean ala Del Mar, but the action was the same.

Backside in the stable area, grooms carefully wrapped bandages around the legs of horses heading for the track. Trainers gave a leg up to exercise riders followed by explicit instructions, anything from jogging to breaking from the gate or breezing five furlongs. Fine-tuning was the object. Mario paid close attention to how that was done. He scribbled notes about stuff even the trainer didn't know he or she was doing.

Grooms were engrossed in grunt work. Horses returning from their duties were washed down and cooled out by walking the shed row. It didn't matter if they were five thousand dollar claimers or million dollar two-year-olds. For the same day rate, each got pampered. Three squares, a bath, a rubdown, music they liked, maybe a friend in their stall.

Good trainers, bad trainers, good jockeys, bad jockeys, good grooms, bad grooms and, of course, good horses and bad horses all existed as neighbors. Mario knew them all and knew them well.

Around ten, activity dwindled to a trickle. The chirp of birds replaced thundering hooves.

He packed up his notes, led the pony home, took a shower, shaved, grabbed a bite to eat and headed for Baltimore . . . off to see the wizard of sauce, again, *wondering how much he knew about women.*

When he arrived, he fumbled his words for a few minutes. He told Geno about Cannonball but Geno sensed he was there for another reason. Geno touched Mario on the arm and said, "You got a problem I should know about?"

Mario walked from his spot beside Geno and visited Secretariat's picture before answering. Finally, he said, "I don't know."

"You don't know if you have a problem or not? What kind of bullshit is that?"

A grin crept out his mouth before Mario spoke. "It's the girl."

"What about the girl?"

"I can't figure her out."

"Hell, Mario. What the crap did you expect? Don't tell Maria I said this but women will drive your ass crazy, send your brain into a tailspin trying to figure out the mood of the day."

"It's not that."

"Then what the hell is it?"

"She keeps telling me I don't want to get involved with her."

"Then don't."

Mario studied Geno's eyes for a moment. He shrugged then said, "But why would she tell me that?"

"How many answers would you like?"

"How many you got?"

"I could give you a few." He patted the bed. It was time for Mario to take a seat and suck in some wisdom.

"Shoot."

"She could be married."

Mario ran his hand across his head before scratching the back of his neck. "Hadn't considered that."

"Where does she live?"

"I don't know?"

"Didn't you pick her up?"

He closed his eyes and shook his head. "She met me at a 7-Eleven."

Geno shot him the old *how-stupid-can-you-be* look. "And you didn't question that?"

"Yeah, but I've had women meet me on first dates before."

"Any of them married?"

Mario smiled. "One."

"Well, this may make two."

"I'll ask."

"Good idea . . . and if you think she's not telling the truth, follow her home and find out for yourself. Maybe she's not married, just lives with a guy." He placed a comforting hand on Mario's shoulder before saying, "Or a gal."

"You mean a roommate?"

Geno shook his head. "Nope."

Mario pondered the possibility, visions of Cassie making it with a woman dancing before his eyes, a scenario he didn't want to consider. "Keep going."

"Maybe she has a troubled past."

"Such as?"

"May be divorced, could be an alcoholic, could be into drugs. Who knows? May have a criminal record, could have been molested as a child or raped as an adult."

"She's hiding something, I'm sure." Mario went on to explain about going through Tommy Dorsey albums and *not* finding a Crawford.

"And how long have you known her?"

"We officially met four days ago. I've seen her at the track every race day for the past four or five weeks."

"So, you've been out with her one time?"

Mario nodded.

"You take her home?"

"No."

"You dropped her at the 7-Eleven?"

"Yep."

"Would you bet on a horse you know nothing about?"

"Nope."

"Then, you need to sniff around, do some handicapping. Check out where she was bred, her sire and dam, take a hard look at her past performance chart. Know where she's stabled."

"You're right." He leaned over and hugged Geno. "You need anything before I go?"

"Legs that work would be good." He shook his head at Mario. "We're a hell of a twosome, aren't we? I can't control my legs." He rubbed his thigh with his good hand then pointed at Mario's crotch. "And you can't control your pecker."

On the ride home, Mario digested all that Geno had said. He decided he would follow Cassie home after the races Wednesday. Maybe he'd borrow a car and be a real sleuth.

12

Joyce Cooling woke him, strumming on her guitar. She made him think he was about to embark on a trip to Malibu, top down, surfboard reaching for the sun. No need to slam the off button this morning. The programmer had a heart or must have known that Mario was thinking of kicking his ass the next time Santana blasted him out of bed.

Mario stood, rolled his neck like a cobra before hitting the john for the aiming contest.

When he stepped from the bathroom, The Rippingtons greeted him with "Crusin' Down Ocean Drive." Damn, he thought, as he glanced in his full-length mirror. He needed to add some color to his Wonder Bread body but sunbathing didn't fit into a horseplayer's schedule. A tanning salon was the only answer. Maybe he'd indulge in one of those fifty-dollar bronze jobs. Music has the uncanny ability to send a guy's mind to some hypnotic oasis, forcing a reaction to the chords and, perhaps, a change in body color. The last time he heard Ray Charles singing "Georgia on my Mind" he visited a veggie stand and purchased a pound of peaches.

Now that the station had him moving and grooving, he decided to continue with the euphoria, listen to some satellite radio on his way to the track. He took the coupe and had the music cranked so high the car got the shakes.

The only beat he heard while walking from his car was the sound of hooves pounding the dirt with a rhythm only a player could appreciate. For the next three hours he focused, wrote down three pages of notes, highlighting a two-year-old prepping for his first start, a sure winner.

Buster's hot coffee and warm smile assured Mario that Cannonball would answer the challenge Saturday. He said his friend's horse had arrived on the grounds and would work tomorrow. Mario offered to buy him breakfast so they headed to the track kitchen on the backside for some greasy bacon, scrambled eggs, biscuits, hash browns, freshly squeezed orange juice and an earful of bullshit coming from all directions. The kitchen was a gathering spot for backstretch personnel: trainers, owners, jockeys and agents. If you accepted what you heard as the gospel, you could buy yourself a broken down piece of shit thinking you had purchased the next winner of the Breeders Cup Classic. Or, you just might know the winner of the sixth today. Separating truth from fiction was the challenge. Mario and Buster dangled their toes and got their feet just wet enough to need a giant towel to wipe away tall tales and visions of grandeur.

When Mario arrived home, he exchanged the G35 for the Pinto and cruised to the Chevy dealership. The salesman took one look at the pony and his sucker-meter came alive thinking he had a live one. In honor of Joyce Cooling, Mario showed real interest in a black Malibu. For the past two days, Chevrolet had been promoting a twenty-four hour test drive with no strings attached. Damn if it wasn't true. Mario took advantage and drove off the lot in a black Malibu sporting dealer tags.

Usually, he grabbed an early lunch before heading for the track but his stomach reminded him of the breakfast he had downed a couple of hours ago. No need for a refill. Not yet, anyway.

He parked in the furthest lot from the clubhouse entrance, close to where Cassie usually parked on weekdays.

Having reviewed today's entries earlier, he wasn't betting but did want to watch a filly run in open company that was eligible for state bred races. She'd probably get beat today but Mario thought she could handle Maryland Breds at the same level if she showed some kick going long for the first time. She was in the hands of a trainer who was good at stretching horses out. Mario had run the dosage figures. Numbers said the horse would like the added ground.

At three-thirty, Cassie hadn't shown. Mario paced and wondered why.

At four, a maiden race caught his attention. Well, actually it wasn't the race. It was the name of a first time starter, California Music. Betting on a name was for amateurs. He was a pro. He bet on the horse. Joyce Cooling and The Rippingtons had convinced him to lay down two dollars across the board—win, place and show. Horse finished dead last. Horse ran like he had eaten too many avocados. Mario laughed and decided to visit the concession stand and celebrate his six buck loss by indulging in a couple of tacos loaded with guacamole.

Just before the last race, he caught sight of Cassie heading to her normal spot. He ducked behind a pole and followed her with his eyes. Five minutes before post time she made bets at eight different windows.

As the horses were coming down the stretch, he didn't know which horse she had bet but as soon as the three got his nose in front at the wire, she turned and headed to collect.

He headed for the Malibu.

Her bug was parked a couple of blocks from the clubhouse gate. He could see it from the Malibu. He stuck an O's cap on his head and tugged it tight to his ears. He looked like a little kid peeking over the steering wheel.

He waited.

Engines cranked up all around. Sounded like the start of Indy, everyone in a hurry to get home and total up their losses. The parade of cars lined up. One by one they pulled onto the main road, beating the oncoming traffic. The Malibu began to get isolation complex, sitting all alone in the back of the lot.

Finally, he spotted her, toting a bag—probably full of money. He slid deeper into the seat and rolled down the window so that he could hear her car start.

She turned onto Rt.197 after leaving the track. He followed, but not so close that she'd notice. Pulling into a Wendy's, she eased behind a three-car line at the drive-thru. He parked in a vacant spot just to the right and, with his window down, heard her order a mandarin chicken salad and a Diet Coke. She drove around the building, pulled up to the window for her order, paid the guy then drove off.

Just past Bowie State College she turned onto a dirt road, kicking up a cloud of red dirt and loose rocks.

He slowed down at the road, caught glance of her about a block into a thicket of woods. He made the decision not to follow. Instead, he pulled into a McDonald's down the street on the opposite side, parked, went inside and ordered medium fries and a Dr Pepper. He carried the bag and soda to the car and perfected his ketchup-dipping while he waited, his eyes never leaving the dirt road.

An hour later he drove home, wondering what in the hell was at the end of that road.

13

Thursday morning he sprung from his pillow and tried to destroy his radio as quickly as possible. Somehow or other a DJ had gone out on a limb thinking that Little Richard had become a smooth jazz artist. The god-awful sound had interrupted his dreams with words he couldn't understand and a piano that sounded like a toddler banging on a pot. He decided he needed to change stations, find some string music, maybe a quartet, with the loudest instrument being a flute. Wake up to a waltz . . . push the snooze button . . . remain horizontal for an extra five.

He was hungry. He had forgotten all about eating dinner last night after the mid-afternoon taco and the late-afternoon fries. After opening a brand new box of Bisquick, he whipped up a ten-stack of pancakes, sprinkled a little powdered sugar and pecans on top, drenched them in about a quart of Aunt Jemima's, and dug in. Within minutes, his white undershirt was covered with sticky stuff that had dripped from his chin.

A half hour later he was standing trackside, sipping Buster's coffee out of a Seattle Slew mug.

Around ten he rushed home, cleaned up and navigated the Malibu to the dealership. He told the salesman that the four-door sedan just didn't fit his image. He wanted to test a four-wheel vehicle, one of those SUV types. This delighted the salesman. The SUV was priced much higher than the Malibu. Mario could see the cash register totaling up behind the guy's eyes.

For the first time in two years, Mario didn't go to the track.

At two, Mario revisited McDonald's and parked in the same spot. Instead of fries, he moved up to a culinary classic, the Big Mac. He washed it down with a super-sized iced tea then went back inside and refilled.

At three-forty, the blue bug rolled onto 197, heading toward Laurel.

Five minutes later, the SUV was bumping along the dirt road. It was an overcast afternoon, humid with a slight mist in the air. Trees hung over both sides of the road creating the eerie feeling of a long tunnel with no light at the end. Mario felt water forming a puddle in the small of his back. He slid around on the seat, trying to release his pants from the grip of the leather. At ten miles per hour, he was creeping yet making progress. His eyes danced, searching for he didn't know what. He rounded a curve that revealed a small opening in the trees about the size of a regulation swimming pool. A recreational vehicle he estimated to be forty to forty-five feet long was parked in the rear near a tree line. Tire marks led to the door.

He parked and slowly stepped from the SUV, closing the door ever so gently. Earlier he had found an old white T-shirt in a drawer with Virginia Beach Campground displayed in bold green letters across the chest. He figured he'd use it as a decoy device if needed. It was a size too small, hugging his body like a wet suit. He wore jeans and three-quarter boots. A hound dog and a rifle would have finished off the outfit but he didn't know any hound dogs nor own a rifle.

Before inching forward he wheeled a three-sixty, not spotting anyone or anything. It seemed to be all clear until a squirrel scooted out of the woods and made his ass pucker. He sucked in a breath and edged close enough to stand on his tiptoes and peek through a window. The first thing he spotted was the dress Cassie had worn Saturday night. It was hanging on a rack. His eyes didn't tell him that a guy lived here or, for that matter, anyone other than Cassie. He did a double take when he spotted an open canvas bag sitting beside a table in the far left corner full of bills, lots of bills. Damn, he thought, she cleaned up in the last race yesterday. He glanced around again before trying the door but it was locked. Breaking and entering wasn't part of the plan. He took another look through the window and noticed nothing unusual.

Just as he opened the door to the SUV a voice hollered at him and, in no uncertain terms, told him to stop right where he was. He turned his head over his right shoulder and spotted a brawny guy, about six seven, toting a shotgun, pointed right at his head. He was about twenty-five yards away at the edge of the woods. Mario raised his hands as he turned. His whole body was shaking.

"What the hell you doing man? This is private property."

Mario fumbled, searching for words of salvation. "I'm lost," he said. "I'm trying to locate Simpson's Campground. I thought it was down this road." Decoy time had arrived. He squared up to the guy so that his T-shirt was in full view.

"You see any tents?"

Mario glanced around. "No."

"You see any people?"

"Just you."

"You damn right, just me."

Mario stuttered, "I, uh . . . I saw this RV, thought it might be an office or something."

Six seven caught a glance at the dealer tags. "Thought you said you were looking for a campground. Shit, that there car is from a dealer down the street."

"Actually, I'm looking for a person staying at a campground. Someone I met when me and the wife camped at Virginia Beach."

"Yeah, what's his name?"

Mario took a shot. "Crawford."

"Well, you can bet your sweet ass he ain't here. Don't know no Crawford."

Mario pointed at the weapon. "Could you please lower that shotgun."

"What? You scared?"

"As a matter of fact I am." At this point, Mario wasn't sure if the wetness along his thighs was just sweat.

The guy smiled. "You ought to be, sneaking up on somebody's private property, peeking in windows. Could have shot your ass as soon as I saw you, which was when you drove in right after she left."

Mario jumped all over that statement. "Who is she?"

"The lady renting this land, one that lives in that there trailer. She showed up a couple of months ago, from Florida. Keeps to herself. Pays with cash. I like cash."

"Yeah, me too."

"You got any?"

Mario swallowed the question before answering, "Not much."

"How much would *not much* be?"

"Fifty bucks and change."

"Might buy me some groceries."

Shit, thought Mario, might buy a horseplayer some freedom. He reached into his jeans and pulled out two twenties, a ten and a handful of dimes and stuck his hand forward. "Here, I shouldn't have been on your property. I'm sorry. Take what I have. Consider it an entrance fee."

The guy walked up to him, shotgun dangling to the side. He shot a wad of tobacco juice between his feet. "More like an exit fee." He grabbed the money and stuck it in his pocket. "Get your slimy ass out of here and don't ever come back unless you want a butt full of lead."

Mario didn't hesitate. He traveled faster than a speeding bullet to the main road, whipped a left and sped off toward Laurel. It started raining like hell. The drops hitting the window were almost as big as the ones popping out on his forehead.

He took a few minutes to shower, refresh his body and his mind before returning the SUV.

"So, how'd you like this baby?" said Super Slick.

"Didn't. It just isn't my cup of tea. I tell you what. I think I'll come back tomorrow and maybe drive one of those Corvettes, a red one. Think you could arrange that?"

"Not a problem. I'll have it ready for you." The salesman could see the commission reaching epic proportions now.

Mario drove the pony home, grabbed a cold Bud, swallowed all twelve ounces in one gulp then collapsed on the sofa. A thousand thoughts played havoc with his mind. He would not visit the Chevy dealer again but, as required for a test drive, the salesman had copied his driver's license. Oh, man, here come the phone calls.

As an investigator, he was a total failure. His ass could be occupying a metal table right now, shot for trespassing. The only thing at the end of the dirt road was her recreational vehicle. Guy said she came up from Florida. So what? Lots of people follow the horses from track to track. But the guy had said he'd never heard of a Crawford. What was with that? Maybe she didn't tell him her name. Maybe it didn't matter to the guy, cash being cash.

What really pissed him off was missing a day at the track and not seeing her up close and personal.

He closed his eyes and took a nap.

14

Rollins paced the floor in front of the map as he listened to Valdez on the speakerphone.

"We got hair fibers, from a damn wig."

"That's it? Nothing else?" said Rollins loudly from twenty feet away.

"That's it, must have worn gloves."

"Didn't see any on tape."

Valdez spoke again but Rollins couldn't hear over the barrage of sirens filling the air from the street. He flopped in his chair and picked up the receiver. "I'm sorry. Didn't catch what you said."

"I said you'd think we'd pick up something useful."

"Nothing from clothes or shoes?"

"Found a small piece of clear plastic, that's it."

"Yeah."

"Probably laid one of those clear sheets over the seats."

"Couple of thorough guys."

"Looks that way."

"We do have an eyewitness who saw them get in the car."

"Anything useful?"

"Only that they were laughing as they sped away."

"They're not going to be laughing when we throw the cuffs on."

"How are you coming on the others?"

"I got a hunch."

"Want to tell me about it?"

"Not yet, I'm still trying to form it into something solid."

15

Cassie eased up beside Mario at the paddock fence and said, "Where have you been for the past two days?" Her hand grazed his bicep, sending an instant message to his heart.

"Had to take care of some personal business for Geno."

"Uh, huh. Which one?"

"The oldest."

"You betting today?"

He cocked his head toward the seven. "I like him, but not to win."

"Good show bet?"

"I think so."

"Me, too. I've already placed mine."

He shot her a questioning glance. "Twelve minutes to go and you've already placed your bet?"

"Surprised, aren't you?"

"A little."

"Thought you had my betting patterns down pat, did you?"

He slipped out a sly smile. "How many windows?"

"One."

Startled, he said, "One?"

She nudged him. "Didn't want to make you follow me from window to window."

Again, he smiled.

She stared in his eyes and said, "Or, anywhere else."

Uh,oh.

"If you wanted to know where I lived, all you had to do was ask. I told Joe to go ahead and shoot you the next time you showed up without me." She grinned. "Where did you get the SUV? I thought you bought a sports car?"

He didn't know what to say so he didn't say anything. He just stood there like a mannequin, displaying his style . . . showing off his white polo shirt, blue khakis and deck shoes.

She added, "I have a security camera. You're now a movie star. You want to see the tape?"

By this time the horses were on the track, leaving them stranded in a pool of distrust.

Mario didn't take his eyes off his shoes. She nudged him and said, "Let's you and I go watch this race and I'll give you a chance to explain." She walked away waving her finger forward over her shoulder, directing him to follow.

He tagged along, searching for something clever to say. She flaunted her stuff and teased him a little. Damn mystery woman had him mesmerized. Looked like Meg Ryan and had an ass like Catherine Zeta-Jones. Nice combination.

When they reached the fence, her peripheral vision caught glimpse of him searching for some answers in zombie land. Despite the stone face, she couldn't mask a smile.

The seven finished second, got beat four lengths by the two and paid $2.80 to show. Finished well but wasn't good enough to catch the winner.

She cocked her head toward the grandstand. "You want to go with me to the window. I bet two hundred and won eighty. I might be nice and use the funds to buy you dinner if the invitation to ride in your new car still stands."

He walked along beside her. "You're not pissed at me?"

"Oh, I'm pissed, but not so much that I don't want to listen to some Tommy Dorsey records."

That got his juices flowing. *He'd take her to his place, play some Dorsey, let Sinatra pave the way and who knows, maybe he'd get lucky.* "Tonight?"

"Of course."

"Do I pick you up at the 7-Eleven or at your place?"

"Your choice."

He made a quick decision. "7-Eleven."

She shook her head. "Scared the crap out of you, didn't he?"

He nodded, checked out the top of his shoes again.

"Tell you what. Just meet me at Buddy's. I'll treat you to some soft-shells."

"Across from the mall?"

"Only Buddy's I know."

"What time?"

"Seven-thirty."

"Thought you wanted to ride in my new car."

"I will." At the window, one window only, he edged to the side as she cashed her ticket. She folded the two hundreds and four twenties neatly and stuck them into a pocket.

"Didn't bet, huh?"

"Didn't have time, got waylaid."

"You wish." She allowed the words to linger before she turned and walked toward the exit.

He observed her caboose again for a few strides before hollering, "Hey, where you going?"

She never looked back but answered, "Got a hot date tonight."

Now, he was really distracted.

He went home.

16

"Hey dumb-shit, you're still not sure about her name. You
don't know where she's from. You don't know what she
does before three during the week. You don't know if she's
married, been married. You don't know if she's just out of
prison or headed that way. You don't know why she's not
interested in getting involved. Bottom line is that you don't
know crap. So, tuck your pecker in tight and cool down
the excitement about tonight. And, while you're at it, clean
the damn place up a little. Take out the garbage. Lower
the toilet seat. Change the sheets, for Christ's sake."

Mario was confused. He could see it in his eyes, the
mirror talking back to him, making suggestions. Damn.
Having a live-in for ten years hadn't prepared him for
someone like Cassie. He was wrapped up like a Christmas
present and tied with a bow. What the hell was wrong
with his brain? He was now on his sixth change of clothes
for tonight's date. He stood in front of the full length
mirror in his bedroom and stared at black dress slacks
made out of that new material that felt like silk but was
priced like cotton. He was fumbling with the buttons on

his sport shirt. It had been a long time since he'd worn anything but a three-button pullover. Finally, he found all the button holes and tucked the shirt into his trousers. He loved the design, a repeated pattern of fish, already filleted, nothing but head and bones showing, cream on a medium blue background. He chuckled thinking the shirt was more of an after dinner design and here he was wearing it to dinner. He had pulled on a pair of socks, too. How about that? And then there was the big prize, his black tassel loafers. The old standbys had been hiding under the bed for months.

Impressive? Yep.

The boy was ready, he thought.

On the drive over to Buddy's he opened the sunroof and soaked up the pleasant early evening seventy-two degree weather. There was no sun to be found, only clouds that would open up and water the grass later. The humidity hadn't made a dent yet but he could already smell the rain. He located big band music on satellite, locked it in and cruised.

He arrived two minutes before the designated time. Her car was not in the lot. The place was crowded. Folks were huddled outside waiting to be called. Mario slipped inside turned on some charm and gave his name to the hostess for a table for two. He stepped outside and joined the rest of the crowd. Slowly names were called and the crowd began to dwindle. He checked his watch and it was seven-thirty. Five minutes later he was pacing.

At seven-fifty, she still hadn't arrived. He had read all the reviews displayed on the wall, talked with a couple of guys he knew from the track and watched a little-bitty one hundred and three pound jockey order two pounds of crab legs to go.

At eight, he saw her car pull into the lot.

She apologized profusely and told him she'd make it up to him. *Whatever that meant.* He hadn't heard much of what she said. His eyes were too busy going bonkers over how she looked. She was dressed in pink pants and a pink sequined top that looked like a jacket to be worn over something else but she wasn't wearing anything else. Buttoned high at the neck, only three buttons held it together from there, allowing her abs to be in full view below. She wore pink open-toe shoes with heels that brought her up to five-eleven or so. He still had her by a few inches but his eyes didn't have to drift far to capture hers.

He heard the whispers as they were shown to their table. *Meg Ryan was in the house.* Guys gawked. Mario gave it his best *yeah and I got her* strut.

She patted him on the rear just as he was about to sit down. He cracked a grin. She winked.

Buddy's was buzzing with activity, voices echoing off the pine walls. Platters of steamed crabs were flying by, held high by waitresses. *All you can eat for $24.95.* Big, thick, fresh Chesapeake Bay crabs. The aroma of Old Bay Seasoning ran up their nostrils providing hot flashes. They exchanged glances. Both shook their heads. They were sticking with the soft-shells. Crabs shed during the full moon and there was a big round face hanging in the air tonight, hiding behind clouds.

Their waitress appeared and immediately flashed her big blues at Mario while asking the drink question. Cassie answered, "Susie, bring us a carafe of white and two glasses." Cassie knew her name because Susie had written it in huge letters on the brown paper that covered the table. Cassie hadn't asked for a wine list. It was a crab house. Red or white was it. But if you wanted beer, that was another story. The selection was longer than a surfcasting rod.

When Susie returned she ignored Mario, which was okay with him because Susie wasn't but so cute. He wasn't sure what he was having for sure until he listened to Cassie order. A dozen steamed oysters for starters. She glanced at him as she spoke, catching the gleam in his eye. Susie scribbled on her pad. Cassie then ordered soft-shell crabs with pecan relish. *That sounded real good, sweet, too.* Side of corn pudding. *Never tried it.* House salad with oil and vinegar and an order of hush puppies. She asked if they had sweet tea. Susie said sure, once you add sugar or Equal.

Just as Susie hustled off, Cassie said, "I spent a lot of time in South Carolina."

Well, thought Mario, some information. "You like shrimp and grits?"

"Love it."

"Next time I'll take you to a place over in Annapolis that has great shrimp and grits, place called The Low Country Café."

"Who said anything about a next time?" Somehow her right foot had escaped from her shoe and her toes were creeping up his leg.

113

Mixed message, what's a guy to do?

"Oh yeah, I forgot. You can't get involved."

She said, "That's right. I can't get involved, but that doesn't mean we can't have some fun." Her big toe had reached his thigh.

Susie showed up and laid a platter of big succulent oysters in the center of the table. Juices were escaping from the shells. Mario didn't hesitate. He picked up a shell, threw his head back and engulfed one of those babies. Cassie used a baby fork for hers, dipped it in clarified butter before Mario saw it slip down her throat.

They laughed and repeated the ritual five times. Good thing Susie had furnished extra napkins.

Cassie's eyes met Mario's. She looked away, brought them back. "I can't."

"What?" He didn't have a clue where she was going.

"I can't get involved." Problem was she was falling all over herself for Mario and she knew he knew it. "I just can't."

"You keep saying that."

"You don't understand. I can't take a lot of steps. It just wouldn't work."

Susie was back, this time with salads. She introduced a pepper mill that approached the length of a baseball bat. Mario told her to grind away. Cassie gave her the no thanks motion with her hand.

"Why do you have to be so damn charming?" she said.

Mario used both hands to point at his chest. "Me? Charming?"

"Yeah, like you don't know it."

He smiled, bit on a cucumber slice. *She's coming around.*

Both piddled with their salads. It was a typical house salad: iceberg lettuce, slice of cucumber, sliver of onion . . . nothing to get excited about. Seafood was the attraction at Buddy's.

Mario spotted Susie heading for the table. He could smell the pecans.

Three small soft-shells, sizzling and drenched in pecan relish, decorated each plate. Susie placed separate bowls of corn pudding to the side, set a basket of hush puppies in the middle of the table then asked if she could get them anything else. Susie stood there for a moment watching two adults attack soft shells as though it would be their last meal before execution. Finally, Cassie cut her eyes in Susie's direction and shook her head.

Minutes later, when Cassie lowered her napkin to the table, she said, "Brings back old memories. I once had a shedder. I sold soft shells to local seafood markets and picked up some spending money."

"So, you grew up near salt water?"

"When my dad played at Myrtle Beach and Charleston he rented a small place for a couple of months near Georgetown. The shedder came with the house."

"You really miss him, huh?"

"Yeah, you and I are two of a kind." She placed her hand on his. "Do you really have all of Tommy Dorsey's records, or was that a pick-up line?"

"Only one way to find out."

Cassie wiped her mouth with her napkin, caught Susie's attention and scribbled in the air. The action confused the hell out of Susie but she showed up anyway with check in hand.

Mario tried to pay but Cassie insisted. It was her treat.

Good thing Mario had two quarters handy. He quickly deposited them in a green metal box hovering just outside Buddy's, grabbed the last *Washington Post* and handed Cassie a section. They both sprinted toward his car, newspaper sections held high soaking up the raindrops.

They sat. Only the pitter-patter of rain broke the silence. She smiled, ran the back of her hand along his face and wiped away a drop that trickled down his cheek. He returned her smile, took her hand and kissed it like she was royalty or something, sending her a message that the evening had just begun, time to move on.

With the turn of the key, Count Basie changed the mood jumping right in their ears, filling the car with horns and drums and Basie's trademark one-note piano. They both laughed. Mario moved his thumb about an inch on the steering wheel and reduced the volume.

"Satellite?"

"Yep, I love it."

"Did you tune it to big band music just for me?"

"Yeah, I went out of my way. It took at least ten seconds," Mario said with a grin.

"So, how would I find some rock and roll, maybe a little Rod Stewart?"

Mario pointed to the scan button, told her to give it a try. She did, didn't find Rod but did find Elton and a song about Philadelphia that made both of them sway.

Mario said, in his best Robert Klein imitation, "I can't stop my leg."

"And I can't stop my booty."

Mario caught a glimpse of her movements as he backed out the car.

They were having fun, enjoying each other's company, way beyond her intentions.

Mario pulled forward and stopped behind her car. "What about the bug?"

He took notice of the local dealer sticker on the rear. She must have purchased it after driving the RV up from Florida.

"It's not going anywhere. The grocery store next to Buddy's stays open all night."

She pointed to the navigation screen. "You need this to find your way home?"

"Only when I've had too much to drink."

Cassie kept her finger busy with the satellite sounds. She found R&B, classical, show tunes, country, opera, hip-hop, oldies but goodies, jazz, alternative and a host of other musical forms before Mario turned into the lot of a small church and parked in one of the hundred or so parking spaces marked off by white lines.

Her eyes followed the steeple to its peak before taking in the stained glass windows on the white frame building before shooting him a stare as if to question his religious beliefs.

"I live here." He shrugged and eased out a smile.

"You're a minister?"

His smile became a chuckle. "Never set foot in this church until I bought it."

"You bought a church? How does that happen?"

He pointed to a Methodist church two blocks down the road, across the street. "They moved. Needed a bigger sanctuary."

"And you just made an offer and bought it?"

"Yeah, but I spent a lot more than the purchase price remodeling it."

She glanced to the side, then at the street. "I don't see the Pinto. You hide it somewhere?"

"It's parked out back."

When he ushered her inside to the vestibule, she leaned back and looked straight up at the bell. Mario had eliminated the walls and stairs, creating an open view of thirty feet.

"That's kind of neat."

"Yeah, I ring the bell whenever I get lucky. Let the neighbors know."

She planted an elbow in his side. "And how often would that be?"

"Haven't rung it yet."

"Uh, huh. And how long have you lived here?"

"Two months."

"After you," said Mario, as he opened one of the two arched doors leading into what before had been a roomful of pews. Mario had stripped the doors of their white paint, replacing the finish with a light stain that allowed the richness of the wood to shine through. A sensor turned on the lights.

Her mouth opened, but she didn't speak.

She slowly roamed the room, fascinated by the transition, eyes darting, hands exploring. The four stained glass windows on each side were now abstract designs, rich with color, graphically expressive. Cone-shaped brushed aluminum lighting fixtures hung from the ceiling casting brightness onto a kitchen equipped like a gourmet restaurant. In the center stood an island complete with a large wood block and double sink. Four wooden stools were snuggled under a counter that hung off the backside. Pots and pans dangled from cast iron rods above. On top of glass front cabinets, wooden boxes were displayed advertising products that no longer existed but were much desired by those appreciative of quality.

Mario watched her absorb the room not knowing what she was thinking.

She sunk into the wraparound palomino leather sofa, looked at Mario, shook her head, smiled then motioned for him to step forward and join her. He sunk in beside her. She discarded her shoes, tucked her legs to the side and got comfortable, easing closer to him.

"You do this yourself or did you hire a designer?"

"Just me and a big day at the track."

"So, where's Tommy?"

Mario reached to the coffee table that really wasn't a coffee table but a converted ammunition chest he had found in Gettysburg at an antique shop. He grabbed a remote, pushed a button and the orchestra filled the room with "East of the Sun." He used the remote to point to a stack of LP's hovering over a turntable sitting on top of a cabinet that contained a JVC amplifier, CD player, cassette player, and what she estimated to be a couple thousand LPs and about five hundred CDs. The man liked his music.

He stood then retrieved two armfuls of record jackets, all Tommy Dorsey.

She viewed each and set seven aside next to her. "I don't have these."

He had to ask.

Pointing to a list of musicians on a cover, he said, "I went through all of these and couldn't find your dad's name anywhere."

She didn't hesitate. Immediately, she stuck her finger on top of the name of a sax player. "That's him, Charlie Lewis."

"I was looking for a Crawford."

She squirmed, glanced away before commenting. "Lewis is a stage name. It was a popular thing back in the thirties and forties. Marilyn Monroe wasn't Marilyn Monroe. Everyone did it."

"Tommy Dorsey wasn't Tommy Dorsey?"

"Well, most everyone." She stood and scanned the room. "Does your church have a bathroom?"

He nodded toward where the pulpit had previously stood. "Up the three steps, door on the right."

At the top of the steps she turned and played preacher, speaking to a congregation of one. Mario waved. She told him not to break into a chorus of "Amazing Grace" while she visited the restroom.

She really didn't have to use the bathroom. She needed a break in the action to gather her thoughts. She blew out a breath as she glanced in the mirror. Yep, she was the spitting image of Meg Ryan, and damn proud of it.

When she opened the door, Mario awaited with a glass of white wine in each hand. He handed her one. She thanked him and swirled the wine in her glass before tasting it.

"I want to show you something," he said, his head motioning for her to follow. Off to the right of the bathroom was another door. He opened it and led her in. The room had no furniture and no windows. Three walls were filled with charts, the other with books from floor to ceiling encased in a spectacular built-in bookcase.

She was drawn first to the charts. She moved from one to the other engulfing the details. Before her were facts on workouts, horses claimed, probable opponents, trainer tendencies, times and distances, jockey statistics, dosage figures, track conditions by date, track bias, speed ratings, trouble in races, horses shipping in, dirt to grass, grass to dirt, off tracks, turf conditions, sire rankings. She didn't say a word before turning her attention to the books, a library of every conceivable handicapping tool ever published. Wall was at least twenty feet long, full of manuals, magazines, sale catalogs and books written about and by prominent names in the thoroughbred industry.

"Impressive," she said. "Very impressive."

"I call it my war room."

She pointed to the charts. "How often do you update?"

"Daily."

She shook her head in astonishment. "Wow! You could promote this and charge admission." She made another round of the info, storing mental notes as she viewed the details.

"Tomorrow, Cannonball will win the feature," said Mario, filling her in.

"I see your check mark. What's this about the speedball shipping in?"

"Cannonball will benefit. Bet him."

She turned, eased up close, now shorter with the shoes off. "I will. You have anything else you want to show me?" She looked up into his eyes, toying with him again.

He couldn't rationalize how to answer her question, what to say. His sexual glands were conflicting with his brain causing a guttural mumble as he walked toward the steps. She followed him, knowing she shouldn't and couldn't get involved. But here he was and here she was. She didn't want to hurt him. She liked him way too much.

He turned and took her hand to help her down the steps, she thought. But she was wrong.

"You want to dance, take a spin and see where Charlie Lewis and Frank Sinatra lead us?"

She answered with a little curtsy before gently placing her left arm around his neck. "Embraceable You" brought their bodies together.

She hummed the words in his ear and kissed his neck as they glided around the room, feeling the words to the music. He ran his hand down her back and edged her closer. She could feel him throbbing. She was wet but it wasn't perspiration.

The song ended and another started. They kept on dancing, right up the steps, down the hall into his bedroom. Lights did not come on automatically. It was dark except for a trace of light beaming from a skylight above the king-sized bed. Raindrops tapped the tin roof, music now in the distance. He undid the three buttons. She gave him a gentle push onto the bed. Slowly they continued to undress each other. She shut her eyes, laid back and allowed him to explore her body from boobs to ankles. It was a delicate journey that caused her shivers but also concern. When his kisses headed north from her breasts, she quickly rolled him over and did some exploring of her own. An hour later, while on her back thinking about what had just happened she listened to the comforting sounds of raindrops as tiny tears slipped down her cheeks.

The question of why or how people fall in love is one that most can't answer. You'll know it when it happens is the standard response, passed along by moms and dads and grandparents. In reality, no one knows. But a heart sends a message until the brain gives in. The words eventually come out, but not tonight, not from Cassie or Mario.

They lingered for another half hour, deep in thought about each other.

Mario slipped out of bed first. Cassie asked where he was going.

"To ring the bell."

"You're not."

"How about some scrambled eggs?"

"I think you just scrambled all the eggs you need to scramble for the night."

Yeah, thought Mario, scrambled my damn brain, too. Now he knew where no man's land was, and he wasn't sure it was a comfortable spot.

17

The warm waters off the Virginia coast swarm with tuna, dolphin, wahoo, king mackerel, and white marlin. The right bait trolled at the right speed in the right spot can assure a fierce battle between man and fish.

Nineteen years ago William Rollins, Hector Valdez, Vince Hopkins, Dave Norris, Paul Spencer and Joe McKnight became close friends while attending the FBI school of hard knocks at Quantico. They rekindled that friendship annually aboard the Four Corners, a forty-eight foot fishing machine captained by Fred Shockey. Captain Fred, as they called him, always found fish. For his efforts he expected no snarled lines, total focus on the task at hand and for the guy with the rod in his hand to be tightly belted into the fighting chair. If either of the six lost a fish by any means, good old Captain Fred would raise enough hell to make the other five wonder why they always booked him. Imagine paying a guy twelve hundred dollars to yell at your ass all day long and harass the living shit out of you. They loved fishing with Captain Fred, the grumpiest charter captain docked at Rudee Inlet in Virginia Beach . . . and, the best.

Each year one of the six was responsible for planning the trip. This year, the honor fell to Rollins who was intent on making this the best trip ever. The guys were friends, but everything was a competition. They bet on first fish, biggest fish, most fish and who got yelled at the least by Captain Fred.

As usual, they would arrive in the afternoon on Friday, fish on Saturday and head home on Sunday.

Early Friday morning Valdez arrived at Rollins' house in Alexandria, parked his car, loaded his bags into Rollins' new six-passenger Dodge van and they were quickly on their way south to Norfolk International Airport where they would hook up with their fishing partners. Hopkins would be arriving from San Diego, Norris from Boston, Spencer from Chicago, and McKnight from Newark.

Hopkins flight was late but by three-thirty they were all piled into the van and immediately engaged in conversation only guys could appreciate. They headed for the oceanfront at Virginia Beach. Just before they reached 16th Street on Atlantic Avenue, Rollins said, "I think you guys are going to like this place." He pointed to the Boardwalk Resort Hotel as the van approached the parking deck.

"We'd better like it or you're fish bait," commented McKnight who was the oldest of the group and true to the image of people from Jersey, in both attitude and accent.

"So you sought out the highest rates on the beach, I see," said Spencer who was watchdog of finances, a tightwad if there ever was one.

Norris didn't say anything, just nodded knowing that when William was responsible, the accommodations would be better than nice and his restaurant selections would be unusual.

"We're eating early, right?" said Hopkins whose stomach occupied a different time zone.

"Got a five-thirty reservation just for you, Vince."

No way would William be fish bait.

In February he and Kaylan had snuck away for a long weekend and stayed in a suite at the Boardwalk where they slipped into the in-room Jacuzzi, fiddled with the jets...and each other. The trip made his wife happy even though she recognized that William was playing advance man for the fishing trip. Together, they tested the she crab soup at Timbuktu and the oysters at Rudee's. They sampled seafood at several other spots near the boardwalk but it was the excursion south of the beach that uncovered the hidden gem.

After edging his way between suitcases and bags on the elevator, William pushed the button for the top floor as he spoke to his buddies. "Here's the deal. I got us two adjoining three-bedroom suites. One of the bedrooms in each has a balcony overlooking the ocean. You guys can fight over it, flip, whatever. Dave, Vince and Paul are in one unit. He nodded at Hector and Joe. "We got the other."

It didn't take but one quick look around for the accommodations to be declared the best in nineteen years. Even Joe patted William on the back. Must have been the giant television screen or the fact he had won the flip for the oceanfront room.

William reached into a large travel bag and tossed a navy blue polo shirt to each of the guys. "Wear these tonight. I have T-shirts for tomorrow."

"So, according to the logo on these shirts we are the FBI Fishing Team?" said Dave.

"Nope," William said. "We are members of the Fishing Buddies International Fishing Team, in case anybody asks."

"Who's going to have the balls to ask?" Hopkins said.

"Captain Fred," Valdez said.

They all laughed knowing that Captain Fred not only had the balls to ask but he just might kick everyone's ass for the hell of it, pending his mood.

"I got a shirt for him and the mate, too," William added.

An hour later the team left for dinner.

William hopped one block over to Pacific and headed south across Rudee Inlet Bridge and onto General Booth Boulevard. Just after passing the Virginia Marine Science Museum Spencer spotted the Hooters' sign, figuring they were going to take in the boob show and maybe eat some wings and a bucket of oysters. But William didn't stop.

A mile later, McNight bellowed, "Where the hell are you taking us, to Po-dunk?"

"Pungo."

"Same difference."

"Nope. You'll see."

A few minutes later he turned left onto Indian River Road then took another left onto North Muddy Creek. Blue Pete's Seafood & Steak Restaurant was just ahead, a beautifully restored old fish camp nestled on the waters of Back Bay. The setting was inspiring enough to entice a guy like James Taylor to write a song.

William had reserved a corner table with a water view but first they'd sit out on the deck and sip a beer, start catching up on family and friends while they kept their eyes on the water moccasin dangling from the tree across the creek. Rule was that no bureau business could be discussed until the long ride out to the deep blue water.

Once they were seated inside, William suggested they order six different seafood dishes and pass the plate. Everyone agreed. They feasted on coconut shrimp, Rajun Cajun catfish, crabcakes, broiled scallops, Blackened Mahi-mahi and bouillabaisse. But, despite the goodness of all that fresh seafood, the hit of the night turned out to be the sweet potato biscuits. They wore out six napkins wiping butter off their chins.

As they walked to the van, Hopkins said, "William, you outdid yourself tonight."

"Yeah, asshole, Pungo ain't so bad," admitted Joe.

No one had asked about the shirts.

In fact, no one vocally acknowledged their presence.

18

Light was edging darkness to the west as the sun peeked over the horizon casting long shadows across Pacific Avenue. Inside the van, six FBI agents were armed with bagels, orange juice and coffee. William's watch said four-forty-two. Captain Fred's boat would leave the dock at five.

At ten minutes before five, they unloaded the van and walked in single file up the pier to the Four Corners, docked in the same spot it had occupied for nineteen years. The engines were running and the mate was busy checking the drag on reels, shirtless. He was either showing off his tan or hours in the weight room, or both. His name was Mike Owens and he had helped them reel in a ton of fish on the previous trip. Worked his ass off and expected a big tip.

As soon as Captain Fred spotted the matching red shirts with white letters, he let out a laugh that woke up two sea gulls, sending them flying into space squawking at each other. He hollered from his perch high on the flying bridge. "So, that's how my tax money is being spent, buying frigging T-shirts that won't help you catch a cold, much less a fish."

William tossed Fred a shirt and a smile. "Hey, catch. This one's for you." Fred grabbed it out of the air, changed into it and immediately started bellowing instructions. "Okay, you landlubbers. Put the damn coolers inside the galley and get the hell out of the way so we can go catch some fish."

Mike shook hands with everyone, welcoming them aboard. William handed him a shirt. He said thanks but didn't put it on. He was already sweating.

Fred eased the boat out of the slip and up the channel, crossing under the bridge.

Three guys waved from the rocky bank on the starboard side. One was busy unhooking a flounder that looked to be about three pounds.

As soon as they hit open water Fred yelled, "Everybody on deck so I can see you."

Six FBI agents obeyed his instructions and twelve eyes looked toward the flying bridge awaiting words of wisdom which Fred instantly barked. "The weather report is so good I shouldn't have to tell you this but if any of you assholes decides to get seasick, it better be over the side and not on my boat. You got that?"

Salutes followed. They knew the drill.

Two hundred yards out of the inlet, Mike suggested that everyone hold on. Fred gunned it, the bow rose and the stern sat like a dog on command. A few minutes later, the boat leveled off on its way southeast. Fred hollered at Mike about rods and reels and bait and gaffs. The guys laughed as Mike kept nodding his head and smiling knowing that the captain was just keeping him on his toes.

It would take two to three hours to reach the blue water. William started the conversation. "You guys get my e-mail about next week?"

"Yeah," McKnight said, while rubbing suntan lotion along his arms. "It's going to do lots of damage to our budget."

"I know, but it's got to be done."

"Mondays and Tuesdays only, nine to eleven, right?" Hopkins said.

For the next four weeks, William had instructed all FBI branch offices to provide two armed agents to cover every bank location in every major market across the country. Agents were to be undercover and not on the bank premises but instead, they were to be directly across the street from the front door, ready to pounce and arrest. Or shoot if necessary.

Each of the eighteen unsolved robberies had taken place on a Monday or Tuesday in the morning hours. He felt a connection with each robbery but didn't know what it was.

"I got a theory," Norris said. "I think we have different robbers but the same leadership."

"Like the mob?"

"It ain't the mob," said Spencer. "But I agree with Dave, I think there is a connection."

William glanced around, "Everyone agree with Paul's assessment?"

They all nodded.

William ducked inside the cabin and came out with a laptop. He pulled up facts on each and every robbery. The computer was nestled on his knees when Fred hollered, "Put that piece of shit away and get in the chair. We got birds diving ahead, tearing up the water."

The boat slowed. The guys leaned over the side and peered at the gulls diving, scooping up the remains of baitfish, filling the air with squawks, scrapping over bits and pieces. There were so many closely bunched that the scene resembled a tornado rolling through the plains.

Mike quickly had released two outrigger lines trolling baits about fifty yards off the stern, reels locked, drag set. Like a cat, he grabbed two more rods and spooled a hundred yards of line off each directly behind the transom, the baits skipping across the surface. All eyes were watching lines. The guys had drawn numbers for the fighting chair. If more than one fish hit at a time, forget the numbers. Grab a rod and start reeling.

Just as the boat got within twenty yards of the birds, all hell broke loose. Four strikes simultaneously jolted the rods. The sound of lines singing pierced the air. Valdez and McKnight weren't quick enough to react. The other four had rods in hand and were pumping and winding. Vince, who had drawn number one, was supposed to be in the chair but never made it. It was a battle of man against King Mackerel and the guys were winning. Mike was gaffing and tossing fish directly into the large cooler at the stern, then unhooking them. Fred was growling at everyone, making sure they hooked and caught some fish. Valdez and McKnight got into the action on the next two strikes. They were bringing them in from a standing position, leaning hard against the rail, using muscles that hadn't been engaged since last year's trip. The action was fast and furious.

Two other boats had spotted the birds and were now in the mix, pulling in King Mackerel one after the other.

As suddenly as it started, it stopped. The birds disappeared to who knows where, and the fish sounded. Fred lost them on the fish finder.

All six were covered with perspiration. Exhausted already and they hadn't made it to the stream yet. They collapsed into deck chairs, forearms glistening with sweat. Fred took one look and smiled to himself. He yelled, again, "Hold on." With a quick motion he pushed the throttle forward and the boat surged, getting up to speed in just seconds. He yelled into the air, "Watch out fish, Captain Fred coming at you."

William asked Mike how many they caught. He lifted the top and counted eighteen. The guys hovered by the cooler and took a look. Every fish was the same size.

"Is there a message here?" asked William to the others.

"What do you mean?" McKnight said.

"They're all the same length, eighteen of them. Stand them on their tails and you could draw a straight line."

"And?"

"The bank robbers. Think about it. Everyone looks different, but in every report the robbers are the same height. A guy about six foot at the teller window and a guy five eight or so at the door."

"There are millions of guys six foot or five-eight. Weights and body descriptions have differed in each case. Hell, the guys in Delaware were black, the others represented the world of diversity," said Valdez.

"I hear you, but for some reason these fish are sending us a message."

Fred had come halfway down the ladder seeking a beverage. "Shit. No wonder you can't catch anybody. The damn fish are so stupid they eat artificial lures but you guys are down here carrying on a conversation with them. What the hell did you wimps bring me to drink?"

William answered, "We wimps got your Cokes, bottled water, orange juice, Coors, Bud, iced tea and lemonade. What's your pleasure?"

"Bottled water. Got a slice of lime to go with it?"

"As a matter of fact we do. Even got some sugar and can stir you up a limeade if you want one."

Fred pointed at him. "Yeah, limeade sounds great. Bring it up."

William poured some bottled water into a cup and then added about a ton of sugar before stirring. Wasn't often old Fred invited you to the bridge. He climbed the ladder and stepped onto the deck. Fred grabbed the cup out of his hand and gulped half of it instantly. "Damn, that's good."

"Well, we're off to a good start," William said.

"Yeah, we're going to slay 'em today. I just got word. One boat left at three this morning, got twenty-seven big tuna and twelve dolphin in the cooler already. Good eating, my man. Good eating." He pounded William on the back with the impact of his two hundred pounds. "You guys going to catch those bank robbers anytime soon?"

"God, I hope so. If we don't, it's going to be my ass."

"You'll get 'em." For a second there, he thought Fred was giving him a compliment, not knowing he was about to be asked for a favor. Fred nodded toward the stern. "You know, Mike finished up this year at Old Dominion, majored in criminal justice. I don't know why but he likes you guys and wants to become an agent."

"Is that so? Seems to be a nice kid, and we all know he works hard."

"Best mate I've ever had. I hate to lose him after this summer but it would be great if you could help him out."

"I'll take care of it."

"Thanks William. Thanks a lot."

"Damn, Fred. You're almost being nice."

Fred looked ahead, saw grass lines riding the rolls of the sea. He jabbed his finger forward. "Nice time is over, time to catch some fish."

Grass lines are like restaurants for dolphin. You see grass, you see fish. It was that simple. Toss out a lure and hungry fish would start dining. William hustled below as Fred pulled back on the throttle. Mike had spotted the lines himself and, as efficient as he was, had baits already in the water. Two minutes later, six dolphin were thrashing around on the deck, mahi-mahi to the politically correct. Fred yelled to Mike to go get the light tackle. With the boat now in neutral, Mike handed everyone a spinning rod with fifteen pound test line and told them to start casting. The feeding frenzy lasted for twenty minutes. Norris and

Spencer lost fish right at the boat. Fred went bonkers, told them to go inside if they couldn't land a damn twelve-pound fish. They shot him the bird and cast again, each bringing in a fish. Old Fred smiled like a coach who knew how to motivate.

The action slowed as quickly as it had started. William brought out the eight box lunches prepared by the hotel. He tossed one up to Fred. Fred said thanks then told Mike to put away the spinning gear and get the big rods ready again.

Everyone stuffed their faces with roasted chicken sandwiches, potato salad, dill pickles and a slice of carrot cake.

William sat down on the stern beside Mike and talked with him about becoming an FBI agent. Mike listened and said he'd do whatever it took. William asked him a lot of questions about his background, his family and his political beliefs then told him he'd be in touch.

An hour later they were trolling at a high rate of speed picking up tuna in the thirty to forty pound range. The first time they had ever gone out with Fred they couldn't believe how fast they trolled but that was how you caught tuna. Tuna were swift and strong. One fish could wear your ass out and make your shoulders ache for a week. They caught fourteen before heading back to land.

The wind had shifted to the north bringing on six-foot swells and a longing for solid ground. It took three and a half hours of fighting the waves before they hit Rudee Inlet. They waved to bystanders and showed off their catch.

As usual, Captain Fred had done his job.

William handed Mike a generous tip of two hundred dollars. Before Mike wheeled the fish to the cleaning station, he hung them up for the annual picture. The FBI Fishing Team smiled. All eight of them.

19

Ten thousand dollars and change occupies a lot of space.

Mario had dumped his winnings onto his bed. The hundreds, tens, twenties and fifties resembled a patchwork quilt. He thought about taking a power nap, pull the quilt over his body . . . and re-live the outcome of the eighth race. Instead, he smiled, picked up a hundred dollar bill and planted a kiss right on Ben Franklin's lips.

Cannonball had rolled by Shooting Star at the sixteenth pole and won going away by two lengths.

He had promised Buster and his wife some sauce if the horse won. The invite also included Buster's daughter and her family. Having added five thousand to her bankroll, Cassie had also agreed to join the celebration. Little Geno had also cashed a ticket, adding three one hundred dollar bills to his college fund but he was passing on the sauce in order to watch a movie on TV, something about a dog named Scooby.

It was time to celebrate. They were all meeting at Geno's except for Cassie. She was riding with him. He was ready to leave but she hadn't arrived at his place. The thought that she wouldn't show up entered his mind but was quickly squelched when he heard the call to the post on trumpet. He didn't possess an ordinary door bell. He hurried to the door, opened it and waved Cassie in and said, "Damn. You sure do clean up nice."

She stuck a finger in his gut. "You don't look so bad yourself, lover boy."

Mario mustered a grin, thinking the nickname was appropriate considering the pre-dawn roll in the hay they had shared. Afterwards, he had driven her to her car. She then followed him to the track and both, along with Buster, had watched Cannonball gallop through darkness in preparation for his afternoon conquest.

The day had been pretty special. He got laid by Meg Ryan. *Well, she looked like Meg Ryan.* Cannonball won the race resulting in his new bedspread. He got to spend another fun afternoon at the track with the eight-year-old. And dinner at his favorite restaurant was still in front of him and possibly, just possibly, the day would end as it had started.

But he was wrong.

After a terrific dinner that all enjoyed, Cassie applied the finish to the day. She thanked him for the meal and the tip on the horse, kissed him good-bye in his car, smiled, reminded him that she couldn't get involved, got out, slipped into the VW, shot him a quick wave and drove out the lot, leaving him sitting in his car scratching his head, seeing if he could cure his love itch.

Yep, the kind of day that added up, but never totaled.

20

At five, Mario was trackside, watching horses work and trainers prep. The sun was creeping up, casting long shadows toward the west. Buster was going on and on about yesterday's race, still celebrating. His excitement made Mario give serious thought to becoming an owner. He ran it by Buster. They talked about going partners and slipping over to the Fasig-Tipton Select Sale at the Timonium Pavilion to check out the offerings.

Mario held up his mug of Buster's coffee and stared at the picture of Affirmed. "I guess old Cannonball is your Affirmed, huh?"

"And my Seabiscuit."

"Seen the movie?"

"Took the family. Brought tears to my eyes. Your uncle and nephew would love it. So will you. They got it on DVD now."

Mario nodded, "That's a great idea. I'm going to go buy it and head for Baltimore this afternoon."

"And miss the races?" Buster said, surprised by Mario's response.

"Yeah, and miss the races."

And miss seeing Cassie, which he thought wasn't such a bad idea. Get her out of his mind for a few hours. Clear his head.

Two hours later, Buster and Mario headed for the track kitchen where Buster became the center of attraction as super owner of the week. Buster was all smiles. He bought breakfast for agents, jockeys, trainers and a couple of other owners.

Mario picked up a hot tip on a horse in the fifth on today's card. He ignored the tip, as always. Didn't matter anyway, he was going to watch a movie.

At one-thirty, he picked up Little Geno at his house. At two, he bought the DVD at Best Buy. At three-thirty, he and Little Geno walked into Geno's Parlor and five minutes later Mario inserted the disc into the DVD he had given Geno for Christmas. Geno touched Mario's arm and said, "I was there."

"You were where?" Mario said.

"At Pimlico, for the match race."

"You never told me that."

"Hell of a race."

Mario leaned over and whispered to Geno, "Don't tell Little Geno who won."

The beginning was a little slow for the kid but nostalgic for Geno and educational for Mario. It covered the depression years, leading up to the purchase of Seabiscuit. For the next two hours, a story of human spirit and a courageous horse evolved.

When the movie ended, Geno made a request. "Can we watch it again?"

Mario patted him on the shoulder then asked the little guy if he wanted to see it again, making sure he could handle another couple of hours. Little Geno was all for it.

After the second viewing, Little Geno asked some pretty serious questions. Soup lines, the depression, and the stock market had captured the little one's mind.

Sometimes a movie can teach a kid more than a textbook.

21

On Monday, Mario was back in Baltimore, his face-to-face conversation with Geno leaning more toward Seabiscuit than upcoming races or the woman he thought *maybe* was in his life.

Tuesday was another story altogether. At sunrise, Buster informed him that Cassie had not shown up for the races on Sunday and that his trackside buddies had speculated that he and Cassie had taken Saturday's winnings and flown off to some island and were busy making love in a hot tub, between margaritas.

"I told them you were taking in a movie, but they didn't believe me."

"She didn't show, huh?"

"If she was here, none of us saw her."

A stocky bay colt galloped down the stretch catching Mario's eye. He nodded toward the horse, his mind back where it belonged. "Looks like Supersuds is coming back strong. The bowed tendon doesn't seem to be bothering him. He's moving smoothly."

"He might hold up for a few races. You never know with a bow."

"He could win us a nice pot first race back. Let's keep our eye on him each day."

"You want to go over, catch some breakfast?"

"Thanks but no thanks. I want to watch a couple more gallop, then I need to get home, catch up on some laundry and update my charts."

"Are you going to call the little lady?" Buster shot him a wink with the inquiry.

Mario soaked up the question, realizing he didn't even have her phone number. "I'll catch up with her tomorrow."

He congratulated Buster again on the win before departing. As he walked to the pony, Cassie and horses were tangling in his mind battling for prominence. He laughed out loud, wondering if she knew he hadn't shown up. How old was he? Little Geno hated that question. Now he knew why.

Two blocks from his house he spotted the tape.

Police were directing three lanes of traffic into one. The entire Central Maryland National Bank branch office was roped off. At least a hundred guys in dark suits were inside the tape walking side-by-side searching every inch of ground from the road to the rear of the bank property. He noticed a white sheet covering a body on the ground about ten feet outside the front door. At least, he thought it was a body. He wasn't sure.

This was his neighborhood, his bank, just around the corner from his residence. He pulled onto a side street and found a parking spot in front of a vacant lot. While walking toward the bank he ran into the guy who lived two doors down from his house. "Joe, what happened?"

"The bank was held up about an hour ago. The FBI shot one of the robbers as he ran out the front door. Apparently the guy wouldn't halt at the FBI's command. He pulled out a gun and started firing at FBI agents. Two agents fired back and the guy ended up drilled with holes. Word is that there were two guys and the other one got away, ran around the back of the building, disappeared into the woods while the exchange of gunfire took place out front."

Mario cut his eyes toward the woods. Another fifty dark suits had their eyes glued to the ground, looking for some kind of clue. Bloodhounds were sniffing everything. He excused himself for a moment and walked five steps and picked a hundred dollar bill from a bush.

His neighbor pointed at the bill and said, "They're all over the place. You should have been here earlier. Apparently, when the robber caught the bullets, the money went flying. People were picking up bills two blocks from here is what I heard. I didn't get any myself."

"I guess I should turn this in."

"Haven't seen anyone else do it and I've been here since I heard the shots."

"You think these are the same guys who robbed all those banks across the country?"

"Could be."

"Think I'll walk up to the tape, turn in the C-note and see if I can sweet talk an employee, pick up some scuttlebutt."

"I'm heading home. Give me a call if you find out anything."

"Will do."

Mario knew everyone who worked at the bank. He had been a customer since the opening eighteen months ago. Still had the calculator and shirt they gave him when he opened his account. Used the calculator all the time, never had worn the shirt.

He handed over the bill to one of the guys in a dark suit who thanked him with a startled look.

His favorite teller, Shirley, spotted him, waved and hurried toward him coming to an abrupt stop at the tape. Shirley had a little thing for Mario, as did a couple of the other female employees. Shirley told him exactly what had happened, and she knew because she was the one who handed over the money. She couldn't stop wringing her hands as the details flew from her mouth. A tall white guy had walked up to her window and demanded money by handing her a note. Another white guy, who was smaller, stood at the door and pointed a handgun at the head of the security guard. She stuffed a canvas bag with bills. The robber grabbed it out of her hands and darted out the door and sprinted to the right. Suddenly, she heard voices scream at him to stop. She didn't know at the time that the FBI had the bank staked out. The robber pulled a gun and started firing. The FBI fired back. Meanwhile the shorter guy who had been at the door took off in the other direction and disappeared around the corner of the building. Shirley blew out a long breath then batted her eyes at Mario.

"Were you scared?" he said.

"I hate to admit it but I wet my pants as soon as I heard the shots."

Mario cracked a grin. "I bet you weren't the only one."

"I threw the panties in the trash."

He smiled, nodded, and added a wink. "I always thought you were sexy, panties or no panties."

A little color blossomed on her cheeks. "It's not the first time I've had wet pants." Quickly realizing what she had just stated, she covered her mouth with her right hand, released it and then said, "Oh my God, what am I saying? You're a customer. I apologize. I didn't mean it that way."

Mario figured she needed a little stress relief so he toyed with her, playing to her sexual being by tossing her a lifeline. "My place or yours?"

She shifted her body and engaged his eyes before belting out a laugh. Mario joined in. Two suits approached, wanting to know what was so funny.

Mario answered, "Nothing. Just trying to ease the tension."

"You finished?" snarled one of the agents.

Mario nodded.

Shirley was escorted away, helped along with a tug on each arm. She turned her head over her shoulder and said to Mario, "Yours."

He headed for his car and seconds later was at home punching in numbers on his phone to everybody he knew. Then he clicked on the TV, found a comfortable horizontal position on the sofa and watched live coverage from the robbery site for the rest of the day. The robbers entered the bank at twenty after nine. A reporter mentioned that one person had turned in a hundred dollar bill found in a bush. It was the only bill turned in. All bills were marked. Mario wondered if the statement was true.

Lunch had passed him by. At six his head did some thumping, notifying him that food was needed. He called in a pizza order, one with pepperoni and another with sausage, peppers and anchovies. He was a big boy. He could handle two.

Mesmerized by the robbery of *his* bank, he gulped down both pizzas and two Coors while continuing to watch the coverage from the comfort of his sofa. Switching from channel to channel, he had seen the same tape about a hundred times.

At nine he drifted off into dreamland. Both cans were horizontal on the floor, the pizza boxes were straddling the table and a couple pieces of pepperoni were fighting him for space on the cushions.

The chirp of his cell startled him. He jumped up, and for an instant didn't know where he was. After shaking the cobwebs out, he checked his watch. Ten after eleven. Who in the hell?

Still a little grumpy, he leaned over and grabbed the cell off the coffee table and answered. "Hello."

"Mario. It's me, Cassie. You sound like I woke you up."

"You did. And you sound like you're in a windstorm."

"It's not the wind. I'm on my cell sitting out on a deck listening to the waves hit the beach. It's pretty rough tonight. That's what you hear."

"Beach? What beach?"

"I'm on the Outer Banks, down in North Carolina. Nags Head area. Have you ever been here?"

Static interrupted the call, sounding like someone cracking walnuts for a Christmas party.

"Can you hear me?" she shouted.

"Barely, but yeah, I've been down that way a couple of times. Went deep sea fishing out of Oregon Inlet."

"I rented a place for a week. Has six bedrooms." She continued with the shouting not realizing the line was now clear. She ducked as a seagull buzzed the deck, the tail of a small fish hanging from its mouth. Another seagull was in chase, determined to get his share of the goody. She ducked again and blurted out, "Damn."

"What'd you say?"

"Nothing. A couple of seagulls are dive-bombing me."

"Well, bring out the big guns and shoot the bastards down."

"They're gone now but I'll try to remember that next time."

Might as well get personal, he thought. She's the one who called. "So what's with the six bedrooms? Are you expecting a lot of guests?"

"No." Silence. "Just you."

"I don't know, Cassie. You don't want to get involved but you're inviting me to your beach house. I don't get it. Help me out here."

"I really want you to come."

Mario sensed tears at the other end and didn't know what the hell to think. His gut started gurgling like a commode that wouldn't flush.

"Let me think about it overnight and I'll call you early tomorrow. Maybe I'll come and, then again, maybe I'll stay and bet the ponies. At least they like involvement."

She allowed the sly comment to pass. "It's a really nice place. We could mess up six beds, two decks, a swimming pool and a hot tub. Besides, you need a tan."

"Yeah, you're right about the tan but look, I'll call you. I promise."

"Please come."

His finger was an inch away from pushing the power button when he reconsidered. "Hey Cassie, did you hear about two robbers hitting my bank this morning?"

"What did you say? I didn't get that."

"My bank was held up. One of the robbers was shot and killed."

"He died?"

"Hell yeah he died, that's what *killed* means. The FBI shot his ass a dozen times, no way he was going to survive."

He heard what sounded like a sigh. "That's horrible."

"You're right. It was my bank, some of my money, the way I look at it."

"I mean about the guy dying. Did he say anything before he died?"

"I doubt it. Twelve bullets will shut your ass up in a heartbeat."

Cassie didn't reply.

"You still there?" he said.

"Please come." She said.

He started to respond but realized she had hung up. Staring at the receiver, looking for answers to a thousand questions, he said, "What the hell is with you, Cassie Crawford? I sure would like to know what's waltzing around in that brain of yours."

He stretched his arms and made a grunting noise loud enough to wake up some horses over at the track. He thought about heading for the bedroom but instead collapsed back onto the sofa.

Two minutes later he was snoring, the phone dangling from his hand a foot from the floor, daring to fall.

22

Rollins got the call from the lab at midnight while playing piano on his desk with both hands. He was still wired from the day's events. He tapped the speakerphone button, wanting Valdez, who was leaning forward from a chair across the desk, to hear what was said. The two of them along with one hundred and fifty-three other FBI agents had spent the day at the Central Maryland National Bank robbery site. Four cups of coffee had added to the adrenalin rush he and Valdez were still experiencing. They were sitting in Rollins' office at the Hoover Building. Their shirt collars were unbuttoned and the knots on their ties hung low enough to compete with the knots in their guts. It had been a long day, and it wasn't over.

From the speakerphone, the lab director's voiced boomed. "His face, his hands, and forearms were covered in latex. I've never seen anything like this make-up job. Guy was a fucking genius."

"Good enough to have been black if he wanted to be?" asked Valdez, sounding like he was speaking from deep in a tunnel.

"Black, Oriental, Hispanic, it wouldn't have mattered. Believe me, this was one talented son-of-a-bitch."

"Is he clean now?"

"Yeah, I'll fax you a photo of the real person as soon as we hang up. I'll send a before shot, too. You're going to shit when you see the difference."

"Have you told anyone else?"

"No."

"Let's keep this under wraps for now. Might give us a little edge and help us identify the other guy."

"Not a problem."

"Thanks for your help."

After hanging up, Rollins stood, turned and stared out the window into darkness, as thunder rumbled off to the west. "Answers a lot of questions," he said as he glanced at Valdez.

Valdez shrugged. "Think we can tie the two into the other robberies."

"No doubt in my mind that they committed the other robberies."

"I agree but proving it is going to be huge, if what our guts are telling us is actually true."

The methodical sound of Rollins' fax machine interrupted their conversation. Both hurried over, stood like early-risers waiting for that first cup of java. It only took a minute, but it seemed like twenty before the paper worked its way out of the machine.

Rollins grabbed the photos as soon as the machine spit them out.

They both stared at the *before* face, then at each other. The face didn't register.

Rollins buzzed his secretary who was, yes, in the office ready to help. He directed her to get the photo on the wire to the Hollywood and New York offices immediately then send a copy to all other offices.

Valdez called New York and Rollins called Hollywood to notify them of the coming photo. Not only did they want to know who this guy was, they wanted to know the names of any guys he had worked with who were in the five eight range, maybe a hundred and twenty to a hundred and sixty pounds. Both offices were told to call in as soon as they had any hits.

At this stage, sleep was not an option other than a possible catnap in a chair.

Valdez spoke, "You think both were makeup artists and did each other or do you think this guy or possibly the other guy was the sole expert?"

"Don't know, could be both, either, or possibly a third party."

"Had to have tons of experience and had to work in Hollywood or New York. Had to."

"Yeah, and that's going to help us, I'm sure. You want some more coffee?"

"Rather have a beer."

Rollins winked, "Coming right up." He walked out of his office and returned two minutes later with two cold bottles of Michelob. As he handed a beer to Valdez, he said, "Got a supply in the fridge for nights like this but one's the limit. Big boss rule."

Before taking a swig, Valdez ran the bottle across his forehead.

"Does that help?" Rollins said.

"It don't hurt. Cools down the wires."

Rollins tried it. "Yeah, I see what you mean. Hell, I might just go get me another one and not drink it."

The phone rang.

Rollins grabbed the receiver instantly. Valdez motioned for him to push the speaker button.

A bellowing voice from California told them that the guy's name was Cal Russo, considered to the best makeup artists to ever work in Hollywood. Had a website. Lots of guys in the five eight range had worked with him over the years. A list would be e-mailed shortly and a follow up list early tomorrow morning. After giving Rollins Russo's web address, he finished up with the fact that Cal Russo had not worked on a picture for the past two years

"Pull the site up," said Valdez.

Rollins swiveled his chair to his computer and typed in the address. "Bingo," he said.

Valdez circled around Rollins' desk, hovered over his shoulder as they both stared at the site, captivated by exquisite samples of Russo's work.

The phone rang, again. It was New York calling. Same info other than the fact no one on Broadway could afford the genius. He hadn't competed for a Tony Award in years.

The phone rang again.

"We got a vehicle." It was Field Agent Chuck Davis calling in from the crime scene.

"Where'd you find it?"

"It's a van, parked in the carport of a house two blocks away on a dead end street. The house owners have been on vacation for the past ten days and own an identical van. Neighbors thought they had returned. A kid told us his buddy, Rick, had e-mailed him earlier from Florida."

"What led you to that particular vehicle?"

"Dogs. The dogs trailed the guy's scent."

"So the other guy must not have gone back to the vehicle."

"The dogs trailed the other scent back through the woods to a used car lot and then lost it."

"Anything else?"

"Oh yeah. The back of the van was loaded with makeup materials covered by a drop cloth. Rouges, mascaras, lipsticks, dyes, pigments, false nails, beards, boxes and boxes of latex, teeth, hair, about a hundred brushes, molds, bald caps, and shit I can't begin to describe. Must have been from Hollywood or something."

"We think he is. You hold tight with that info until we get the vehicle towed in and have the lab go through it. See if we can come up with some prints."

"Truck is here now."

"Good. I love efficiency."

"I'm an efficient kind of guy." He laughed. "Oh, and I got something you're really going to love. Under the front seat I found a bunch of city maps from all across the country. I'll call in with anything else. You going to be there?"

"I'll be here. Valdez is with me."

"Tell that old fart I said hello."

"You just told him. I got you on speaker."

"Oh, shit."

"Hi, Chuck," said Valdez. "I am an old fart. Good job."

Rollins hung up. He and Valdez exchanged cool, reserved expressions.

"Progress," said Valdez.

Rollins nodded. "Remember the eighteen King Mackerel?"

Valdez smiled, held his hands apart indicating the size of the fish. "All the same size."

"I told you they were sending us a message."

"Identical, but different."

"Exactly."

23

Mario heard piano music off in the distance. Nice and melodic. Somebody was in his house fingering notes on a Steinway he didn't own.

Slowly, he opened his eyes. The piano was in his bedroom hiding in his clock radio. He sat up, went to rub the crud out of his eyes but instead conked himself in his left eye with his phone. He yelled a couple of four letter words just to let the neighbors know he'd hurt himself. Then he stood and made his way to the bedroom as the piano melody ended and Natalie Cole started singing a duet with her dad, who was dead, which reminded him to call Cassie. He hit the off button and picked up the phone beside the bed. That was useless. She hadn't left a number. Off he went to retrieve the phone that tried to knock him out. It had caller ID.

He found the number and made the call. It was five after five. Roosters were still asleep at this hour. She answered on the third ring and spoke before he could utter a grunt. "Please tell me you are coming. Please."

Actually, he had decided not to go but he changed his mind at the sound of her voice. "Yeah, I'm coming. I hope I don't regret it."

She brightened up immediately. He could hear it in her tone. "Great. Can you leave right now?"

"That I can't do. I have to go over to the track and watch one horse work then I'll come home, pack up some things and head south."

"Make sure you bring a couple of bathing suits and some fishing rods if you want to fish. A guy caught a whole bunch right in front of the house yesterday."

"I'll buy surf stuff down there if I want to fish. How about clothes? All casual, right?"

"Right. God, I can't wait to see you. I need you."

What the hell did that mean coming from a woman who didn't want to get involved? Maybe he should stay home a couple of afternoons, catch up on the soaps. Probably find a few women just like her messing up a guy's space. Suddenly second thoughts jumped into his mind. "Cassie, I uh---"

"Hey Mario. I bought you something."

"What's that?"

"A thoroughbred."

"Yeah, right. What is he, plastic?"

"I'm not kidding."

"Bullshit, look I'll see you late today. Give me some directions."

"Once you cross the Wright Brothers Bridge turn left just past the McDonalds onto Route 12. You'll come into Duck in about five minutes. Turn right just past the tennis courts and indoor pool at the entrance to Four Seasons. Stay on the road all the way to the end where the road curves to the right. The house I rented faces the ocean. It's blue, like my car. And Mario, stop and eat some oysters on your way. You're going to need them." She hung up.

"Jesus." He dialed the number again, but she didn't answer.

He brushed his teeth, ran a brush over his hair, grabbed a quick orange juice and headed for the track, a place where the fillies didn't screw up your brain.

Buster was waiting for him. He filled Mario's John Henry mug as he spoke, "Man, that's a nice horse you bought."

"What?"

"Shellcracker." He nudged Mario and cracked a grin. "Aw, come on Mario. We're friends. Damn horse has already won over six hundred grand in New York this year."

"I have no clue what you are talking about. Fill me in."

"You got to be kidding. The four-year-old. Shellcracker."

"I know Shellcracker. He won a stakes two weeks ago at Belmont. I saw the race on the deuce."

"Well, he's standing in stall seven next to Cannonball this morning. Chuck said he belonged to you and he told me to send you over to the barn as soon as I saw you. Said the horse and papers in your name showed up at four-thirty this morning. The security guard called him at home and told him to get his ass to the barn in a hurry. Guy who delivered the horse had to pick up another horse from a farm over in Frederick and deliver him to Delaware Park.

Mario was looking for answers at his feet but none materialized. Cassie had just told him she bought him a horse but he thought she was joking.

He nudged Buster. "You are putting me on, right?"

Buster shook his head. "Chuck said forty thousand in cash accompanied the horse to cover training for a year or so. He wants to know what's going on."

"Me, too. I'm heading over."

"Hold up. I thought you wanted to watch Thunder Ridge go three this morning." He pointed across the track to the three-eighth pole. "He's breaking off now."

"Yeah, I need to watch him go."

Thunder Ridge was prepping for a stakes race a week away. Mario liked the horse at decent odds pending other entries but he wanted to make sure the horse was ready to run big before making the bet. The horse was in hand, moving comfortably working with another horse. At the eighth pole, the rider gave him his head and asked for another gear. Jock didn't get it. Mario didn't like what he saw. Thunder Ridge would not get the dough, from him or the purse.

Buster shook his head. "I didn't like that, not at all."

"Me neither. I'm going over to the barn to see Chuck and this horse you say I own then I'm heading to the Outer Banks for a little R&R. Cassie invited me. She's rented a place. I'll see you in a few days."

"So, are we still going partners on a yearling in the fall?"

"Yeah, and we'll name him Mario's Bus."

Buster laughed. "Nah, we'll name him The Sauce."

Mario pointed at Buster as he hustled away. "I like it."

Sure enough, Shellcracker was standing in the stall. His halter identified him. Mario said hello, talked some trash to the four-year-old before he heard Chuck Coleman coming around the corner saying, "Probably the best horse in the barn based on his past performance."

"Hi Chuck," Mario said. "I heard I own him. That true?"

Mario had met Chuck seven years ago standing beside the fence one morning in a pouring rainstorm watching horses work. Ridiculous? No. Chuck is one of Maryland's most respected trainers and Mario is one of the state's most respected horseplayers. Both earned their reputations by doing their jobs through rain, sleet and whatever else the good lord threw down. A friendship blossomed, drenched with a work ethic only successful people could understand or appreciate.

"That's what the papers say." Chuck said as he reached under the horse's chin and started scratching. The horse nickered, letting Chuck know he had hit the spot.

"I didn't buy him."

"I know. An unidentified lady paid one mill in cash for him and threw in another forty thou for training fees." He paused, moved his hand from below Shellcracker's chin to behind the horse's ears and continued with the scratching. Mario took note. Chuck kept his eyes on the horse as he talked. Both of his hands were into the scratching now.

He shot Mario a sly grin. "Maybe we should send you to Kentucky. You must be some kind of stud."

"Yeah, I think I'm going to change my name to Super Mario."

Chuck grinned. "The Jockey Club wouldn't approve it. Name's already taken, but speaking of the Jockey Club, you need to get yourself over to the commission office, fill out the papers for an owner's license so we can run this money machine and get our picture taken."

"I'll take care of it. Are you taking him to the track this morning?"

"Hell yes. He's about to kick the wall down, wants to strut his stuff. I think he's taken a look around and figured out he can beat the rest of these suckers."

"For a million dollars, he'd better."

"I can get him tacked up now if you want to stick around and watch him gallop."

Mario considered staying but decided he needed to hit the road and find out about his love life and exactly why he had become a horse owner . . . and how Cassie, who bet horses to show, had come up with a million bucks. His intuition told him something was amiss. He just didn't know what, or who, the something was.

"I'd love to watch him go but I need to motor. I'm heading down to Duck, North Carolina. See if I can add some color to my Wonder Bread body. I'll catch up with you in a few."

"Bring back some fresh shrimp, for your trainer." He held his thumb about five inches from his fingers. "Big boys."

"I can handle that."

Mario decided to gamble before departing. He slowly reached up and scratched under Shellcracker's chin. When he removed his hand, the horse nuzzled him, asked for more. The horse already liked his new owner.

Despite the early hour, the commission office was open. Mario quickly filled out the papers. He had his picture taken and was fingerprinted then he received a parking sticker and a clubhouse pass. Wow, he thought, for a million dollars an owner gets free parking and a freebie through the gate. Hell of a bargain. He smiled. Wasn't his million, but he had forked over fifty bucks for the license.

He went home, showered, dressed and packed some clothes and a cooler into the car. He was sporting navy blue shorts and a T-shirt that extolled the beauty of Margaritaville. He opened the sunroof, slipped a Jimmy Buffet CD into the dash, punched some buttons on the navigation panel and headed for a suntan.

Somewhere along the way he'd stop for lunch, grab a cheeseburger.

24

Bellevue, Idaho is a small quiet community, a nice place to live especially if you like to fly fish. The population of rainbow trout exceeds the human head count. Rumors have it that the first word out of a baby's mouth is "hatch." Just rumor, of course, a little local lore.

Cal Russo owned a home in Bellevue that he had purchased a little over two years ago. Its glamour rested in its rustic stature and tranquil setting amongst stately pines that provided shade and seclusion. A porch about ten feet deep stretched across its width offering a place to rock away the hours engulfed in a view of the countryside. A hundred yards down the slope, Big Wood River flowed south between mountains, meandering through meadows, spilling the runoff of melting snow from the peaks of Sun Valley. Behind every rock, under every ledge and in every deep hole, a rainbow trout waited, ready to pounce on a Griffen's Gnat or a stimulator with a nymph dropper.

As the sun crept over the mountains, six FBI agents entered the front door armed with a search warrant. A simple picking of the lock had gained them access. The agents had driven from the Boise field office having been instructed by a call from William Rollins to search every square foot, dust every inch and gather every piece of evidence they could uncover, especially anything on fellow make-up artists. They were looking for photos, names, addresses, phone numbers, bank accounts, and possibly some cash. Any relevance to banks or locations where banks had been robbed in the past twenty-four months would be a momentous discovery.

For fifteen hours, they searched.

They found lots of fingerprints, unfortunately all belonged to Cal Russo.

They found a roomful of makeup supplies, enough to open a small store.

They found photos of movie stars, after Cal had dazzled them with his handiwork.

They found a little black book of phone numbers. Prominent names in the movie industry were listed along with names they didn't recognize. The names and numbers of two banks in the Cayman Islands were included along with a bank in Zurich.

They found hundreds of flies each identified by name and separated into clear plastic compartments. One of the agents, a dyed in the wool trout fisherman, pointed out the Tricos, PMDs, Baetis, Callivbaetis, Yellow Sallies and Pink Alberts as the reigning champs for enticing rainbows. A dozen boxes of feathers along with an array of thread in a thousand different colors was evidence that Cal was just as handy at fooling rainbows as he was at fooling the public. Tiny tools occupied a workbench equipped with a vice and magnifying glass. Above the bench, six bamboo fly rods hung like trophies.

The big surprise was the four million dollars they found bundled up in plastic bags hidden below solid blocks of fish, filet mignon, and a variety of vegetables in a large floor freezer.

But, they didn't find any evidence of a five eight male accomplice.

Meanwhile, agents in California contacted every guy who had ever worked with Cal. Each had an airtight alibi for Tuesday. None could believe that Cal had robbed a bank. All were shocked and saddened by his death. According to those in the industry, Cal was one of the *good guys*.

Back at headquarters, agents had determined that the van used in the robbery had been stolen from the Christiana Mall parking lot just off I-95 in Delaware on Monday night. The plates were heisted from the same mall lot and belonged to a math teacher at Elkton High School who lived just across the state line in Maryland. Both vehicles had been parked side-by-side about forty yards from the entrance to Macy's.

At the end of the day Rollins suspected that the other guy was not in the makeup business. He had to look elsewhere. It was imperative that they capture the guy, alive. He had to be assured that all nineteen robberies were committed by the same twosome so that he could close the books, put his mind to rest and take his wife on a long vacation.

He left the office at midnight lugging a box of videotapes. Somewhere on one of those bank tapes he knew there was a clue. He just hadn't recognized it, yet.

25

Mario's demeanor changed as soon as he crossed the Wright Memorial Bridge. It happens to everyone who visits the Outer Banks. That's why tourists return year after year.

It had been fourteen years since he last ventured offshore with five of his college buddies in search of billfish. They had raised one, lost him at the boat when the white marlin made a last second dive and escaped by cutting the line on the engine shaft. They settled for a cooler full of bull dolphin which was a pretty tasty settlement.

Much had changed since his last visit.

He sat at the red light waiting to turn north to Duck. He remembered the area, known to him as Nags Head, to be block after block of one-story beach cottages on stilts between the ocean and the by-pass with a few scattered homes on the western side around Sea Scape Golf Course. He was surprised to see a huge Home Depot to his right and wondered if the area could support it.

He found out in the next five minutes.

He could hardly keep his eyes on the road as he eyeballed home after home on both sides of the road as he approached Duck.

When he pulled into the entrance to Four Seasons, he parked, deciding to make a quick tour of the model, take a look around, and out of curiosity ask the price. He went into momentary shock when he heard the figure. The sales agent showed him some rental numbers, told him what homes were bringing from Duck to Corolla.

As he slowly guided the silver machine around and down the gentle slopping road to the oceanfront his mind was formulating questions for Cassie. He needed some answers. On one hand she was living in a RV and driving a Volkswagen. On the other, she was buying him a million dollar horse and renting an oceanfront house that was worth a small fortune. What a contrast. He didn't know if she had a job or just played the horses. From what she had said about her father and mother, he didn't think a trust fund was in the picture. He simply did not know. Perhaps she had a rich grandparent or maybe she had hit the lottery.

He spotted her car in the driveway of a house that belonged on the cover of a magazine. It was enormous. As he stepped out of his car, she came hustling down the steps from the wraparound deck on the first floor. She jumped into his arms, straddled his hips and planted a big one on his lips, digging for his tonsils with her tongue. The only thing she had on was a bright lime bathing suit with a turtleneck top and a string bikini bottom. Made him want to see the master bedroom in a hurry and forget about the questions and lack of involvement.

She grabbed his hand. "Come on. You got to see this place."

He didn't bother with his bags.

Instead of going in the front door, she led him around back and up the stairs to the deck overlooking the Atlantic. He stood in awe at the sight. He knew England was out there somewhere beyond the sand, the osprey and the feeding gulls, but at this moment he had no desire to cross the ocean. He just wanted to admire its vastness. It was a pure day, not a cloud in the sky. A warm breeze flowed from the southeast. Couples were holding hands walking the beach. Kids were building castles, occasionally running to the surf, giggling and running back. And here he was, holding the hand of a woman who looked like Meg Ryan. Damn. He didn't know if he was in heaven or a step closer to feeling a little heat.

She waved her hand in front of his face. "You coming out of that trance anytime soon?"

"Huh?" He slowly turned and looked into a face as innocent as a baby who just escaped the womb.

She doubled up with the hand waving. "Hey, don't look so happy to see me!" A love tap to the gut followed, seeking some radiance, hoping for a smile.

He engaged her eyes, searching for answers, before slipping out a grin. "Just wondering where you got a million dollars to buy me a horse?"

She lowered her head and watched her toes wiggle away some sand pebbles.

He added, "And why?"

She responded to the why question. "Can't a girl buy a guy a gift every once in a while?"

"Yeah, maybe a shirt or dinner or a ten-dollar win ticket, but a million dollar horse?"

"Just wanted to let you know how much I love you." She ran her fingers into his side, tickled him.

He didn't know if she was playing or serious about what she said. Warning signs flashed before his eyes. What happened to no involvement? He didn't respond, deciding instead to play a little cat and mouse and see what developed.

"What? You don't like the horse? He's a major stakes winner."

"Oh, I love the horse but where you got a million dollars to buy him has me baffled. You live in a damn RV on rented land."

She laughed, grabbed him by the hand and led him indoors for the nickel tour. "Baffled? I haven't heard that word in a long time. You just don't know how good a handicapper I am. You think I just make show bets but that's not true. I make all kinds of bets. And I win a lot of money. I've been winning for years, at a lot of different tracks. The RV takes me from track to track. You're not the lone ranger with charts and rules, by the way. I got in early on Funny Cide. I put down a bundle in future bets in Vegas, probably twice as much as the owners. I cleaned up."

The Funny Cide statement shocked him. What did she know about Funny Cide in advance? How did she know?

Her demeanor evoked a tone of bravado. He bought the betting angle but wasn't sure about the love comment. He decided it was time to inquire.

"So, you buy me a horse then you invite me here and now you tell me you love me. What happened to no involvement?"

"I canned it and decided to follow my heart." She shot him a puppy dog look and awaited a response.

Mario turned and walked away from her. He ran his hand through his hair, scratched the back of his head and tried to figure out what the hell was really going on. He wanted to believe what she said but for some reason he had doubts and it ate at him, chewed at his brain, nibbled at his heart. He decided to test the waters. From twenty feet away, he glanced toward her over his right shoulder as he opened the fridge door. "Well, in that case, let's find us a Justice of the Peace, get this show on the road and become a couple of married folks."

"Okay."

Oh, hell. He searched for a beer as he awaited an addition to the "okay" response.

She started laughing. "You're so full of shit. You don't want to marry me. What kind of a proposal is that, you with your head stuck in an ice box?"

Here we go again, more of her hocus-pocus. Ice box? She must be from the south.

"Just trying to cool down," he said as he turned and chucked her a Bud.

She tossed it back. "You hot and bothered?"

"Nope, but I am hot and thirsty." He returned her beer to the top shelf.

"Tell you what. Let's go to dinner, come back to the house and discuss your proposal under the sheets when our bodies are touching and not twenty feet apart."

He tossed her word back at her. "Okay."

Yep. He was about knee deep now and the water was rising.

She led him through the rest of the house. The great room included every toy known to the electronic world. As soon as she picked up a remote and pushed a button, he was surrounded by music, big band of course, with Frank singing and Tommy playing. The rich sound continued throughout the house. Mario figured the place had more than a hundred speakers. He strolled through six bedrooms, all big, all exquisitely decorated in beach motif, lots of shells, ceramic fish and driftwood. Place had seven bathrooms, one adjoined each bedroom, another catered to the great room crowd. A sauna occupied a corner in the master bath. He looked for an indoor tennis court but couldn't find one. Owner probably didn't think of it. The kitchen, where the tour had started and ended, was so big that Emeril wouldn't be able to find a big wooden spoon.

A few minutes later he was out the door and back down the steps. He checked out the pool and hot tub, shaking his head with every step, wondering what the long-term outcome of all this opulence would do to the laid back image of the Outer Banks.

After unloading his car, he ended up in Cassie's. He slid low in the passenger seat. Being chauffeured around in a blue Volkswagen messed with his ego, the rebirth of the bug known to the guys as a lady's car. He endured the trip and actually waved back to a couple of heavily endowed bikini-clad teenagers who had waved to him while jogging on the bike path. They apparently didn't know about the car's image and thought he was cute or something. Cassie didn't know what was going on in his head and caught him with a right to the shoulder, figuring he was flirting, or turning into a pervert.

She whipped a left into the lot at The Waterfront Shops, then turned right and found a parking spot behind Tommy's Market.

After stepping out of the bug, she motioned with her head and up the steps they went. As soon as Mario hit the top, he gazed at the sun flattening out on the horizon over Currituck Sound, the water still, a tinge of orange on the surface announcing the end of the day.

Cassie had told him that The Blue Point Bar and Grill was her favorite Outer Banks' restaurant. Her opinion was obviously shared by many. A line about twenty deep awaited a table. She assured him that it was worth the wait of forty-five minutes to an hour. She gave her name to the hostess, requesting a table for two overlooking the sound.

Next door a small gift shop loaded with T-shirts, trinkets, cookbooks and puzzles welcomed the Blue Point crowd. Cassie scanned the puzzles. She bought one of a porpoise rising, posing in mid-air, about to dive and enjoy some dinner. She told him that they'd work it piece by piece when they got back to the house. He had visions of a more seductive evening. He didn't need another puzzle.

He was still working on the one standing in front of him in a pink turtleneck sleeveless cotton sweater and white shorts. As he glanced around, a T-shirt caught his eye that he thought would mess with her mind. He dropped a twenty down on the counter then held it up for her to see. She shook her head when she read *I'm Available* boldly displayed. A good looking girl wearing a University of North Carolina shirt held up the same shirt in a different color and said directly to him, "So am I."

Cassie gave the girl the eye and said, "He's not."

Mario smiled. Mission accomplished.

With shirt in hand they walked out of the shop. The sun had escaped. Reflections of the moon were scatting across the ripples. White lights lined the deck that ran in front of the waterfront shops. With gulls and osprey providing the music, it couldn't have been any neater or more romantic.

The line was dwindling. Wait time was about to end.

She snuggled up to him as though reacting to the setting. He sensed it was more than that. She was there but she wasn't. She'd drift off like her mind was taking her on a trip someplace she didn't want to travel then she'd suddenly become all lovey-dovey again, confusing the hell out of Mario.

"Crawford, table for two," said the hostess. Cassie raised a hand and they followed the hostess to a booth where a view of the sound welcomed them to the world of warm and cozy.

"I don't have any relatives who own this place but I think you'll find that the quality rivals Geno's," Cassie said as plates heading for other tables paraded by, the aromas floating through the air grabbing Mario's attention.

He looked across the table at Cassie. "You dine here often?"

"Every time I visit the area," she answered, never looking up from the menu.

"So, what's your recommendation?"

"The Saute of Lump Crab, Country Ham, Lima Beans & Corn on Toasted Corn Bread with Roasted Jalapeno Cream is my favorite."

"What about the Mahi Mahi with Italian Sausage, Tomatoes, Herbs and Linguini?"

"I thought that might catch your attention. It's delicious. How about we order both and share."

"I'll buy that."

"I'm doing the buying. I invited you, remember?" She winked and all of a sudden her toe was climbing one of his legs, again.

"Okay." Lots of okay's happening.

"We can share a salad too, if you want?" she added.

"Which one?"

"Shaved Fennel with Walnut Oil, Lemon Juice and Romano Cheese sound good?"

"Sounds great."

Dinner was a big hit with Mario. Both dishes rivaled Geno's without question and actually may have been better than any of the Baltimore restaurant's seafood offerings. He asked their waitress if the chef, or the owner, was around. She mentioned that two guys owned the place and said both were in the back. She'd see if Sam had a moment to say hello.

A few minutes later Sam visited their table. Mario complimented him on the food then told him about Geno's before asking some questions about the preparation of the fish. Sam told him the recipe was included in the Blue Point cookbook. He said he'd tell their waitress to bring him a copy, compliments of the house.

Turned out everything they had ordered was in the cookbook.

Cassie suggested they walk off dinner with a stroll on the beach. Mario wasn't much for strolling but he agreed to join her, not wanting to kill the moment.

They changed into bathing suits. Mario sported the knee long Hawaiian look and Cassie strutted around in another turtleneck with a bikini bottom. This one was black.

The temperature had dropped, cooling the air to the point that a two-bodied- cuddle-walk was required as their feet dug into the wet sand near the breakers, water washing up pebbles with each incoming wave.

The rumblings of a storm at sea caught their attention. Flashes of lightening were striking at the horizon many miles offshore. It looked to be moving south and was getting stronger as it picked up warmer water.

Twice they stopped and groped each other like a couple of college kids who had just met on spring break.

An hour later they were back at the house in the hot tub making their own waves, causing a stir, feeling the heat. Hoping no one was watching.

From the tub they hurried to the master bedroom. His bathing suit hit the floor in seconds followed by her bikini bottom. She didn't bother to remove her top as wet bodies quickly turned into sweat, exploring, trying different positions, going for . . . a love fest at the beach.

"I don't think you love me at all," Cassie said as she straddled him, grinding slowly, purring the words. "I think you love Meg Ryan. You want to be Mr. and Mrs. with Meg, not me."

Water was creeping up his ass now. Soon he'd drown, be dead from lust if he didn't get some solid answers, something he could believe.

"Then tell me who you are."

She kept on slipping and sliding, back and forth, driving him crazy.

"You want to know who I am?"

"Yes."

"I'm Cassie Crawford. My father and mother are dead. I do free-lance evaluations of real estate sites for financial institutions and oil companies in the mornings. I go to the track in the afternoons, play the ponies and have a lot of success. I'm thirty-five, never been married. I move from track to track as I do my free-lance work. Four years ago I hit the pick-six at Santa Anita for over a million, giving me a nice stake that I parlayed into a considerable amount of money." She lifted up, back down, up again, back down. Beads of sweat covered her body. Sticky. She was in a rhythm, her knees pressed into his flesh, urging him, pushing him to the brink, talking fast. "Right now, right this instant, I'm about to have another orgasm because the guy I'm with sends me to places I've never been." She closed her eyes, tossed her head back, screamed God's name, her body giving in to the spasms, tightening, releasing, as did his.

A dead heat, photo finish and all.

Testing time was over. Water crept over his head and he swallowed it.

She had collapsed in a pool of togetherness, sweat on sweat. He held her, feeling her heart find a lower gear while his raced, controlled by his mind, finally forcing a response. "I think I'm serious about Mr. and Mrs."

She backed off a couple of inches and looked him in the eye. "Think?"

He smiled. "Yeah, think."

"Me too." She got up, headed for the bathroom before adding, "I have a lot on my mind right now. We've only known each other for a couple of weeks. Let's give it another week and see if we still feel the same way."

"Okay." That word again.

"And, I want to know more about you, especially about your ten year love affair."

"Who told you about that?"

"I have my sources." She smiled before shutting the door.

He stared at the ceiling, rolled all she had said around in his head, played some bumper pool. A red flag kept popping up saying, "Whoa."

He fell asleep wondering why.

26

William and Kaylan owned three televisions. One was so huge it captured an entire wall of the family room. To William it was the fifty-yard line for Redskins games. Another faced the bed in the master bedroom, one of those thin plasma jobs that hung on the wall like a painting. The third was one of those little bitty units with a self-contained tape deck and 12" screen requiring up close and personal viewing. Most of the time it resided in the study, although it was light enough to be toted around to just about anywhere a plug resided.

For the second night in a row, William was entrenched in a big soft black leather chair in his study, five feet from the little bitty screen, his feet protruding onto a matching ottoman, his eyes glued to the action. Looking for a clue, anything that would help him in his quest to identify and capture the second bank robber. He had been at it for four hours and fatigue had raised its head. He ran the back of his right hand over his eyes hoping to displace the red lines before ejecting the tape and inserting another. B.B. King provided background music, blues stretching the depth of the speakers. Rollins couldn't sing a lick, but his humming was top notch. Sometimes he imitated Ella, introducing a little scat to change the mood but tonight it wasn't working. Blues, blues, blues, nothing but blues. Maybe he should stick Aretha in the slot, let her liven up the joint and bring on the R-E-S-P-E-C-T. She'd make him stand, shake his booty and forget about bank robberies for a few minutes. But no, the blues were in control.

A novel rested on the table beside his chair, the latest by Michael Prescott featuring FBI special agent, Tess McCallum. It was one of three hundred books that filled a wall in the study, suspense genre for him, romance and classics for Kaylan. A bookmark indicated he was at the halfway point, but he hadn't read a page in the past three days.

He raised the coffee mug to his mouth, took a sip. It was his third cup of the evening, brewed extra strong to fit the task at hand. He spilled a little on his shirt. It matched fifteen years of other spots on his old Randolph-Macon white football jersey carrying the number forty-four in black, outlined in gold. His coach had given him his home and away jerseys when he graduated. The other one was black with white numbers trimmed in gold. He never wore them anywhere but in the house. Both brought back fond memories. For some reason, the jerseys made him want to kick some butt. He needed to, now.

He'd rewind, hit pause, then play. Again and again he viewed the tapes from the robberies.

Last night he fell asleep in the chair at three-thirty with the robbery in Tampa frozen on the screen.

He was watching the Tampa tape again when Kaylan brought him a fresh cup of coffee, kissed him on the neck and slid onto the arm of the chair, deciding to keep him company for a few minutes. She had not watched any of the tapes previously, always allowing him his space when he brought work home from the office. She knew he had to concentrate, do his job. But tonight was different. He was suffering, feeling defeated and it was obvious to her that William needed some TLC.

"What exactly are you looking for?" she asked.

He lifted his eyes, "Some tiny touch of a clue, something that will lead me to the second robber, the one at the door."

She cut her eyes to the screen. "You mean the girl?"

"Girl?" he said, astonished by her comment.

"Yeah, the one with the gun in her hand standing beside the security guard." She got up, walked to the TV, and stuck a finger on the robber's head. "Her."

"That's a guy."

She shook her head, "Nope. It's a female. Watch her move. Check out her rear. You like to do that anyway." He cut his eyes at her and smiled then rewound the tape and concentrated on the robber by the door.

"You really think that's a female?"

"Let me see another tape."

He stopped the tape, ejected it and replaced it with the tape from Newark. She watched, still standing close to the TV. He slid his eyes back and forth between the screen and his wife.

Three minutes later she said, "Got another one?"

He ejected Newark and replaced it with Boise then pushed the play button.

"It's a girl," she said, emphatically.

"You're sure?"

"Absolutely."

"Damn. Russo is beyond genius if what I see is really a female."

"Who?"

"The guy we killed, Hollywood makeup artist." He jumped up, stepped towards her, cupping her face in his hands. "And you're a genius, too."

"If I'm right," she said. "But I know I am. Take it to the bank."

"Cute. We'll soon find out if you're right." He hurried to his desk, picked up his cell, called Vince Hopkins, his fishing buddy, in San Diego. Vince answered after the first ring.

"Vince, William. Hope I didn't wake you."

"Watching the Padres . . . down by three in the sixth."

"The second bank robber may be a female."

"What?"

"Kaylan watched tape with me and spotted it immediately. She swears that the *guy* at the door is not a *guy*."

"With everything we've learned about Russo, I'm not surprised. He could make Robin Williams look like Denzel Washington."

"We need to roll."

"Right away. I'll call you as soon as I get anything. You'll be awake, I assume."

"Oh, I'm wide awake now, that's for sure."

Kaylan kneaded his shoulder muscles, whispered in his ear, "I'm going back to bed now."

He turned and wrapped his arms around his wife. "I owe you one."

"Yes. And I plan on collecting."

"Jamaica?"

"Aruba."

"Aruba it will be." He kissed her on her forehead.

Immediately, he went back to viewing tapes with his concentration strictly on the body movements of both robbers, ignoring everything else. After six tapes he was convinced the same two robbers held up all six banks. They looked entirely different, but in each robbery the body movements were identical. He had just inserted a seventh tape when the phone rang.

Vince said, "It didn't take long to come up with some very interesting information. I called a security guy over at Paramount who knew Russo well. He said Russo's top assistant was a female, a gal by the name of Sam, short for Samantha. Last name Sullivan. He gave me the number of a producer, Sid Goldstein, who, by the way, is a total asshole. Mad as hell I had his number and had called at such a late hour. I identified myself as a FBI agent but it didn't faze him. He called me a 'fucking degenerate' but went on to tell me that Sullivan was as good if not better than Russo and the two of them had worked as a team for at least three years but no one had seen them for the past two. Told me they got pissed and left town, something about the Academy Awards and not getting paid enough for their talent."

"Damn."

"I've been online since talking with Goldstein. I discovered several pictures of Samantha Sullivan. I'm going to e-mail them to you. Call me back on your cell to confirm."

"You have her address or phone number?"

"I have an address and a phone number but she moved out two years ago. I'm going to interview some neighbors first thing in the morning. See if anyone has a clue as to where she is."

"Good." He stepped to his computer and within seconds was online.

Kaylan had heard the phone ring and had appeared at the door in a sexy robe from Victoria's Secret. She was leaning against the frame, listening to William's end of the conversation when she said, "Was I right?"

"I think so."

"You coming to bed now?" She unbuttoned the top, exposing her cleavage, enticing him.

His eyes smiled and he said, "I think so."

She pointed to the computer screen. "Looks like you have a message."

He turned, still standing, read a short message from Vince then used his mouse and clicked on the attachment icon. A page with color photos rolled up the screen.

"Shit."

"What's the problem?" Kaylan said.

"He sent me the wrong photos. I need to call him back."

"Now?"

"I got to, Hon, I got to. Then I promise I'll come to bed."

"Uh, huh. Well, I'll be waiting, for five minutes. After that the restaurant is closed. You get my drift?"

"Loud and clear."

He dialed and Vince answered immediately.

"You must be drinking. You sent me pictures of Meg Ryan not Samantha Sullivan."

"That *is* Samantha Sullivan. She's the spitting image of Ryan except for the mouth. You can see a slight difference if you look close."

"Jesus. Meg Ryan is not going to be a happy camper."

"Yeah, but the press will love it. Sullivan's picture will dominate the tube, be on the front page of dailies, maybe a couple of weekly magazines."

"You think you can come up with a private number for Ryan?"

"You going to call her?"

"Yeah, out of courtesy, before we release anything."

"You think we're on the right track?"

"Absolutely. I'm convinced the same twosome committed all the robberies."

"But are you convinced Samantha Sullivan is involved?"

"Convinced enough to pursue the hell out of her to find out."

"Yeah, her connection to Russo and the timing points right to her."

"Talk to as many people in the industry as you can, as soon as you can. We need to nail a few things down before releasing an APB."

"Will do, keep your cell on."

"It's on."

He hung up and headed for the bedroom.

"Is the restaurant still serving?"

"Full menu, but you can start with an appetizer."

27

The temptation was too much.

Sitting on the deck watching a guy bring in fish after fish from the surf while the sun was making its morning appearance sprung Mario into action. He wasn't sure Bob's Tackle Shop was open but he took a shot, grabbed his keys and drove the three blocks to Duck Road.

Four Jeep Cherokees were parked in the lot. A kid was testing new rods by casting toward the road with no line and reeling with no reel. The kid picked up one rod after another from the display of surf rods leaning against the building beside the door. Play fishing. Mario parked, joined in the fun and selected an eight and a half footer, broke it down, went inside and had the guy behind the counter help him select a suitable reel, then fill it with twelve pound test line. He bought two packs of number four hooks, half dozen three-ounce sinkers, a dozen bloodworms and a half-pound of fresh shrimp, a package of squid, a filet knife and a sand spike. Whatever he caught would end up costing a fortune by the pound.

He was ready, raring to go.

He cruised back to the house with the rod reaching for the sky through the sunroof.

Cassie had her head half buried under the sheet facing away from him when he snuck into the room and gathered his bathing suit, yesterday's T-shirt and a tube of Coppertone.

He spotted a small cooler in the kitchen, filled it with ice and was on his way, barefooted with a brown bag in one hand subbing for a tackle box. He dropped the rod twice while hustling down the boardwalk to the beach, and on top of that, stubbed the same toe three times. He laughed at his sudden lack of coordination which scared the hell out of a dozen gulls, sending them flying and squawking. Sky was clearing, the result of a slight breeze out of the southwest. Nice day, very nice.

The guy he had watched earlier had a cooler full of fish. He told Mario that he had been catching fish since five, mostly on shrimp.

Mario stuck his spike in the sand twenty yards down the beach, tied on two hooks about fourteen inches apart and a sinker six inches below the bottom hook, threaded a shrimp on each hook, walked into the surf up to his knees and made his first cast. He heard a loud snapping noise. Two hooks and a sinker flew through the air looking to bomb a foreign country. He had failed to flip the bail. Embarrassed? Yep. But he didn't give up. Hurriedly, he went through the whole process again. This time he made a nice cast, back-walked up the beach, tightened his line until there was no slack, set the drag, turned around and shot a smile at the other fisherman who had just brought in a double-header of sea mullet. That's when something attacked his shrimp. He lifted his rod tip-- showing the other guy he knew a little something about fishing--stuck whatever was on the other end and fought the fish until it was bouncing around on the beach gathering sand. He locked his reel, hustled to the water's edge, grabbed the line and lifted a sea mullet big enough to eat. He removed the hook, walked back up to where his sand spike awaited, stuck his rod in the holder, deposited the fish in the cooler, re-baited and made another cast.

An hour later, he had ten sea mullet close to a pound each, one speckled trout about a pound and a half, and a decent sized croaker in the cooler.

He was having so much fun he hadn't missed the ponies. With water up to his knees he spotted a school of porpoise, watched two pelicans scoop up some baitfish and saw a small whale flop his tail a few times about two hundred yards off shore.

As the morning progressed, people appeared from behind sand dunes carrying blankets, radios, books, buckets, coolers and umbrellas. Guy with a gray beard hanging down to his chest walked up and asked him if he was catching anything. Had a Marlboro in one hand and a Bud in the other, one of those good old boys in a T-shirt promoting NASCAR. Walkers were walking. Joggers were jogging. Beach was like a highway, traffic moving in both directions. It cleared out each time he was about to cast.

Cassie showed up and tapped him on the shoulder from behind. "You catching breakfast?"

He eased his head around and said, "If you can come up with some cracker meal." He figured she must have spent two, three hundred dollars on bathing suits, all the same style, different colors . . . turtleneck top, bikini bottom. This one was red. He checked her out, knowing that what he saw was as good as it looked.

She touched a finger to his arm and quickly released it. "You should have used some lotion."

He raised his shirtsleeve about an inch, "Oh man, I brought a tube down but it's still in the bag."

The other fisherman had disappeared, worn out from catching more than he could eat.

Mario glanced at the sun. "What time is it?"

"A little after nine."

"They've slowed up a little so I think I'll go clean some fish. Are you out here for the rays?"

"Going to walk up to the pier and back, get in a couple of miles. Captain wafers are in the pantry. Use the food processor and you'll have your cracker meal. Eggs are in the fridge along with orange juice. I made a pot of coffee."

"Good. I'll have breakfast ready when you get back." He patted her on the rear as a send off.

He gathered his stuff, headed for the fish cleaning station he had spotted on the ground level under the house.

After cleaning the fish he sensed an unpleasant odor in the air, quickly realizing he was it. He stepped into the outdoor shower, turned a knob and cold water welcomed him. But it felt good on his sunburned body. Not having a towel, he dripped himself up the deck stairs and into the house to find one and dry off before embarking on chef duties.

A few minutes later Cassie walked in, perspiring, a little out of breath. He urged her to hit the shower letting her know that fresh fish would be on the table in ten minutes.

She lifted the top to the electric skillet, took a whiff of four sea mullet coated in cracker meal, just starting to brown.

"Are we having anything else with these fish?"

"Potatoes are roasting in the oven, all cut up and loaded with salt, pepper and olive oil. Oven fries."

"No grits?"

He stared and shrugged.

"We are in North Carolina, you know."

"Tomorrow we'll have grits."

After she quickly showered, they dined on the deck, relishing the delicate flakes of fresh sea mullet while carrying on a conversation about people they spotted on the beach. Skinny people, fat people, young people, old people, and lovers who may or may not have been married, engaged or knew each other yesterday. Lots of dogs were spotted too, doing to pieces of driftwood what they usually did to fire hydrants.

While cleaning up the kitchen, Mario asked what was on schedule for the remainder of the day. She reminded him he was at the beach. Plans didn't exist.

A few minutes later, she was lounging on the deck reading a novel by Fern Michaels about horses and romance while he had his face buried in a vacation guide and was busy flipping pages, discovering all kinds of stuff he didn't know about the Outer Banks.

"What's Corolla like?" Mario said, interrupting her concentration.

She read on for a few seconds before answering, "Neat. It's a neat place. You might have to stop the car while a wild horse crosses the road."

"Can they run?"

"I wouldn't bet on them to beat you in a hundred yard dash."

"That slow, huh?"

She smiled. "Want to take a ride up that way, see the sites, grab a cup of coffee, buy a house, or something?"

"I don't think I can afford a house down here."

"But, I can." She shot him a wink, slapped him on the leg with her book. "Come on, let's go."

She drove again, putting his image at stake.

As soon as they traveled past the new Comfort Inn, which to him seemed totally out of place, his eyes doubled in size. The size of the homes in Pine Island blew his mind. He couldn't believe it. House after house lined the oceanfront, the backsides providing a view of the sound. You could wake up to a sunrise, turn around and go to sleep to a sunset. While still gawking, he asked Cassie, "Are these private homes or rentals?"

"Mostly rentals." She pointed to a humongous pink house. "That one rents for ten grand a week in peak season, thirty-five hundred now. I tried to lease it this week but it was already rented. Has nine bedrooms and an indoor pool."

"You're kidding."

"I've stayed in it before. Place is unreal."

"Yeah, so is the price."

"Twenty-five years ago you could have bought all this land for peanuts."

Mario saw a plane land over to his left behind some trees. "They have an airport up here?"

"Yeah, small private field, and tennis courts, too. A couple of movie stars own homes close by. They fly in, fly out."

"The only thing missing is a golf course."

"Coming up on your left."

Mario didn't play a lot of golf but he liked it when he did. As soon as he caught sight of a couple of holes at The Currituck Club he was itching to tee it up. Thought he might see if he could rent some clubs, play the course sometime later in the week.

Despite not seeing any wild horses, he loved the feel of the Corolla area with its stately trees, lagoons and unique stores. Cassie pulled into TimBuck II, a quaint shopping village with most of the stores located in two buildings on stilts. They walked hand in hand and visited all the shops. Mario splurged and bought a hammock chair after sitting in it. He told Cassie it would fit the décor of the church. She was hoping it would fit in the car. Then he bought a kite at Kitty Hawk Kites that possessed giant wings that made it look like Big Bird ready to fly the Atlantic. All excited, he said he'd get it airborne, run up and down the beach and make it do some tricks until he found a kid who wanted it. Then he'd hand it over, make a kid happy. With that thought, he changed his mind, deciding that the little kid he'd make happy would be Little Geno. The kite would travel to Baltimore.

Cassie purchased a three-piece outfit at Mustang Sally's at Corolla Light, flowing black pants with a white shirt and black open vest. Had a horse motif, very casual but very classy. Mario liked it. Liked who bought it too . . . liked her more minute by minute. Still hadn't figured her out though. There were moments when she'd stare off into space as though she expected someone from Mars to make an appearance.

Breakfast had been pretty heavy so they decided to lunch at Steamer's and share a dozen steamed oysters and a spinach salad with roasted red peppers.

By the time they got back to the house, Mario was enthralled with the Outer Banks. Despite a little sunburn on his arms, he stretched out on the deck beside Cassie and soaked up more rays. This time he was covered with Coppertone, courtesy of Cassie. He offered to reciprocate with the lotion but she informed him that her tan was already in place.

No TV, no radio, no phone calls; just the sound of the ocean filled the afternoon.

Cassie watched Mario doze for two hours. Couldn't take her eyes off him, wanted to reach out and touch him, hold him close. A tear trickled down her cheek, her emotions churning, spitting out conflicting messages.

At five, Mario opened his eyes and immediately felt the heat from his body. He shook his head. For a smart guy, he was pretty stupid. He stood, stretched, made a couple of weird noises then walked around the deck and peeked over the railing. Cassie's car was gone. He ventured inside and searched for a note but didn't find one. She must have gone to pick up some groceries or something.

He took a shower, washing off the lotion and sweat. The burn didn't budge.

He walked out of the bathroom naked except for the white towel he was using to dry his hair. He hadn't heard Cassie come in. She startled him with a whistle and a drawn out "Hmmmm." He never lowered the towel, just smiled. She laughed, which is something a naked guy does not want to hear. "Your Wonder Bread is showing. Cute, but boy are you sunburned. I'll get some lotion, rub it on you."

"You see me naked and you want to rub lotion on me. That's it?"

"For now." She turned and walked out of the room, grinning.

She returned with a bottle of HAWAIIAN Tropic Cucumber Melon, rubbed it gently on everything but Mario's white parts. "This stuff is soothing, contains aloe vera." He winced as she applied the lotion. "While you slept I went up to the Roadside Bar and Grill, got us some grilled shrimp and a couple of orders of slaw for dinner."

"They didn't have a pool of ice I could jump into, did they?"

"No." She brushed the back of her hand across his member causing an arousal reflex. "Better keep that thing under control. I don't think your body would appreciate any heavy contact right now." She brushed him again, teasing, having some fun at the beach. Taking advantage of the time they had.

He slipped on some khaki shorts and a colorful T-shirt with a picture of Secretariat winning the Belmont. She was dressed in lime green shorts and a sleeveless peach top with a high neck, looking very tropical.

She suggested they eat at the kitchen bar and avoid the sun even though it was late in the day. He had no trouble agreeing.

Earlier she had brewed some iced tea and sliced some fresh lemon. She poured two glasses. He added two spoonfuls of sugar and a wedge to his. She added two packets of Equal to hers.

"You need to taste this sauce," she said, dipping a shrimp, offering him a bite.

He chomped down. "Damn, that's good. I think I like this better than cocktail sauce. What's in it?"

"They won't reveal the ingredients exactly but I know it's a mixture of orange marmalade, grainy mustard and horseradish. At least, that's what a waiter told me when I ordered it for the first time a couple of years ago. And I was flirting with him, trying to get him to spill the beans."

"I would have given you the recipe."

"Oh yeah, then how about revealing the recipe for Geno's sauce."

"That I can't do."

"I'll flirt with you."

"Won't help."

"I bought you a horse."

"I'll talk with Geno."   A sly grin accompanied the statement.

With an hour of sunlight remaining, she suggested they walk off dinner, dip their toes in the ocean, maybe exchange some spit here and there. The wind had picked up, now blowing from the northeast, dropping the temperature enough to suggest sweatshirts.

28

It took most of the day.

During the morning Rollins and his staff at headquarters researched Samantha Sullivan. Found a Samantha Anne Sullivan who resided on the west coast. Home address listed as 724B Rolling Hills Drive in Los Angeles didn't exist. Phone number of 310-555-4823 was bogus. So was the Social Security number.

At ten-thirty, Rollins dialed Meg Ryan's agent to fill him in on the situation. The agent told him that Samantha Sullivan had appeared as a double on several occasions. He added that he had been absolutely stunned when he met her for the first time, wondering if Meg's mom had held out on Meg regarding a twin sister. Rollins said he had both of their pictures sitting in front of him and if he didn't turn them over and read the identity he wouldn't know which photo was the real Meg Ryan. He apologized in advance for what was about to take place but he assured the agent that it was necessary, adding that if she encountered problems from any law enforcement agency to contact him immediately. Before hanging up, Rollins supplied the agent with an emergency FBI code number.

As of eleven o'clock, Samantha Sullivan's photograph had been dispersed to FBI offices throughout the country, wanted as a suspect in nineteen bank robberies. An APB had been issued worldwide.

At noon, a press release and photo was issued to all television networks, daily newspapers, and weekly magazines. Included in the release was a toll-free number to be used by anyone with information regarding Samantha Sullivan.

Within thirty minutes over four hundred calls had been received. Many from Hollywood and surprisingly, to Rollins, a large number from people who said they had seen the suspect at a racetrack. The very first call received came from Sonny Claven, a security officer at Laurel Park in Laurel, Maryland. Said he had seen a female who looked exactly like her at the track just about every day for the past month or so but hadn't seen her this week.

The calls from racetrack personnel and patrons intrigued Rollins. He went online and printed a list of U.S. racetracks from the *Daily Racing Form*. With the list in one hand and a fistful of black pins in the other he inserted a pin where a track existed near any of the robbery sites:

> *Turf Paradise (Phoenix, Arizona)*
> *Playfair (Spokane, Washington)*
> *Beulah Park (Columbus, Ohio)*
> *Les Bois Park (Boise, Idaho)*
> *Louisiana Downs (Shreveport, Louisiana)*

Penn National (Harrisburg, Pennsylvania)
Centennial Race Track (Denver, Colorado)
Del Mar (San Diego, California)
Tampa Bay Downs (Tampa, Florida)
Arlington Park (Chicago, Illinois)
Finger Lakes (Canandaigua, New York)
Fairmount Park (St. Louis, Missouri)
Santa Fe Downs (Santa Fe, New Mexico)
The Meadowlands (Newark, New Jersey)
Ak-Sar-Ben (Omaha, Nebraska)
Suffolk Downs (Boston, Massachusetts)
Gulfstream Park (Miami, Florida)
Delaware Park (Newark, Delaware)
Laurel Park (Laurel, Maryland)

"Damn!" he screamed. "Fuckers laundered the money at racetracks." Everyone in the outer offices heard his voice explode. His secretary came rushing in, concerned, wanting to know what was wrong. He pointed to the map, told her what he suspected.

"Maybe they lost most of it," she said.

"I don't think so. Our guys uncovered over four million in cash plus phone numbers for three offshore banks at Russo's place in Idaho. Nope. I think maybe one or both knew a little something about handicapping. Instead of losing money they may have added to the pot using stolen money as a stake." He lifted a note off his desk, handed it to her. "E-mail Mr. Claven a photo of Cal Russo. See if he recognizes him. Ask him to respond ASAP."

"Okay. Hey, calm down a little. You're going to nail her."

"I hope so."

Rollins took another look at the board then he smiled and nodded as he said, "I gotcha."

He called Valdez and brought him up to date explaining that several calls had come in from the Wilmington area. Told him to take some pictures of Samantha Sullivan over to Delaware Park, spread them around and see if anyone there could identify her.

Ten minutes later, his secretary walked in and told him that Mr. Claven didn't recognize Russo. She handed him a tuna sandwich and a Coke from the café.

He smiled. "Thanks." He always said that Lisa Johnson was the best secretary a guy could have and he made the top dogs aware, making sure she was compensated for her efficiency and effort, and especially for her consideration of others.

"Thought you might take five minutes and eat something, drink a Coke. You look a little rattled," she said before turning to leave the office.

"Hey, Lisa, how's your grandson doing in little league this year?"

"Best player in the league."

"Would you mind if I tagged along with you to a game one day? I'd love to see him play."

"I'd like that. I'd like that very much."

He gobbled his sandwich, swallowed his Coke and was out the door heading for Laurel Park within five minutes.

When he arrived at the track, Mr. Claven escorted him to the fence on the grandstand side and pointed out a few regulars who might know something about her.

Rollins thanked him then headed where Claven had pointed. He held up his badge as he approached four guys who were huddled up not too far from the finish line. He didn't waste any time on small talk. He whipped out the photos and asked if they had seen the woman in the pictures.

"Yeah, practically every day," Gimpy said, answering for all. "We know Cassie."

"Cassie?"

Gimpy took the Watermelon Mania Twizzler out of his mouth, held it up. "You want one? I got four flavors. Yeah, her name is Cassie."

Rollins wasn't interested in a Twizzler but he was very interested in the name.

"Crawford," injected Toteboard. "Cassie Crawford, but as you can see, she's the spitting image of Meg Ryan, the movie star."

Rollins said, "Have you seen her today?"

"She's not here," Toteboard answered.

"Do you happen to know where she is?"

Gimpy took a couple of steps forward and stood directly in front of Rollins. "You mind me asking why you want to know?"

"She's wanted as a suspect for bank robbery."

"You're shitting me."

"No. I'm very serious and if you guys have any idea where she is you need to tell me and tell me right now."

"Gone to the beach," Gimpy answered then hollered over to Buster who was in deep conversation with a jockey's agent. "Hey Buster, where did Mario say he was going?"

"The Outer Banks, down in North Carolina."

"Yeah," said Gimpy to Rollins. "Cassie rented a house and invited Mario down."

"Who is Mario?"

"Friend of ours, been coming to the track every day for years."

"And what's his connection to this women you guys know as Cassie Crawford?"

Gimpy laughed. "Mario thinks she's hot. He finally talked her into going out with him a couple of weeks ago."

Before Rollins said anything else, Buster walked over, wanting to know what was going on.

Rollins told him then showed him Sam's picture.

"And you think she robs banks?" He laughed. "Hell, the wife and I had dinner with her and Mario Saturday night to celebrate my horse winning a stakes race. She's a doll baby. Nice as can be, although Mario keeps telling me he can't figure her out."

"Probably because she's a thief."

Buster stared at Rollins, surveyed the guys then cut his eyes back to Rollins, "You're serious, aren't you?"

"Serious enough to take you guys in if you don't give me some straight answers right here, and right now."

"Does this have anything to do with the bank robber that was killed Tuesday?"

"It has everything to do with the robbery Tuesday and eighteen more that have been committed across the country. Does that make it clear enough?" Rollins' nerves were frayed. And it showed. No more Mr. Nice Guy.

Buster said, "He told me Wednesday morning that Cassie called him Tuesday night from the beach and invited him down. That's all I know. But, his trainer, Chuck Coleman might know more." He pointed toward the paddock. "There he is now, guy in the light blue shirt. Has a horse in the next race."

Rollins glanced at the paddock then back at the guys. "Everyone remain right here. I'll be back." He sprinted to the paddock and quickly showed his identity to a security guard standing at the paddock entrance. He asked to speak with Chuck Coleman, saying it was an emergency. The guard told Rollins that it was not a good time to bother a horse trainer. Rollins held up his credentials and said, "Get him."

Chuck was not happy about the interruption, quickly informing Rollins that Mario said he was heading to Duck, North Carolina . . . that Cassie had rented a house and invited him down. Then he turned his back on Rollins and walked away to saddle the favorite.

Despite Rollins' request, everyone except Longshot had headed to the windows to get something down on Chuck's horse. He didn't like the odds.

Rollins flipped open his cell and called in as soon as he departed the paddock. He told his secretary that he wanted every real estate agency in the Outer Banks area contacted immediately, looking for details of a rental by either a Cassie Crawford or a Samantha Sullivan. Then he requested a copter.

"Where are your friends? I told you guys to wait right here," Rollins said to Longshot as soon as he arrived at the spot where the guys had been standing.

"Have we committed a crime?"

Rollins didn't like his tone. "Not yet."

"Then don't treat me or my friends like we have. We're here to bet the ponies and my friends went to the windows. You got a problem with that?" Longshot was showing some balls, getting a little testy.

Rollins smiled. "Nah, I don't have a problem with that."

Longshot nodded toward the grandstand. "Here they come now."

Gimpy did the explaining, if you can call it that. "We went to make bets. Did Chuck say his horse was going to win?"

Rollins shook his head in amazement. "I didn't ask him about his horse."

"You finished with us?"

"What's Mario's last name?"

"Bozzela," Buster said.

"Spell it."

"B-O-Z-Z-E-L-A"

"And you guys don't think he's involved with any bank robbery?"

Buster answered, "I can tell you this. When the bank got robbed Tuesday morning he was standing right here beside me watching a horse work." He pointed emphatically to the ground. "RIGHT FUCKING HERE. Is that a good enough answer for you?" He shot a stare at Rollins as if to add the word asshole to his statement. This coming from a guy who didn't appreciate four letter words.

"For now," Rollins said, ignoring the obvious arrogance. He whipped out a pad and pen. "I need your names and phone numbers in case I have any other questions."

Everyone hesitated.

Rollins raised his eyes from his pad. "You guys are reporting all your winnings to the IRS, right?"

They all nodded then reluctantly gave Rollins the information.

Rollins thanked them for their cooperation and took off running. He didn't hear Gimpy call him a prick.

Buster walked away from the group, dug in his pocket for his phone and dialed Mario's cell but the call didn't go through. He tried again with the same result and got one of those *out of the calling area* messages.

When Rollins arrived back at his office, his secretary handed him a note containing the address of a house in Duck, rented for a week by a Cassie Crawford. The fact that the rental had started on Sunday and she had called Mario on Tuesday night concerned him but didn't prevent him from pursuing her with all the might of the FBI.

He called the Norfolk and Richmond FBI offices requesting twenty agents from each. The office met his request and in addition he was told that the top dog in Norfolk would meet him with a car at the Pine Island airstrip.

He called the Coast Guard, requesting their cooperation with a couple of patrol boats in the Atlantic off Duck. They responded in the affirmative.

He called his buddy Valdez on his cell, told him to line up a copter or small plane and meet him on the ground at the Pine Island airstrip.

On his desk was a folder with background information on one hundred and seventy-eight females named Cassie Crawford, along with maps of the Outer Banks and a note saying that the copter was on the roof, blades rotating, ready for takeoff. Lisa knew what he needed and made sure he had it.

Time was tight.

Valdez was already in the air aboard an FBI turbojet.

FBI cars and jeeps were rolling down Rt. 168 from Norfolk and Richmond, trunks full of weapons, bulletproof vests, night goggles and technology the public had never seen.

Rollins ducked his head and slipped into the shotgun seat. The copter was airborne in seconds. He opened the map and liked the fact that only one road ran from Southern Shores to Corolla. He analyzed escape routes before spending time with a hundred and seventy-eight profiles, his gut telling him Cassie Crawford was not her name.

The turbojet was faster than the Bell copter. On approach he spotted Valdez and Joe Wingo, from the Norfolk office, sitting on the hood of a black Crown Vic, engaged in conversation.

He told the pilot to be ready to get back in the air in about an hour. Another agent would be aboard with coverage details.

He hustled over to the car, shook hands with Wingo while nodding to his buddy, "Let's go."

They drove south on Duck Road and took a left onto Four Seasons Lane. The house was easy to find. A blue Volkswagen Beetle and a Silver Infiniti G35 were parked in the driveway.

"Looks like they're here," Wingo said.

"Or out fishing or sunbathing, or they could be playing tennis up at the courts we passed," said Rollins.

"It will be easy to block the cars," Valdez added.

"I just hope we can do this without violence," Rollins said.

"If she is guilty she has to be on edge. I don't know about the guy," Valdez said.

"Yeah, I ran a check on him while flying down. Nothing there to indicate he's involved, or would have any inclination to be involved, but you never know, shit happens."

"I think I should call and have a couple of my guys keep an eye on the cars while we're meeting. We can fill them in by phone," Wingo suggested.

"Good idea."

Lisa had booked a meeting room at the Comfort Inn, back up the road toward the airport, just a few minutes away.

The hotel had placed a sign on an easel in front of the meeting room: *Bank Meeting, 5pm.*

Everyone was dressed casually, for now. Light jackets, dark blue with large gold letters spelling out FBI, would be worn when the plan went into action. Cans of Coke and bottled water were buried in a cooler of ice off to the side. Most of the agents had a drink in hand when Rollins walked in and greeted everyone. He grabbed a bottle of water, unscrewed the top, took a swig and re-screwed the top before addressing the troops.

"Okay. Let's see if we can't execute this capture without anyone getting hurt. Everyone should be up on the suspect, physical description, location. We need to capture her alive. I can't stress that enough. We don't know if the guy knows anything so handle any situation with him with some care, but stay alert. He's new to the ballgame, we think." Rollins stopped, gulped down some more water. He pinned a map of the area on an easel supplied by the hotel. "We got lucky with the one road in and out. If we don't make the capture and she's on the run, I want a roadblock at Rt.12 and Chicahauk Road to the south and another at the very end of Rt. 12 to the north. The road turns into sand at that point. With a four-wheel vehicle you could drive to Virginia from there. So, cover the beach north of Ocean Hill and also cover it south to Southern Shores. The Coast Guard has two boats off shore. You'll see them when you leave, one will be a mile or so out from the Corps of Engineer Pier and the other will be just outside of the breakers in front of the house. A copter will cover from the air. You'll also see a small plane flying back and forth along the beach towing a sign that says *New York Pizza Pub*. One of our guys will be a passenger. And I've arranged for Dare County police to work with us by patrolling the sound with boats." He took a deep breath and nodded toward Wingo, "Joe, are the cars still at the house?"

"Sitting pretty."

"Guys, you have the radio signal. Everybody keep me informed. Let's get this done."

29

A volleyball game was in progress to the north, an empty beach to the south.

Mario and Cassie chose the southern route for their early evening stroll. Both sported lightweight sweatshirts over bathing suits. Mario had slipped his feet into a pair of water shoes and Cassie had tied on low quarter Nike's. Word of their attire was transmitted via FBI radios. Clouds had rolled in with the change in wind, making a spring evening feel like fall which accounted for the lack of bodies. To the two horse lovers, it was perfect. Crisp and romantic, a chance to dart about, splash some water and stop for some body to body contact, eye to eye, reaching into each other's mind, searching for that special connection.

For the first block or so the two lovebirds walked in the heavier sand closest to the dunes. Mario suggested that the going would be much easier if they went shoeless and walked alongside the surf where the sand was packed. Cassie agreed. With shoes in hand, the sand felt cool between their toes as they strolled for forty-five minutes southward.

When they made a u-turn and started back, the northeast wind had kicked up the surf. Birds were diving all along the beach gulping up leftovers from feeding fish.

Mario elbowed Cassie. "Should have brought my rod."

"I thought you did." She reached and gave him a little tug which made him forget about hooking anything but her.

He pulled her close and wrapped his left arm around her shoulder. She snuggled up, made him feel wanted, made him sense she had changed her mind about involvement.

They were within three blocks of the house when she abruptly stopped, leaned down and toyed with some shells, casting her eyes ahead, seeing a group of men leaning over the deck on the house. She could feel their eyes, knew they were aimed in her direction. She looked out to sea, spotted two Coast Guard cutters lingering offshore. She spun her head and caught sight of a half dozen men jogging up the beach with a purpose. She heard the helicopter overhead but never looked up. She knew why it was there.

Mario said, "You becoming a shell collector all of a sudden?"

She slid her eyes upward and the words poured from her mouth. "Mario, listen to me and listen closely. There is no doubt in my mind that I am in love with you. But, when I told you I couldn't get involved, I meant it. I was serious."

Her emphatic tone startled him slightly but he liked the part about her being in love with him. "And . . ."

"I am going to walk away from you now, in the direction of the dunes to my left. DO NOT FOLLOW ME. In fact, do not move. Just stand here and wait. It would break my heart to see you get hurt."

He leaned, lifted her chin with a finger and looked into her eyes. "What the hell are you talking about?"

"The FBI."

"FBI?"

"The FBI is here, right now, at the house, behind us, in the copter overhead, on those boats. They're coming after me." She was speaking rapidly, fear raising its ugly head. "Don't tell them about the horse. Please. I bought him with money I won in California. He's my gift to you. He's yours, fair and square."

Mario squirmed, his eyes capturing the fear in hers before he looked northward toward the house and spotted guys in matching jackets pointing in his direction.

Cassie didn't say another word. She tossed the shoes and sprinted toward a path between the dunes.

A searchlight from the copter popped on and the area suddenly became a stage. The group from the south yelled at her to stop, screaming, "FBI, FBI, FBI." They held guns pointing toward the sky as they tried desperately to catch up with her, the deepness of the sand causing them to struggle but they kept on coming and were no more than a couple of minutes from following her between the dunes.

Mario stood there dumbfounded, his head swiveling, his eyes dancing, his heart pounding, his body frozen to the spot.

He didn't know what to do as the group was fast approaching from the north, six guys sprinting on the firmer wet sand closer to the surf, hollering at him to halt, guns in hand. Halt? What the hell did they mean by that? Jesus. He was about to piss in his pants. This was some serious shit. Theses guys had guns. What the hell had Cassie done? He tried to swallow but the fear in his throat wouldn't go down.

As soon as she was out of sight, Cassie ripped the Meg Ryan disguise from her face and the Meg Ryan wig from her head. She jammed both into the sand to the right of the path then hurried down the street for twenty yards rapidly peeling off the sweatshirt as she ran. Spotting a trash can in front of an empty house, she lifted the top and stuffed the sweatshirt as far down into the can as she could push it. She knew she was down to seconds now. Using both hands, she quickly wiped away any remaining residue from her disguise. She turned and started walking back toward the path to the beach in her bathing suit and bare feet, sucking in a deep breath then easing it out slowly. She didn't look a thing like Meg Ryan . . . or Cassie Crawford . . . or Samantha Sullivan. She was whistling "Over a Rainbow" when six FBI agents stormed onto the street.

She stopped in her tracks, threw her hands to her mouth then screamed, "Oh my God!"

One of the agents grabbed her by the shoulders and held her strongly as the other agents pushed forward in search of their prey.

She kept on screaming to the man upstairs, her body trembling.

"Settle down, lady. We're FBI. We're looking for a female who just ran this way. Blonde hair, dressed in a sweatshirt. Did you see her?"

She stared at the agent, buying time to think about her answer.

"I asked you a question, lady. This is urgent. DID YOU SEE HER?"

She nodded then turned and waved a finger down the street, excitement in her voice, "I did see her. She ran by me and I saw her turn into the wooded area past that blue house on the left. Oh my God, what did she do?"

The agent didn't answer and she didn't care as he pushed on by her, yelling to the other agents to head toward the fourth house on the left.

She stood there for a moment and watched the action with a smile on her face. Not only was she a good makeup artist, she was also a pretty damn good actress. She turned and stepped toward the dunes. Voices made her hesitate. Carefully, she slid into an area close enough to listen. Dropping to her knees she parted blades of the tall grass with her fingers and saw Mario standing exactly where she'd left him. She felt safe for the moment knowing that the other agents were up the street in search of Samantha Sullivan. The copter was inland, working in conjunction with the agents on the ground. Six FBI agents were approaching Mario yelling for him to hold his ground. She suspected that they were the agents she spotted hanging over the rail at the rental. Her body was still, her eyes and her ears tuned to the action around Mario.

She saw one agent hold off the five who were with him by holding up his hand like a traffic cop as he approached Mario. He showed his badge and said, "I'm William Rollins of the FBI. Are you Mario Bozzela?"

My god, she thought, they were looking for Mario as well.

Mario nodded, his toes doing a tap dance in the sand as he stood there nervous about he didn't know what. He stared at the five guns pointed at him and eased out a long breath before speaking, "What in the hell is going on?" Beads of sweat had broken out on his arms, little pools of water from his brain reminding him that he was scared shitless.

Rollins calmly said, "You can walk back to the house with us or we can cuff you and escort you with force."

Mario responded instantly, "Cuff me for what? I'll walk."

He felt like a caged animal with Rollins in front, a guy on each side and three guys behind him. "Will somebody please tell me what this is about, why Cassie ran and why you are after her?" After two steps, he stopped in his tracks. "God, you're not going to kill her, are you?"

"Her name's not Cassie," Rollins said.

"What?"

"Her name's not Cassie, nor is it Crawford."

Astonished, Mario responded, "Then what is her damn name?"

"Look, let's just get back to the house. We'll sit down and do some talking. You tell me some things. I'll tell you some things."

Those were the last words she could hear with clarity. She checked behind her and saw no one then stood and watched Mario being led to the house. Tears slipped from her eyes. Slowly, she walked the path to the beach and stepped onto the sand.

To Mario, it seemed like forever before they reached the boardwalk. While trudging up the steps, Mario glanced back to where he had last seen Cassie. He wondered if she were still alive. He saw a lone person in a bathing suit walking along the surf but it wasn't Cassie.

Just as they stepped inside the rental, Rollins got a call from Wingo who stated, "We lost her."

"You haven't lost her, you just haven't found her. She has to be holed up. She's barefooted and has to be right under your nose."

"She may have stolen a car or forced someone to drive her."

"In two minutes time? I don't think so. But, if she did, we'll nail her. All exit roads are covered."

She was aware of the distant scurrying of men, loud voices, the low flying helicopter humming along, searchlights scanning every inch of the area. From a distance, she spotted people out on decks stretching their necks, gawking at the action, anxious, nervous and scared out of their wits. *This was the Outer Banks, an oasis. How dare anyone interfere and change that landscape.* She said out loud, "I'm sorry."

Mario absorbed Rollins' end of the conversation not knowing which side to cheer for, his emotions percolating on overload, drumming up a hundred visions.

No question she had lied. His heart was now in a tailspin.

Rollins motioned for Mario to take a seat on the sofa. Rollins tapped the power button on the television, tuned it to CNN then pulled up a wooden kitchen chair. He placed the back facing Mario and straddled it. He motioned toward the screen. Now, it was just Mario, Rollins and two agents, one standing guard by the door, the other down by Cassie's car. The other three had taken off, joining the chase three blocks away.

Cassie's picture filled the screen. The name Samantha Sullivan was displayed in large white letters. Obviously the press had been notified and was on top of the situation. He figured that the FBI wanted her picture out there for all to see. He listened carefully to the reporter as shots from Tuesday's robbery of *his* bank were broadcast. He remembered her calling him from North Carolina that evening. He had been told that she hadn't shown up at the track on Sunday. Nothing made sense to him. His ass was confused, tangled by a female.

Rollins watched him view the screen, looking for any tics or gestures that might indicate involvement. But what he saw was a guy who was overwhelmed, shocked and downright flabbergasted.

Mario massaged his brow, sweat dribbling down his face, his breath escaping in short spurts.

"You know anything about this?" Rollins said while motioning toward the TV.

"No."

"Nothing?"

"I said NO!"

"What do you know?"

"Obviously, I don't know shit."

"How long have you known her?"

"Two, maybe three weeks. I spotted her at the track earlier, followed her around for about a month before finally getting to talk with her."

"You telling me you stalked her?"

"Jesus. No. I thought she looked like Meg Ryan and that got my attention. She's a damn good-looking woman and I'm a single guy."

"Looking for some action."

"Yeah, I guess you could say that."

"Well, I think you found it."

Rollins continued presenting a friendly front, wanting Mario to warm up to him.

"So, did you ever go to her place?"

Despite the intenseness, Rollin's question brought on a smile. "I followed her one day, curious about where she lived."

"You're pretty good at stalking, aren't you?" Rollins said, tapping Mario on the knee, shooting him a little grin.

"I wasn't stalking. I was curious. We had been on a date. She met me at a 7-Eleven, for Christ's sake. Wouldn't you have wanted to know why? I mean, hell, she could have been married or something. Husband could have shot me. I had to find out."

"And did you?"

"I didn't find out anything about a husband but I did find out where she lived."

"And."

"Down a dirt road off Rt. 197 across and down the street from a McDonald's near Bowie State College. She lived in a damn RV . . . rented the land. I know that because the guy who leased the land threatened my butt with a shotgun when he caught me looking in a window."

"Snooping?"

"Whatever. I tried to wiggle out of the predicament by telling him that I was looking for a person named Crawford."

"And what did he say?"

"He didn't know any Crawford."

"I assume that got your attention?"

Mario nodded, "I confronted her about it later but she laughed and told me she told the guy not to tell anyone her name, said she had me on tape from a surveillance camera."

"Did you ever see the tape?"

"No, why?"

"Maybe she didn't have one."

Mario let out another long breath, shook his head. "Probably not. I'm an idiot."

"Did you see anything interesting when you looked through the window?"

"Lots of cash."

"What was your reaction?"

"She won it at the track."

"She bet a lot?"

Mario went on to tell him about her betting patterns, explaining more about why he followed her around the track, trying to figure her out.

Rollins said, "I suspect she was using bank money as a stake, betting it. You know, laundering it in case it was marked."

"How come the track didn't call you guys?"

"It wasn't marked."

Mario grinned.

"What's funny?"

"Oh, nothing really but it does explain her winning all the time making show bets on favorites."

"Anything else you want to tell me?"

"The guy who owned the land told me she had come up from Florida."

"That's interesting since the robbery before Delaware took place in Miami." He paused and gathered his thoughts before continuing, "Route 197, right?"

Mario nodded.

Rollins got up, strolled around, opening cabinet doors in the kitchen, searching as he made a cell call to headquarters requesting the RV story be checked out.

Meanwhile, Mario continued to watch the news, CNN now announcing that the FBI had Samantha Sullivan cornered in Duck, North Carolina.

"It was my damn bank," Mario said.

"What?"

"She robbed my damn bank, two blocks from my house."

Rollins tried to maintain his composure but lost it, couldn't help but laugh.

Mario joined him, laughed a little, shaking off some tension.

"Did she ever give you any money?"

Mario ran his forearm across his mouth before answering, "No. She didn't give me any money, but she did buy me dinner once." He didn't mention the horse.

The agent standing by the door walked over and whispered into Rollins' ear.

Rollins eyes moved in the direction of the agent.

The agent returned to his post.

Rollins leaned in, got a little closer to Mario. "You happen to be kin to Geno Bozzela?"

"He's my uncle. Why?"

"Excuse me a minute. I need to make another call." Rollins got up again, this time he walked outside, hung his arms over the deck after dialing a number on his cell.

Mario glanced at the agent by the door. The guy smiled and tossed him a slight nod.

Mario heard the pitter-patter of rain. Northeast winds about to bring down some moisture, dampen the Outer Banks. Little drops followed by big drops followed by a downpour.

Rollins rushed back inside, his hair now wet, water dripping down his face, phone still to his ear.

Her hair was wet, too. But she didn't hurry anywhere. The rain was the least of her worries. She had been standing in the surf allowing the waves to kick over her feet as she watched Mario through the windows wishing she could hear the conversation. Her house was another few blocks ahead. She hadn't invited Mario there because it would have been way too revealing, a house full of memories and what she *really* did for a living. That was for another day down the road. She'd committed to the rental knowing that she was going to invite him to Duck, convinced that he would come once she mentioned the horse. She didn't know that the robbery was going to tangle her plans but she sure was sorry that it had. She had no idea how she would rectify any of her actions with God and she knew damn well that Cassie Crawford's relationship with Mario was down the tubes. The whole bank robbing scenario had caught her at a vulnerable time in her life. Damn Cal Russo. She shook her head, the rain pounding down not making a dent in her thoughts. She saw Rollins close the phone and use his hands like a wiper blade on his face before she started sloshing through the surf toward her house. Every step or two she glanced back toward the rental as the tears came again.

Rollins opened his cell and punched in another number.

Mario listened attentively picking up bits and pieces.

"Damn," Rollins said as he folded his phone then pointed it at Mario. "Your girlfriend is still on the loose."

"Ex-girlfriend," Mario said, curious as to how she was avoiding an onslaught of FBI agents.

"If you say so. Look, you want some water or something, maybe need to use the head?"

"Both," said Mario, his bladder full and his mouth so dry he couldn't juice up a baseball.

Rollins motioned with his head. Mario headed for the john. When he returned, Rollins handed him a can of Coke.

"One of our agents is a close friend of your uncle, known him for years. He and his wife eat at the restaurant at least once a week."

"Yeah, what's his name?"

"Lou Capella."

"Short guy, stocky, has a Jersey accent?"

"Uh, huh."

"Yeah, I know who he is."

"He's on the phone with Geno right now, checking you out."

Mario smiled, knowing this would be positive. "Geno had a stroke."

"Lou told me."

"But he can comprehend and communicate. His mind is still sharp."

"Let's hope he says good things about you."

Rollins went to the fridge, grabbed a Coke for himself and tossed one to the agent at the door. Mario thought about the guy by the car, wondering if he had sense enough to come in out of the rain and find a spot under the house.

Larry King's guest was John Walsh. Appropriate.

Rollins' phone chirped. He answered then ducked into a bedroom.

Mario listened to King and Walsh, his thoughts turning to Cassie. Ten minutes later, Rollins was back in his seat.

"Geno said he warned you about the girl."

"Yeah, he did. That's why I followed her to where she lived."

"Says you're a good boy, wouldn't steal from anybody but would bet your life on a horse. That true?"

"Afraid so."

Rollins turned to the agent, "We need to dust, get some prints."

Mario chuckled.

"What's funny?"

"Oh, just the fact that probably a thousand different people have stayed here."

Rollins pondered the statement for a moment. "Yes, but we have her car."

"Right." He stopped laughing. "Her prints, my prints and I don't know who else's prints."

"And we have your place."

"What do you mean, you have my place?"

"We need to search your house. We have the address. Agents are parked in your driveway right now, waiting for my call."

"What? You need my permission?"

"I can get a warrant in two minutes or you can give me permission. It's your decision."

"And, what exactly are you looking for?"

"Prints." He leaned in, stared into Mario's eyes. "And any involvement by you."

The last statement grabbed Mario by the throat, pissed him off. "Yeah, you can go in, mess up my house, but I'm not involved with any damn bank robberies. And you better leave the place the way you find it."

Rollins grinned. "You wouldn't be threatening the FBI would you, Mario?"

Mario considered Rollins' question carefully before responding with a hint of arrogance. "Take it any way you like." He swigged down some Coke, had his eyes on Rollins, awaiting his response.

Rollins stood then walked away and whispered something to the other agent before turning and speaking. "You got a key hidden anywhere? We wouldn't want to get you all riled up by damaging your front door."

Mario smiled, knowing his statement had made some impact. Maybe, just maybe, they would not destroy his house. "It's around back hanging on a nail in a tree with a note attached that identifies it as the key to my front door." He smiled one of those forced smiles.

"I think we need to put the cuffs on you now, maybe stick a piece of tape on your smart-ass mouth," Rollins said while walking toward Mario.

"The key is hidden underneath my lawn jockey, painted in the silks of Seattle Slew, my favorite horse."

"One of those stone jobs?"

"Heavy as hell."

Rollins made the call, told the agents where the key was located and to proceed with the search. As soon as he hung up, his cell chirped again. He carried on a brief conversation. Mario assumed he was talking with headquarters.

Rollins closed his phone and said, "The RV is gone. Your friend who owns the land told our office that a guy drove the vehicle away early Saturday morning. Said the girl followed in her car. Didn't know where they were headed, didn't give a shit, he had two month's rent advanced in cash."

Mario shrugged. What could he say? He wondered what was happening down the beach. Again, he had mixed emotions, his heart interfering with his brain, scrambled eggs and stupidity doing a two-step. He could hear the copter flying back and forth. He could hear tires screeching, voices screaming. He hadn't heard gunfire.

The guy from downstairs came up, grabbed a Coke out of the fridge then lifted a bagel from a bag. Mario wanted to tell him to ask. The FBI didn't have the rights to raid the refrigerator, drink her drinks, eat her food, but they did.

Rollins disappeared, gone to chase down Cassie or Samantha or what's-her-name. Left Mario in the hands of two agents. The agents told him he could go to bed if he wished. Mario wished and he did hit the sack but never closed his eyes.

Early the next morning Rollins walked into the house carrying a plastic bag. He whispered something to the agent still on the premises. The agent nodded and headed out the door. Mario was already up and back in the same seat again watching CNN reveal photo after photo of bank robbers from nineteen thefts across the country. Thirty-eight different faces appeared onscreen but they were all disguises created by two former Hollywood makeup artists. One of those individuals was Samantha Sullivan, the other Cal Russo. Russo was killed in the robbery attempt in Maryland and discovery of his real identity led the FBI to Samantha Sullivan. To Mario, Rollins said, "Enjoying the show?"

With his eyes still on the tube, Mario said, "Unbelievable."

Rollins eased out a slight smile. "It gets better." He stepped in front of Mario, blocking his view of the screen, and said, "What does she really look like?"

Startled by the question, Mario said, "Meg Ryan. You have her picture. Hell, it's all over television."

"I assume you had sex with her."

"Couple times, that's all. We weren't going at it hot and heavy. She was difficult to get close to."

"You notice anything about her face that was strange?"

"Strange? Not really. Hell, she looked like Meg Ryan and that was good enough for me."

"You sure?"

Hell, thought Mario, he wasn't sure about a damn thing at this point. "Obviously, I don't know crap about her when you come right down to it."

Rollins yanked a handful of stuff from the bag and said, "Here's your Meg Ryan."

Mario said, "What?"

"Meg Ryan is right here in my hands, hair and all. What you fell for was a disguise. But I'm confused as to how you wouldn't have known that having slept with her. I mean, you did kiss her, didn't you? Maybe ran your hands all over her body?"

Mario grabbed the evidence from Rollins, sat there and stared at it, shaking his head in disgust. Suddenly, he threw it against the television. "She wore turtlenecks."

"Turtlenecks?"

Mario wrapped his index finger and thumb around his neck just below his chin. "Up to here."

"Please don't tell me she owned a turtleneck bathing suit."

"She had several. Wore one last night under her sweatshirt."

"What color?"

"Black."

The veins in Rollins' neck suddenly bulged like an explosion was about to take place. He screamed, "Goddamn it! We had her." He whipped out his cell and while shaking his head, he quickly made a call that was picked up immediately. Rollins said, "Didn't you tell me that the woman you ran into last night when you first went through the dunes had on a black bathing suit with a turtleneck?"

By the look on Rollins' face, Mario knew the answer.

"Did you get a reading on her height?" He looked at Mario, one hand holding the phone to his ear, the other moving up and down like an elevator.

Mario held up eight fingers.

Rollins said to the agent, "Mario says five eight, too. Any distinguishing features?" He looked at Mario, expecting some help.

Mario said, "How in the hell would I know?"

Into the phone again Rollins said, "How about hair color?"

He got a short answer then said, "Well, shit, there have to be millions of five eight brunettes . . . anything else?"

Another short pause as Rollins listened then said, "Yeah, I know your focus was on finding a female who looked like Meg Ryan. Call me immediately if another vision pops into your head . . . nose, teeth, ears . . . whatever." He then closed the phone and said to Mario, "She's smart."

Mario chuckled, nodded. "I was just thinking. You're a guy so you know where I'm coming from. Man, when we got naked, so to speak, I was busy, excited as hell, paying attention to the parts of her body I was most interested in at the time. Yeah, we kissed but I didn't notice anything strange. To me it was all good."

"I hear you. The area around the mouth is pretty wide on the disguise." Rollins walked over and picked up the evidence from the floor then showed Mario what he was talking about. "See."

Mario stared at the disguise then said, "I swear to you that every single day I saw her she looked like Meg Ryan . . . every fucking *fool my ass* day."

"She sure did get your attention, didn't she?"

"Yeah, but the goddamn strange thing is she didn't want it?"

"What the hell does that mean?"

Mario ran the story of what he'd gone through to get a date emphasizing that she'd constantly told him she couldn't get involved.

"But you kept after her, correct?"

Mario nodded. "Used every bit of charm I could come up with but it wasn't my charm that got the job done. An eight-year-old took care of that."

"Explain."

Mario spit out the details about Little Geno then added, "She loves the horses."

"I finally figured that out. Every bank that was robbed was near a race track. I'm pretty confident she's still here on the Outer Banks laughing her ass off about fooling the FBI last night, but I think she'll stub her toe somewhere along the way and we'll nail her."

"But you don't know what she looks like, or her name."

"Neither do you."

30

Emma Frederico's image looked Emma Frederico in the eye and Emma stared back from the mirror. She wasn't happy with what she faced. It wasn't the look of exhaustion or the whiteness of her skin but the guilt that that had permeated her mind. The guilt wasn't visible but it was floating in the air like a balloon waiting to be popped. What the hell went wrong with her life? Cal Russo was what was wrong. He had taught her so much and she'd come to totally admire and respect him. What a mistake that was. His reaction to being snubbed at the Academy Awards was childish. Just because all the actors in the movie had scored statues was no reason to go off half cocked and start robbing banks just to prove to the world how good he was, and she was, at fooling people. In his mind the two of them were responsible for the awards, not the actors. She shook her head at the mirror and said, "Just because your dad's funeral was the day before the Awards show was no reason for you to feel sorry for yourself and agree to his shenanigans, no reason at all. It was just your damn excuse. You caved in to an idiot. You didn't need the money. But you went along and now look where you are? Like a foolish teen you allowed yourself to get talked into one robbery, promising yourself that you'd walk away if you weren't killed but you kept on going, all wrapped up in the euphoria. You're a great artist and you know it. You need to walk out of this bathroom and stroll through this house and take another look at the equine paintings you've executed, be proud of the New York Racing Association commissioning you to design the posters seen by millions and purchased by the thousands. Be proud of the paintings *not* hanging on your walls but on the walls of racing fans and art lovers throughout the country. Hell, throughout the world." She wiped a tear from her face then used the mirror again for a sounding board. "And then there's Mario. Look what the hell you've done to a guy who you'd marry in a heartbeat. He had two NYRA posters decorating the walls in his living room, your stylish M signed boldly in the lower right hand corner. You couldn't even comment because you were hiding behind a disguise. I ask you, Emma Frederico, what in the hell were you thinking? Your dad, your poor dad, died in a nursing home from an inoperable brain tumor just miles south in Nags Head thinking you were the daughter that any man would be proud to have." She stepped back from the mirror, tears rolling down her face before easing forward, her face inches from the mirror, the back of a hand wiping away the teardrops as she said, "Dad, I'm sorry I disappointed you. I'm in trouble now. I may end up in prison but I promise you that I will do everything in my power to make amends." Then she turned and walked from the room.

Ten minutes later she was back looking into the mirror again thinking she couldn't make amends of any kind as a locked-up felon. She flipped her hair with both hands while thinking about last night. The hair color must change along with the style. She'd go from brunette to dirty blonde, add some curls and let it grow to shoulder length. Surely that FBI agent would recall something about her. Yes, he was glancing past her while holding tight to her shoulders but he was a *trained* agent, and the FBI was not going to be happy that she had escaped. Without a doubt agents had turned every sand pebble, every rock, and every blade of grass in search of a clue to her whereabouts. They *would* find the disguise in the sand. And, if smart, they would determine that Samantha Sullivan wasn't her name. They'd know she no longer looked like Meg Ryan. Then a smile drifted across her face along with a hint of confidence. The FBI did not know her name or what she looked like other than what the agent could provide and that wouldn't be much. Her thoughts drifted to Susan Atwood. A little over four years ago the economy had tumbled and the art market had dried up. Her dad had made the suggestion to get together with Susan and learn a new trade in case she needed it. Makeup, like painting, was a creative endeavor so why not? Susan was the person responsible for turning her into a great makeup artist, taking her under her wing and teaching her the ropes before she died of cancer. She left a note suggesting that contact be made with Cal Russo in Hollywood, knowing that Russo was looking for an assistant. She'd flown to Hollywood, met with Russo and he turned her down but she returned the next day looking exactly like Meg Ryan, so much so that Russo thought she *was* Meg Ryan. It was the first time she'd ripped off the disguise. He hired her on the spot and tagged her with a new name saying it was how Hollywood operated. That's when she became Samantha Sullivan in both name and looks. Russo assured her that opportunities would come forth for her to be Ryan's double in some movies. Only two people knew the Samantha Sullivan story and one of them was dead.

Despite a night of little or no sleep, her adrenaline stepped forth and provided the energy for her to push onward. The storage area below the house was a fantasyland. Photos lined the walls, movie stars with bigger noses, smaller noses, new wrinkles, cuts, bruises, scars, bald heads, added pounds, facial hair, females who were males, males who were females. Each photo was a display of her artistic talent. She looked around at the silicone and wigs and tools of the trade wondering if she should dispose of it all or keep it. Not knowing what was in her future, she decided that she'd retain it all for now. There might come a day when she needed to become an entirely new person again although she dreaded the thought. She examined several photos before deciding that the hair color and cut of a character actress named Kristy Morrell was perfect. She grabbed the picture from the wall then filled a small cardboard box with scissors, a styling blade, and several boxes of hair color.

Three hours later, a new Emma Frederico appeared before her mirror. No comments were made. She slipped into knee-length shorts and a casual top, stuck her feet into a pair of yellow Crocs, grabbed the keys to her Jeep Grand Cherokee then hustled down the steps to ground level. She popped into the Jeep then backed out the driveway, stopping suddenly as she approached the street. As were most houses on the Outer Banks, the two-story structure carried a name. When her dad had purchased it years ago, he had stuck Saxy Girl on the house. After his death, she'd changed the name to Musical Memories. She stared at the wooden sign that matched the cedar shake structure and shook her head, her mind not allowing her to put what she'd done behind her. The sax part of the original name was all about her dad and grandfather. The girl part was all about Emma. She'd told Mario stories about the family history in the music business but had not given up real names. Something else she was sorry about. Someday maybe she'd be able to tell him the truth. That would be nice.

She drove out to the main road and turned south. She was itching to drive by the rental but knew better. When she passed the Scarborough Lane Shops, a G35 coupe pulled into traffic two cars behind her. Mario was behind the wheel and a kite was riding with him. Two black four-door Crown Vics pulled out behind Mario. Her heart skipped a few beats and her breathing picked up speed. She told herself to calm down. Neither Mario nor the FBI knew what she looked like or what kind of vehicle she drove, other than the blue bug. The Jeep had been around a few years. It was her beach buggy and used to tote large pieces of art. The bug was a goner as far as she was concerned. The FBI had it and they could keep it.

Maybe she'd buy another one but that thought quickly dissipated based on it being an absolutely stupid decision under the circumstances. She kept her eye on the three vehicles as she made her way toward Seamark Foods to stock up on some groceries. She'd bought plenty three days ago but the rental was now home to her purchases. When she stopped at the light near the fire station, she tapped the scan button on her radio in search of some news about Samantha Sullivan. She got it on a talk show. Guy by the name of Neal Boortz was commenting about one of the bank robberies, the one in Spokane, Washington, where one of the thieves looked exactly like the mayor resulting in the mayor being arrested. Boortz and the guy chuckled about it but then Boortz went into a tirade about people's decision-making being the cause of most of society's problems. She heard him make comment after comment about the choices people make and where those choices led. She hung her head knowing that Boortz' words certainly applied to her.

She tapped the radio off then turned into the shopping center at the light in front of McDonald's. Her eyes were on the rear view mirror. Mario went through the light and headed west toward the Wright Memorial Bridge. She assumed he was headed back to Maryland. She didn't know if he knew he had an escort. After the three vehicles were well out of sight, she tossed Mario a little hand wave murmuring, "I miss you already."

31

Rollins stared at his coffee cup, his mind detached as the jet bucked a headwind while fighting its way cross country to Los Angeles. Before leaving the Outer Banks he had instructed a dozen agents to continue the search for the person he still referred to as Samantha Sullivan. Nothing had been released to the press about finding the disguise. He had also laid out a plan for agents from the Baltimore office to keep their eyes on Mario, not as a suspect but as a possible lead to Sullivan. The lady obviously loved the ponies and so did Mario. On the other side of the aisle Valdez was asleep, head leaning against the window, mouth open, making a few gurgling noises. Both were dressed in navy blue pinstripe suits, looking more like bankers than FBI agents. An hour later they landed at a private field west of downtown Los Angeles. Vince, along with Rick Jablonski of the L.A. office, greeted them as they stepped from the plane.

Around a table in the small terminal, Rick filled everyone in on Sullivan's bank, her last home address, business associates and any friends outside of the entertainment business. Rollins made the decision to split duties. He'd take the bank, Rick the business associates since he had local contacts, Valdez the home and neighbors, Vince the friends. Each was to conduct extensive interviews, looking for anything that led to her whereabouts or personal history. The L.A. office had provided cars. They agreed to meet at eight that evening in Rollins' room at the Marriott Courtyard in Marina del Rey.

Rick opened a map and pointed out the destinations. Her home and bank were within a mile of each other near the hotel where Rollins booked rooms for himself, Valdez and Vince. After handing Vince a list of names and addresses, located from Santa Monica to Long Beach, he circled intersections with a red pen to help him find the streets. He drew a larger circle around the Century City/ Beverly Hills area where he would spend the day.

The sky was blue but invisible as Rollins traveled west on I-10 to I-405 south, bumper to bumper traffic whizzing eighty miles an hour, seeing who could zoom in and out the most without playing bumper cars. He shook his head, thinking he might not fuss as much about Washington traffic when he returned.

Marina Community Bank's main office was located at the corner of Lincoln Boulevard and Admiralty Way, a three-story building with great views of the bay. Place looked more like a movie star's home than an office with its spectacular open foyer, expansive glass and bright red railings. Before making the trip, Rollins had contacted the bank and scheduled a meeting.

Executive Vice-President Elizabeth Payson welcomed him into her corner office located on the third floor. She motioned for him to take a seat in one of two leather chairs near the windows then offered him coffee or orange juice. Since he was in California, he sprung for the juice. She buzzed her secretary who brought in a pitcher and two glasses and placed them on the table between the two chairs. She filled the glasses before departing.

Ms. Payson handed Rollins Samantha Sullivan's account information. "It's difficult to believe that Miss Sullivan would be involved in robbing banks," she said.

"You never know about people. Priests prey upon children. A mother drowns toddlers. Millionaires embezzle. And, occasionally a President decides he's way above the law. Nothing surprises me." Rollins never lifted his eyes from the folder as he spoke, very matter of fact, very focused. "I'm going to need copies of several items."

"No problem."

"Did you know her personally?"

"Somewhat. She was a good customer, in and out of the bank several times a week."

"Conducting what type of business?"

"Making cash deposits mostly. I assume you know that she liked to bet on the horses."

"I'm well aware of that, yes."

"She must be good at it. Several times she made deposits of over five hundred thousand, and once well over a million."

"In cash?"

"In cash. Gave our tellers tips all the time on horses running down at Del Mar in San Diego. Once, she rented a bus and took the whole staff. Had a caterer from the movie business load up the bus with food and drink. She paid for everything and gave each of us a fifty-dollar bill to use for betting money. We all had quite a day. Folks around here still talk about it."

Rollins took a sip of orange juice realizing immediately that it was freshly squeezed. A second sip followed before he said, "What you are telling me is that you think she had plenty of money."

"I know she did. Up until a couple of weeks ago she had close to two million in her money market account. She closed the account, said she had sold her condo, was leaving California to start a new life."

Rollins stared at the figure of one million, eight hundred thousand and seventy-nine dollars before easing out a breath. His eyes slid to the withdrawal date, the morning after the robbery in Delaware. He glanced up, "How were the funds dispersed?"

"In cash."

"Really?"

"Yes. She called me the day before, around nine-thirty and made the request. I told her it would take a few hours to get the cash together. She wanted to know if she could pick it up when we opened the next morning."

"And you were able to accommodate her?"

She nodded. "It's not an unusual request here in California, you know, movie stars and all, big balances."

"Did she mention where she was calling from?"

"No, but as you know we are required to keep extensive phone logs. You need a copy of that, too?"

"Yes. My guess is the call came in from Delaware, probably a pay phone."

"I don't know about that but she did show up the next morning. We met in my office and chit-chatted for a few minutes."

"Did she say where she was moving?"

"I did ask her as a friend, but she was vague, told me she wasn't sure yet, had several places in mind. Said she had met someone. I assumed she meant a guy."

Rollins nodded, "Probably."

"You'll notice on her account record that her last deposit by check was over two years ago, a paycheck she received from a studio."

He shook his head in disbelief. "I've never seen one like this."

"What do you mean?"

"It makes no sense. She has money. Why would she take off and start robbing banks?"

"Are you absolutely positive she's the bank robber?"

Rollins chewed on the question before answering, "Everything points to her."

"But are you one hundred percent sure?"

"At this point, we are quite confident she's the guilty party."

She said, "Well, it's awfully hard for me to believe."

"What's the last address you have for her?"

"The address on the account, it's just a few minutes from here." Rollins recognized the address as the one

Valdez was investigating as they spoke. "The last time I saw her in the bank before she closed the account she mentioned she'd be gone for several months. I had the impression she was headed overseas to work on a movie. Used to be that all the movies were made right here in Hollywood but today a film could be made anywhere."

Rollins pointed to the social security number. "Is this the number she gave you?"

"Yes, why?"

"Name and number don't match."

"We haven't been notified."

He got up and walked to the window. Smog had cleared. "Hell of a view."

"Yeah, we paid dearly for it. California real estate is not cheap, especially when water is a factor."

"Did any of your employees have a personal relationship with her in any way?"

"Not really, although I believe Natalie Sanchez did have drinks with her one day after work. She's one of our tellers. In fact, now that I think about it, Ms. Sullivan did most of her business at her window."

"I'd like to talk with her for a few minutes." It wasn't a demand, more like a request.

"Sure. I'll get her and you two can use my office. Just let my secretary know when you need me again. She'll find me."

Three minutes later Natalie Sanchez entered the room and introduced herself, all bubbly and wide-eyed, not the least bit intimidated by the situation. She was a little bitty woman, no more than four eleven, hair the color of a raven with eyes full of energy and skin tanned to perfection.

Each captured a leather chair. She sat forward, anxious to participate.

"You know why we are meeting, correct?" he said.

She nodded. "Sam."

"Ms. Payson mentioned that the two of you went for drinks once."

"Oh, more than once, she was teaching me how to do makeup. Took me over to her condo after work and showed me some tricks of the trade."

"Is your interest in makeup personal or professional?"

"I'd love to become a makeup artist like Sam. She was unbelievable, could make you look entirely different in just a few minutes. One Sunday, she made me look exactly like Madonna then four hours later had me looking like Spike Lee. I went from being Mexican to white to black within hours. She was just incredible."

"That good, huh?"

Wide eyed, she responded, "A bona fide genius is what I would call her."

"So tell me, did she ever talk about her family or where she had grown up?"

"She told me she didn't have any real roots . . . that her dad moved around all the time, that her mom had deserted them a long time ago."

"Was he in the service, Army, Navy?"

"She didn't say. She always changed the subject when things got personal. But it was okay. I really liked her. She was kind and warm and generous. Did Ms. Payson tell you she took us all to the horse races one day on a bus?"

"Yes, said you had a great time."

"Yeah, and I won a whole bunch of money."

"She told you what horse to bet?"

She nodded, smiled.

"Did she have interest in anything other than horseracing?"

"Music, she liked music. Played old stuff the whole time she worked with me on makeup."

"Old stuff?"

"Lots of horns, singers like Frank Sinatra, Ella. The day we all went to Del Mar she had a CD player with her and listened to music while the horses were running."

"Did she ever say why she liked that kind of music?"

"Said she grew up with it, that's all."

"I can relate to that. My mom would have left my dad for old blue eyes."

"Old blue eyes?"

"Sinatra, they called him old blue eyes." Rollins squirmed in his seat, the generation gap touching a nerve.

"Oh." She smiled, revealing a look of innocence.

"Can you think of anything else, anything at all that would help us find her?"

She glanced at her feet, raised her eyes toward Rollins . . . came up with a whole new attitude. Emphatically, she said, "She didn't rob a bank."

"We think she robbed a lot of banks."

"No way. She had all kinds of money, probably could have started a small bank."

He stood, walked to the window and admired the view again. The water was dotted with hundreds of sailboats. He wondered what kind of jobs these people had, or if they worked at all.

"When you say all kinds of money, you mean here in the bank?"

"Here, and at home. She had gym bags full of money shoved under her bed."

"She showed you."

"Yeah, joking around one day, said it was for her dad."

"Mr. Sullivan."

She nodded.

He said, "Did she mention where he lived?"

"No, just that he was sick and needed the money."

"You mean like in a hospital?"

"I don't think he was in a hospital, no."

"She had a checking account, right?"

"A money market account. She could write three checks a month."

"I need to ask Ms. Payson to get me copies of the cancelled checks."

"I don't think she ever wrote checks, just made deposits and cash withdrawals. She was in and out of the bank all the time."

Rollins figured Ms. Sanchez would be unaware of checks written. He made a mental note to ask Payson.

"I'll let you go back to work now. Thanks for your cooperation."

As she started for the door, she said, "She's a good person. She had no reason to rob banks."

"Did you see her the day she closed her account?"

"Yes."

"What did she say to you?"

"She handed me a manila envelope and told me the name of a school in the Beverly Hills area that taught makeup. She suggested that I enroll in night classes."

"What was in the envelope?"

"Ten thousand dollars."

32

Rollins returned to the Marriott earlier than expected but he wasn't the only one. Valdez, Rick and Vince were sitting in the lobby gobbling down popcorn. He approached and held up four bags from Baja Fresh. With a head nod he said, "Come on, let's head upstairs and we'll eat between the words of wisdom I know you have."

Rollins had a suite with a sitting area. They each grabbed a spot. He passed around the bags, the aroma of cilantro rising from each.

"Let's go one at a time, don't embellish . . . just spit out the nuts and bolts. Hector, what you got?"

"Fish taco." He lifted the taco, took a small bite, chewed, and realized that the big boss wasn't interested in what he'd pulled from the bag. "Oh, you mean about Sullivan." He placed the taco on a napkin. "She sold her condo about a month ago but it had been empty for two years. Neighbors who knew her said they couldn't believe she would rob a bank, said she was friendly, had nice things to say about everybody and was generous as hell, always contributed to any cause, put up money for pool parties, sometimes talked a big time movie star into coming over and joining in the festivities. No one has heard from her and no one knew where she was from or anything about her family. A couple of people mentioned that she liked old music. Bottom line is I didn't turn up anything we can use."

Rollins lifted a shrimp taco from a bag while nodding at Rick, saying, "Your turn."

"Omaha came up as to where she went when she left California. Nobody knew for sure, it was all hearsay. Everyone she worked with said she was the best, better than Cal Russo. One small time actress by the name of Carolyn Simmons told me she was sure that Sam's dad had taken sick, that Sullivan confided in her one day after work that she needed to find a place for him, where he could get some care." He paused, nodded. "It's an angle we should look into. And, no one could believe she was involved in bank robberies but they did say it didn't surprise them about Russo. Seems he had a reputation of not always being on the up and up. But they did emphasize that Sam idolized Russo's work and he treated her like a daughter. They were close."

"A love connection?" quizzed Rollins.

"No indication of that at all. I asked everyone that question."

"How about addresses or phone numbers? Anybody have anything other than what we already know?"

"No. In fact, every job was with Russo. Producers contacted him."

Rollins took a healthy bite of his shrimp taco, chewed for a few seconds then directed his eyes at Vince. "Go."

"She made friends with a caterer named Karen Waltz who told me Sullivan was from the northeast but traveled every summer with her dad from New York to Miami. Also said she learned about stage makeup from her dad's girlfriend who had worked at one time on Broadway."

"Did you get a name?"

"No, Sullivan had never mentioned the woman's name."

"We should follow that up."

"She's dead according to what Sullivan told Waltz. Sullivan told her that her dad was, in a sense, her only family. Without a name, I don't see it as a lead.

"We could check out the Broadway scene, do some research on past employees and see if we can't come up with something."

"According to Waltz, Sullivan never actually worked as a makeup artist on Broadway."

"I'll give the New York office a call anyway. They may be able to run down something. We'll take a crumb at this point . . . anything."

"It's a real long shot but you're right, we should run it down."

"Okay, it's my turn, and I can't add much to the situation other than she withdrew almost two million dollars from her money market account the day after the Delaware robbery."

"Stolen money?" Hector asked.

"No. Turns out she is obviously quite the handicapper. In the past she's made deposits of five hundred thousand a couple of times and over a million once. Vice President of the bank said she was constantly in and out of the bank making cash deposits and withdrawals. A teller, who she took under her wing to teach her the makeup business, said she never wrote checks."

"Then she must know something about where Sullivan is," Rick said.

"Has no idea, but get this. Sullivan gave her the name of a school that taught makeup and ten thousand in cash to attend."

"When?" Vince asked.

"The day she closed her account."

"So, you're telling us that Sullivan was pretty much loaded before she started robbing banks."

"Looks that way." He shot a glance at Rick, "You mentioned her dad being sick, needing care, right?"

"Yeah, why?"

"So did the teller." Everyone exchanged glances, thinking that had to be a lead.

Rollins swung his eyes from agent to agent. "Without a name does anyone have a thought on what we could do with that information?"

Everyone shrugged then Hector said, "That's a tough one but the fact that she liked old music came up in my conversations, too. Apparently she's a Sinatra fan. That could lead to something."

Rollins interpreted nods from Rick and Hector to mean that they agreed. He said, "Probably worth a little work. I'll contact Mario, see what he says. If she liked Sinatra, they probably did the horizontal to "All the Way."

Hector laughed. "Yeah, but we'd be better off if she liked Lynyrd Skynyrd."

Vince said, "What the hell does that mean?"

Hector shot him a grin and started singing the lyrics to "What's your Name?"

Everyone chuckled then Rollins said, "You know what I think?"

He paused and his eyes searched the room to grab attention. "I think she's so good at makeup that she turned herself into another person and is sitting on a deck somewhere in Duck right now getting a tan. That's what I think."

Vince shook his head. "Why would she do that when all she has to do now is be who she really is, no disguise needed?"

Hector said, "Then where does that leave our agents who remained in Duck?"

Rollins slowly shook his head. "Don't know really, just trying to cover all the bases. She could stub her toe. I told them to keep their eyes open for any females her height and body shape and age who looked to be alone. The area is a family vacation spot and most females are going to have company of some sorts."

"Age?" said Hector. "How in the hell do we know her age? She could be a lot older than we suspect when you come right down to it."

"True," Rollins said. "But her body indicates that she's not. Let's face it, we need a break here. She's going to be tough to find but, damn it, we are going to find her."

Hector chuckled.

Rollins shot him a glare. "What the hell is so funny?"

"I was just thinking, she's so damn good, maybe she's not in North Carolina but right here. Heck, one of us may have interviewed her today, asked her questions and stared right into her eyes. She's probably downstairs sitting by the pool, having a martini, laughing her ass off."

Rollins shook his head realizing that what Hector had said was not out of the question, as far fetched as it seemed. He said, "Yes, she could be anywhere right now. She has her own identity, whatever that may be. And she obviously has plenty of money. I think we need to concentrate our efforts in two specific areas, music and horses. One, or both, will lead us to her."

33

There wasn't a baseball glove in the world big enough to catch all the crap Mario knew was coming his way. He didn't care. He was a big boy. He'd catch the crap if he could, let it bounce off otherwise. No question about it, he *was* showing up at the track.

Gimpy hit him first. "Damn, Mario. Where's your girlfriend, stuck in a vault somewhere?"

"Or maybe she's changed her looks again, coming out as Goldie Hawn, giggling her way to the windows," Toteboard added.

"Could be that I'm actually her, thinking about jumping your bones right here at Pimlico," Railbird laughed. "Two guys doing it at the track in front of a crowd."

Longshot added, "Must be nice to have a girlfriend who can be anybody. One night you're screwing Meg Ryan. The next night it's Sharon Stone. Hell, you could get lucky and screw Marilyn Monroe, wouldn't that be something?"

Mario said, "Damn. You guys actually read something other than the *Racing Form*."

"We keep up," Gimpy said. "You want a Twizzler? I got a new flavor just for you . . . lemon, one taste and everything goes sour."

Mario blew each a kiss. "I look at you guys and wonder why I hang out with a bunch of smart-ass, no-good track bums who couldn't get a date with a hooker."

"So, her name is Samantha, not Cassie." Gimpy said, after removing a Twizzler from his mouth, his lips taking on a yellow tint.

"Whatever." Mario looked down, displaced some ants with his right foot. He wanted to cough up the truth about the disguise but had been told by Rollins not to tell anyone until he gave the go-ahead.

Noticing Mario's demeanor, Gimpy said, "Yeah, whatever, I'm with you. You okay, good buddy?"

"I'm here, ain't I?"

Toteboard elbowed him in the arm. "Yeah, back in heaven with your buddies."

Heaven was now Pimlico Race Course in northwest Baltimore. Maryland racing bounced from track to track throughout the year. Mario was so caught up in his own mess that he had forgotten about the change and had driven to Laurel, the empty parking lot waking him to reality.

Despite the fact that he'd have to make the drive to Baltimore each day he'd bet only on horses he had watched work at Laurel. He wouldn't deviate. He had his rules and he was bound and determined to follow them. With his distraction left behind in North Carolina, he knew he was about to get back on track and make some serious bucks.

Horse named Skeet's Best was entered for the third. He'd watched the horse prep several times, thought he had a chance although he had missed his last work because of his little vacation at the beach. At 7-1, he'd play him to place, wasn't sure he could beat the four. Turned out he was wrong. The horse finished off the board, costing Mario a hundred. His buddies had all bet on the winner. He hadn't done his homework, taken a good look at how the race set up for a closer like Skeet's Best. It didn't. Race had no speed up front. He realized it afterwards and would have kicked himself in the ass if he could.

He glanced at his program and saw that Chuck had a first time starter in the next race. He wasn't looking to bet. He just wanted to catch up with Chuck and inquire about Shellcracker.

Buster spotted him, came over, tugged on his shirt, pulled him to the side. "Wow, Mario. I couldn't believe what I read and heard. Her picture's been all over television. What's up with the Samantha Sullivan name?"

"That's her name according to the FBI." He thought about the situation for a second then added, "But who knows? That could be an alias."

As horses were making their way to the gate on the backside, Buster said, "Chuck thinks his filly has a big shot. I bet her across the board, five bucks." He and Mario watched the race standing side by side just like watching morning workouts.

Chuck's filly got beat a nose but ran great. Mario made a mental note. She wins next time, probably odds on.

After Chuck finished a deep conversation with the jock--that included some hand gestures as though riding--Mario caught up with him. Chuck suggested that Mario walk with him over to the receiving barn on the backstretch. Mario dug in as they made their way around the clubhouse turn on the main track, memories of deep sand at the beach screwing with his mind.

Nodding, Mario said, "Your filly ran big."

"She may turn out to be special."

"How's Shellcracker doing?"

Chuck said, "The bank robber the one who bought the horse for you?"

It was a straight question and to the point. Mario figured Chuck deserved a straight answer. "Yes."

"Does the FBI know?"

"It didn't come up."

"They'll find out."

"Probably."

"No probably about it."

"Why do you say that?"

Mario was hustling to keep up as they approached the receiving barn. Chuck said, "Feds might think the horse was bought with stolen money. It's the federal government. They may issue some kind of order not allowing him to run."

"You mean like a restraining order?"

"Maybe."

"She told me right before she bolted that she bought the horse with money she won in California."

Chuck shrugged. "I guess we'll have to see what happens, but meanwhile I'm going on with him. He's a talented sucker. I entered him for Sunday, couldn't get in touch with you."

"What kind of race?"

"Allowance, forty-six thousand, going seven furlongs. It should set him up for the Jacobs Handicap two weeks later, hundred and fifty grand, mile and sixteenth. If he runs big Sunday, I look for him to be high weight in the handicap."

"If the FBI doesn't interfere."

"Well, I'm not going to tell anyone how you got the horse. That's up to you. But if the FBI comes around, that's a different story. I'm a horse trainer. I like what I do."

"Buster knows."

"I know."

"You, me, and Buster."

"And the guy who sold him."

Mario nodded, continued walking beside Chuck to the barn, observed the groom cool out the filly, stayed for a few minutes until she was washed down and in a stall awaiting the van ride back to Laurel on a shuttle service between tracks. Since both tracks and the training center at Bowie were under the same ownership, vans continually hauled horses back and forth at no charge. Good for owners, good for the track.

He felt a sense of relief just being around the ponies, sort of like eating comfort food, stuffing down mashed potatoes and meatloaf, banana pudding for dessert. But he didn't stick around. He had another comfort zone waiting for him in Little Italy.

As soon as Mario arrived, Geno shook his head slowly and patted the bed, an invitation to sit, time for a heart-to-heart. Geno said, "I know you didn't have anything to do with robbing a bank."

Mario didn't respond.

"I also know you got a real case of the *hots* for this girl."

Mario shrugged.

"I got the inside word that the FBI will be keeping an eye on you."

"I figured as much."

"Well, now you know for sure. I also know about the name and the disguise, more inside scoop. It's time for you to focus on the horses and the horses only. You got that?"

Mario nodded.

"Okay. I'm going to ask you this one time and I expect a straight answer."

Mario had no idea what was coming but he was all ears.

Geno said, "Do you know where she is?"

"No."

Geno allowed Mario some time to reconsider his answer, but Mario stood pat.

"Do you know her real name?"

"No."

"Do you know what she really looks like?"

"No."

"Do you think she will contact you?"

"Maybe."

"Why? She got the *hots* for you, too?"

Mario smiled, "I think so."

"Mario, Mario, my boy. She's trouble, big, big trouble."

"She bought me a horse."

"She did *what?*"

"Shellcracker."

"Shellcracker . . . the New York horse, won a stakes a few weeks back?"

Mario nodded and he couldn't hold in a grin.

Astonished, Geno said, "So, let me make sure I understand exactly what we have here. She bought you a horse with money she heisted from banks?"

"She said she bought the horse with money she won out west several years ago."

"And you believe her."

"Uh, yeah, I believe her, I think."

"And how many lies has she told you?"

Mario rolled the question around, pondering it. He couldn't come up with a number but knew it was a hell of a lot more than a couple. "A few," he said.

"A few. Jesus, Mario. The woman is a thief and a liar. Wake up."

"I'm awake."

"Yeah, you're awake all right, your eyes are open but you can't see shit."

Mario stood then roamed the room, glancing at some photos before commenting, "What should I do about the horse?"

Geno laughed, "What should you do about the horse? What the hell kind of question is that?"

"A real serious one. He's in my name. I'm licensed. Chuck Coleman is training him. He's entered for Sunday. Yeah, what should I do?"

"You know how much she paid for him?"

"A million."

"Holy crap, I can't get Maria to give me a twenty to make a bet."

Grinning, Mario said, "I'd like to make arrangements for you to come see him race, Little Geno, too. We'll get our picture taken in the winner's circle, all together, a family shot."

Geno studied Mario for a minute before commenting, "Does the FBI know about the horse?"

"Not yet."

"All hell is going to break loose when they find out. You know that, right?"

"It's why I asked you."

"You want to keep the horse?"

"Wouldn't you?"

"I don't know, maybe. But it doesn't seem right."

"What's wrong with it?"

"Two words, stolen money."

"I think she was telling me the truth about buying the horse."

"It would be the only truthful thing she's told you."

"I know, but deep down, I think she's a good person who got caught up in something for all the wrong reasons."

Geno let Mario's last statement linger knowing Mario had good insight. "Let me call Sal, bring him up to snuff, get back to you."

"Okay." Mario paused, stood and looked at the Secretariat picture. "Chuck thinks the horse is pretty special. I'd really like for you and Little Geno to come out Sunday."

"Let's see what Sal says then we'll make a decision." Sal Luppo was Geno's attorney and a very close and dear friend. "You want to take home some sauce?"

"I'd love some."

"I'll get Maria to . . ."

"No need to bother her. I'll pick up a quart downstairs."

Just as he was about to walk out the door, Geno said, "The horse going to win?"

Mario turned, nodded, "Bank on it." He grinned, astonished by his cleverness.

34

Emma eased back from the easel and shook her head thinking that the last few brush strokes were not quite right. Using a palette knife, she worked a dab of burnt umber into a dab of black then dipped her brush into the darker mixture and carefully applied it to the nostril of the thoroughbred. Leaning back again, she nodded approval. That was better. The darker tone created a richer depth, the nostril flaring, adrenaline visually leaping from the canvas.

She loved painting in the early morning hours, the sun creeping into the day over the Atlantic's horizon, the beach still quiet but stimulating her creativity. It was all right in front of her as she sipped freshly brewed coffee from a mug Mario had given her. The mug was appropriate to her task, A. P. Indy in full stride racing around the white porcelain. Indy, as she called him, was her favorite horse. Not because of his racing record but because of his influence in the breeding shed. Leaning against the wall to her left were four completed paintings in a series of twelve for a show to be held at a gallery in Lexington,

Kentucky next summer, each painting of a prominent current day sire. The Keeneland and Fasig-Tipton summer select sales would be in action and buyers from around the world would drop millions on a well bred yearling at the drop of a hammer. The gallery owner and Emma were confident that those same buyers, along with some sellers, would also drop considerable dollars on equine art, especially a painting of the sire of a yearling they'd just sold or purchased. The show had been in the works for over a year. She'd been working on the paintings for months, flying back and forth from wherever she was to Norfolk, Virginia then renting a car and driving to her home in Duck.

Her studio was full of light shining through large windows facing the ocean. With both hands wrapped around the mug, she stepped back to gain a better perspective of the painting. Happy with what was now on the canvas, her eyes drifted to the waves lapping onto the sand, her mind shifting to bank robberies, the FBI . . . and a guy she'd fallen in love with despite her efforts not to.

On her trip to the grocery store, she'd seen signs of FBI presence up and down the main road. She had no idea how many agents were still in the area but she knew she should keep a low profile even though she was quite confident that they didn't know her name or what she looked like. Having stocked up on fresh seafood, vegetables and bread, she would spend her days inside in front of her easel. She hated to admit it, but she was a *wanted* criminal.

After cleaning brushes, she refilled her mug then stepped into her office which was a room very similar to what Mario had at his place. Two walls were covered with charts on horses, trainers, jockeys, sires and broodmare sires. A third wall was not a wall at all but a built in bookcase, floor to ceiling. Everything in the room related to thoroughbred racing and winning money at the track with exception of her computer and a desk which took up most of the space in front of the fourth wall. But even the usage of the computer and desk skewed toward the ponies. She subscribed to several sites devoted to the thoroughbred and within seconds the coffee mug found a spot on a table beside the computer. Quickly she entered the Equibase site, clicked on Entries then scrolled down until she again clicked, this time on Pimlico where she pulled up entries for Friday, Saturday and Sunday. A smile crossed her face when she saw that Shellcracker was entered for Sunday, Mario Bozzela listed as the owner.

Her eyes were glued to the horse's name as she brought the coffee mug to her lips. Could she risk going to the track to see Shellcracker run?

Her head told her no.

But her heart spoke another language.

35

Mario was on his way out the door heading for morning workouts at Laurel when the ringing of his phone stopped him in his tracks. He started to ignore it but considering all that had taken place in the past few days, he figured it would be a good idea to pick up the receiver.

There was no hello, just Rollins identifying himself, immediately saying, "We need to talk."

A shudder shot through his body. This could be bad news on several fronts. He said slowly, "I'm listening."

"I think it would be best if we talked in person."

"Look, I know you have a job to do but so do I and I've been lax in mine. I need to get back on track and I mean that literally. I was on my way over to Laurel to watch morning workouts, something I need to do. Be a couple of hours and then I can meet you wherever you wish."

"Where exactly would I find you?"

"You mean at Laurel?"

"Yes."

"On the grandstand side near the finish line but by the time you get there, I'll probably be at the track kitchen eating breakfast with a fellow horseplayer." He started to say *owner* but had sense enough to swallow that message.

He heard a chuckle from Rollins and then the words, "I'm parked in the lot at Laurel right now."

"Up kind of early, aren't you?"

"I need to catch a thief."

"Cary Grant."

"What?"

"Nothing. Do I need a lawyer for this conversation?"

"Not unless you're hiding something."

A touch of moisture found a spot on his lower back as he said, "I'm on my way."

Mario spotted Rollins standing at the clubhouse entrance when he pulled up in the Pinto and parked. He sucked in a deep breath and stepped from the car then walked toward Rollins, greeting him with a head nod.

Rollins grinned, pointed over Mario's shoulder toward the Pinto. "Man, you really like horses, don't you?"

With his nerves on edge, Mario said, in a matter-of-fact tone, "It's a pony, not a horse." Mario continued walking, passing by Rollins on his way to the rail. Buster was already in his spot.

Slightly taken back by the move, Rollins quickly caught up. "Tell me about your girlfriend's affinity for Sinatra."

Mario ignored Rollins' comment for the moment, tossing a good morning nod Buster's way, before pointing across the infield to the backstretch. From a few yards away, he added, "Are you clocking the chestnut filly?"

Buster nodded.

Mario said, "I'll catch her, too." He pulled a stopwatch from his pocket, checked it, pushed the button on top and was all set.

Rollins said, "What kind of time are you looking for?"

Mario turned his head to Rollins, quite surprised by the question and his obvious knowledge. "Thirty-six and change would be good."

Rollins nodded.

Thirty-six and two-fifth seconds later, according to Mario's murmur, the filly galloped out around the clubhouse turn. He shouted at Buster, "What did you get?"

"Thirty-six and three."

Rollins said, "How could that happen?"

Mario smiled. "I'm younger, have a quicker thumb." Then he said, "Now, what was that about my *ex*-girlfriend and Sinatra?"

"Music."

"What about music?"

"Heard from some folks in Los Angeles that she's a music buff, likes the old stuff, big bands, Sinatra . . . that true?"

Mario nodded.

"Like to hear about it."

Mario spilled it all, from seeing her at the track with a CD player on her hip to the grandfather and father stories to listening and dancing. When finished, he added, "That's everything I remember. I have no idea how much of it is true other than what I personally witnessed."

"You think she simply loves the music itself or does she have an emotional attachment to the era?"

"Both."

"But you have no idea where she lived?"

"Not really. She mentioned New York and Belmont Park a lot in conversation so that would be my guess."

"Okay, Mario, thanks for your help. If you think of anything else I need to know, give me a call. Here's my card."

Mario looked at the card. "You have a home number?"

"Yes, but that's private. You call the office and they'll find me, day or night." Rollins shot a nod Buster's way then headed toward the gate.

Buster walked over to Mario and said, "The filly was all out to get that time."

"Yeah, she just got crossed off my betting list."

"You doing okay?"

"Getting there."

"FBI, right?"

"Yeah."

"Did you tell him about Shellcracker?"

"Didn't come up."

36

Saturday morning Mario watched Shellcracker gallop before the sun made its appearance. The horse was on his toes, ears pricked, looking for competition.

He stuck around for an hour more, back in his groove, watching horses breeze, looking for an edge realizing he hadn't made any money for over a week. Before heading home to clean up, he used a pay phone behind the grandstand to call Geno. Found out all kinds of interesting stuff. Geno had friends in high places. Sal had told Geno that the FBI had nothing on him, legally, regarding ownership of the horse. It belonged to him regardless of who paid for it or from where the money originated although the FBI might indicate otherwise. If there was any talk of confiscation flowing from a fed's mouth, Sal was to be called immediately. The FBI had obtained a warrant to tap Mario's phone based on his association with the alleged bank robber. He needed to be aware of that situation and just remain vigilant. But the seriously good news was that Geno wanted to attend the races if Mario could make arrangements for ambulance service. Little Geno would be tagging along also and was more excited than he'd been on Christmas Eve.

Mario hung the phone up and a wide smile graced his face. This would be the first time that Geno had agreed to leave the house since his stroke. He stuck another two quarters into the machine then called Judy's Tack Shop which was located just a half mile down the road. He was told that his silks were ready. When he arrived at the shop and Judy held up his silks for a quick look, he blew out a breath. Something inside him said that he was about to add some spice to his life, a little salt and pepper, a taste of what it was like to be an owner. He smiled at his own thoughts. Spice he already had but it was more like cayenne than salt and pepper. He hustled the silks to the barn and left them with Chuck's assistant then had a long talk with Shellcracker. The horse listened to every word as Mario scratched him behind his ears.

He spent the balance of the morning making arrangements for Sunday.

He saw it coming. An hour before post time, the guys were huddled up reviewing the *Form*. Gimpy held up the paper as he approached, "You holding out on us?" Obviously, Gimpy and the boys had read the article on tomorrow's feature race naming Mario Bozzella as Shellcracker's new owner.

"No. I meant to tell you yesterday but I just couldn't spit it out. You guys hitting me with all those cute remarks." He shot a wink at Gimpy, "Bet the house."

"A million dollars?"

"If you got it."

"Seriously, did you pay a million dollars for this horse?"

"Not exactly."

"What are you, a Hertz commercial?"

"Ex-girlfriend bought me the horse."

"You got to be kidding."

Mario revealed the facts, as he knew them, shrugging when finished as if to say, "What's a guy to do?"

For the rest of the day they called him *ladies man*, got in his shit all day long, not letting up for a second. He had some comebacks but allowed them to dissolve in his mouth, like cotton candy.

37

For years Mario jumped out of bed early, often beating the sun in its quest to brighten the landscape. Today was different. Today was race day. He pictured *his* horse strutting, anxious, dumping a little fertilizer on the track, ready to rock and roll. He envisioned it all in his mind as he listened to wake up music, little ditty about a Mrs. Jones, Billy Paul at his best.

Usually, he'd bounce out of bed, empty his bladder, brush his teeth, throw some water on his face and be out the door in five minutes. Today, he lounged and stared through the skylight. Stars and a hint of daylight stared back.

No matter what a horseplayer proclaims, deep down he'd rather be a horse owner, and get his picture taken in the winner's circle rather than cash a ticket. Mario could see it happening but his gut went to work, spilling every conceivable thing that could go wrong. Horse could break poorly. Jockey could fall off. Hole could close up. Horse might not like the track . . . too loose, too firm, whatever. Some unknown party could inject the horse with something to slow him down or speed him up resulting in a trip to the spit barn after the race revealing an illegal foreign substance. And the horror that another horse in the race was quicker . . . had more heart, more class. Damn, he thought, horse ownership is a bitch, will tear your insides apart, send your adrenaline on a trip to the moon. He smiled. Exciting, that's what it was, unadulterated excitement, as pure as it gets. And he couldn't wait.

He eased off the bed, did a little two-step with Mrs. Jones on his way to the john, adding a twirl for emphasis before entering.

The *Washington Post* awaited him at his door. He picked it up on his way out, the sun now sparkling off the asphalt as he navigated his way to the Silver Diner in search of a giant stack of hotcakes, side of hash browns and a large orange juice, cup of java.

The long line at the entrance surprised the hell out of him. What's wrong with these people? Don't they know it's Sunday and way too early to be out and about? Glancing through the window, paper stuck under his arm, he spotted empty seats at the counter, excused himself to the front of the line, asked the hostess if he could grab a vacant stool overlooking the coffee maker. She ushered him in with an arm wave.

For the next hour he indulged in more food than he had consumed for breakfast in ten years. Read every article in the sports section, starting with the racing column, his name in print twice. An old geezer sitting next to him went on and on about golf, said he was a fan of the senior tour, didn't give a happy damn about the snot-nosed youngsters batting the ball around on the PGA tour. Said Arnie, Jack, Gary, and Lee would kick their butts every Sunday. Mario took it all in, thinking the guy must not have ever seen Tiger play. Mario changed the subject, brought up the Orioles. Not a good idea. Guy was a lifelong Red Sox fan celebrating another championship, the green monster being the best thing since sliced bread. Guy honestly said that while Mario stuffed a three-inch-high homemade biscuit into his mouth.

Before sliding off his stool, Mario couldn't help himself. He mentioned Shellcracker. "Won't win," the guy said, shaking his head. "New owner and new trainer . . . maybe next time."

Mario eased a little elbow against the guy's arm, shooting him a smile, "I'm the new owner."

"No shit? Is he going to win?"

"You just told me he wouldn't."

"Yeah, but what do I know? Good luck, hope you do it."

"Why don't you come on out, put a few bucks down."

"Love to, but the wife won't let me, got a honey-do list longer than my arm."

"Well, I don't have that problem."

"What, no wife?"

"Not yet."

"Lucky you." The guy winked at Mario, letting him know he was kidding.

As he walked out, the line had lengthened, guys in coats and ties, women decked out in their Sunday best, heading for church a little later, on a full stomach.

The coat and tie guys got him thinking as he eased his car onto Route 1. He hadn't thought about what an owner should wear until then. He went home, opened his closet door and pulled out a blue dress shirt, a white button down, and a white with black pinstripes. Laying out gray slacks, black slacks and tan slacks on the bed beside the shirts, he searched his tie rack for three or four designs that would match. It wasn't easy. He hadn't done this number since leaving his day job. Damn, being an owner was harder than he expected. Maybe he should be his own person, wear his usual polo shirt and slacks. If you own a million dollar horse you wear what you damn well please. A couple of hours later, he walked out the door dressed in a sharp looking red three-button polo and black casual slacks, colors that matched his silks.

When he reached Geno's, the ambulance guys were already toting him down the steps, Maria right behind. Standing in front of the restaurant were Geno and Maria and Little Geno. Seems that Papa had talked them all into going. Little Geno spotted Mario's car, came running and jumped into his arms. "You own a horse and I'm betting on him."

Mario squeezed off a giant hug. "Sounds good to me. How you doing?"

"Great. Did I tell you I got two hits the other night in the little league game?"

"Nope. You should have called me, I would have come."

"I did, but you weren't home."

Won't happen again, thought Mario.

Little Geno rode in the ambulance with his grandfather, said he wanted to keep him company, talk some horses. Didn't mention how excited he was about the ride itself.

The guys had beaten Mario to the track and hovered over a spot near the rail, good angle for Geno to see the stretch run. Had it reserved by placing a half dozen lawn chairs in a circle, theatre in the round.

Little Geno took charge of introductions, remembered everyone, and in great detail explained the reasons for some unusual first names before asking Mario where Cassie was. Mario said he didn't know, didn't expect her to show. He wanted to explain, but couldn't and wouldn't. He tried his best to rub away Geno's disappointment by attacking his hair with both hands.

Mario knew it would happen.

One of Geno's old friends spotted him and quickly brought a couple of other old friends over, expanding the circle. Geno's face lit up like someone had cut on the lights at Camden Yards. Geno told them about the horse. Mario figured even money would drop to 3-5 by post time. Geno had friends with deep pockets. He and Junior headed inside with a mindful of food orders wondering if two sets of hands were enough to carry it all.

That's when he spotted Rollins. He was sure he was there to ask about the horse, not to see him run.

With both hands full and his teeth gripping a drink cup, Mario slowly walked back to the even larger crowd now gathered around Geno. Junior was right behind him, arms wrapped around a ton of food, a bag full of condiments tied to his belt.

While chomping on a burger, Mario cut his eyes at Rollins several times. There was nothing strange about FBI agents frequenting Pimlico. J. Edgar was known to place a bet or two on a regular basis, Old Hilltop being his favorite track and a nice place for lunch. If he were alive today, sure enough there'd be senate hearings, a bunch of politicians screaming about how he abused his office, took off anytime he wanted, used taxpayer money to play the ponies. He'd probably tell 'em to go fuck themselves, have a couple of the bastards shot, stuff their bodies into a bag and dump their asses in Chesapeake Bay. Or drag them along to the track . . . find them a spot under the table where he knew they were most comfortable.

Mario had one bet for the day, his horse to win.

Little Geno had other ideas, big bucks floating in his eyes. He'd bet Shellcracker to win and put him on top of every other horse in exactas, hoping for a long shot to come in second. *If he had any money left.*

He bet the four across the board in the first race, following Gimpy's advice, which was not always sound. The kid liked Gimpy and took a shot. The two of them stood side by side, screaming as the horses roared down the stretch. Four got beat a nose, finishing second. But, at 6-1, Geno got his money back plus $2.80.

Papa Geno called the kid over and convinced him to save up for the big race.

At five minutes to five, Mario walked into the paddock. He had Little Geno by the hand, wanting to introduce him to Shellcracker. The groom brought the horse around and backed him into stall three. Shellcracker was cool, calm, and collected. That was a lot more than you could say for Mario. He couldn't stand still. Luis Gomez, the track's leading rider, showed up at the same time as Chuck. Little Geno compared his own size to Gomez's, tugged on Mario's sleeve, pulled him lower and whispered in his ear, "How old is he?"

All the stuff Mario worried about while stretched out on his bed earlier flew out the window when the gates opened. Shellcracker was on top within two strides and just kept on trucking, leaving the others behind to fight it out for second. In horse racing parlance, it was a laugher. He won by twelve, in hand, not turning a hair.

This was nothing like betting.

Mario never realized his emotions could explode so feverishly. He kissed everybody as Shellcracker hit the wire, surprising the hell out of Gimpy. He wanted to kiss the horse and would, just as soon as he could.

"I got it! I got it!" Little Geno was holding up his tickets, doing the pogo stick thing. Despite the fact that Shellcracker had gone off 4-5, the horse finishing second was 35-1, resulting in a $90 exacta. The little guy loved this game.

Everyone headed toward the winner's circle, including senior, the guys from the ambulance pushing him along.

Instead of positioning Geno's wheelchair inside the circle, they pushed up to the rear fence where his mug would be proudly displayed right behind Mario's in the photo. Gimpy and friends packed closely around Geno each holding up winning tickets, big smiles in full display. Before turning toward the camera, Mario caught sight of the emotion escaping from Geno's eyes. He gave Geno a nod, happy that he was there to enjoy the moment.

Mario kissed Shellcracker on the nose. The horse glared at him, much preferring a scratch. He tried to kiss Chuck and Gomez but they brushed him off, laughing like hell.

The photographer had to take a couple of steps back to get everybody in the photo. Mario ordered copies for everyone.

There is nothing in racing like an owner's first time winner.

When Mario stepped from the winner's circle, high fives greeted him from fans he'd never met. And then there was Rollins, standing there with a look on his face that didn't have a high five in mind. He asked Mario to step aside for a little chat. Mario turned and saw that the ambulance guys were taking care of Geno. He didn't see Little Geno until Maria pointed toward the grandstand where Gimpy and Little Geno were hurrying to cash tickets. Both were dangling red Twizzlers from their mouths.

Rollins said, "Read an interesting article in the sports section of the *Post* this morning. Horse cost a million dollars according to the writer. I couldn't keep myself from running some IRS numbers on you. Couldn't come up with any figures that would indicate you had that kind of money, so I'm a little curious as where the funds came from since your lady friend robbed banks."

Mario thought about Sal's comment and without hesitation said, "Actually, I do have that kind of money. I'm a very successful handicapper. I *could* have purchased the horse. But I didn't. She did buy me the horse, as a gift. She assured me that she bought the horse with money she'd won at Del Mar."

"Uh, huh, and you believed her, right?"

"With her and all that has happened, I don't know what to believe but the horse was purchased by her in my name and that's where we are."

Rollins held off making an issue of the purchase. From what he had learned in California, it was not inconceivable that the million dollars came from track windows and not teller windows. His job was to find her, arrest her and prosecute her. He said, "The paper said she bought the horse in New York from a trainer named Cappy Ludwig. That right?"

"Yes. He was the trainer and also the owner."

"I'll run that down." He wondered if she was listening to a CD player when she made the purchase.

From the last row of the grandstand seats, Emma held binoculars to her eyes and had taken in the entire scene. She would have liked to have been standing beside Mario in the winner's circle. Seeing the joy on his face was worth the purchase price of the horse. She had no problem identifying Rollins, having seen him up close and personal at the beach. She figured he was aware that she had bought the horse and was confronting Mario. She expected Rollins to be at Pimlico. She was counting on it. Rollins was her enemy and perhaps had now become Mario's enemy. She aimed to put a stop to that scenario. Her binoculars followed Rollins. He was talking with a couple guys and one gal, each dressed in the uniform of the FBI. She recalled walking by that group near the grandstand entrance earlier in the day thinking they were feds. They hadn't turned a head her way although she was quite confident that she was the reason they were at the track.

Rollins headed toward the exit, obviously not staying for the last race. She packed the binoculars away and hurried to the escalator. A few minutes later she tailed him to his car then hustled to the Jeep.

She followed him.

Home.

38

Rollins drove straight home after the race, his thoughts separating the FBI from his personal life. He called Kaylan from his car and suggested they head over to Old Town in Alexandria, hit the 219 Restaurant for some Creole cooking, dive into a bowl of bouillabaisse and hopefully find some bread pudding on the dessert menu. His pocket was full of extra money having bet on Shellcracker, a *hunch* wager that paid off.

He hadn't frequented the track in a long time. He and Kaylan used to spend a few afternoons trackside at both Laurel and Pimlico. Every once in a while they'd run up to Charles Town in West Virginia and catch the ponies under the lights. That was before he was put in charge of the bank robbery division at the bureau.

Two months ago they moved into a new house about a half-mile from where George Washington used to pick cherries. They were the only residents on Twin Trees Lane, living at the end of a dead-end street in a two-story transitional with lots of glass and a lawn seeking some green. For now, they had lots of privacy. Four houses were under construction on their block, two with see-through walls, one with a foundation in place and the other under roof awaiting finishing touches.

When he turned onto Twin Trees, Emma hung back and slowed down, not turning onto the street. Before reaching the corner she tapped the brake pedal, lowered the driver's side window and leaned slightly forward for a clearer view through a stand of trees. Rollins pulled into the driveway, stepped from his car, and headed to the front door. She watched him disappear into the house. Easing her foot off the brake, the jeep rolled forward on its own. She touched the gas pedal gently and made a left onto Twin Trees and came to a stop. Before backing out to turn around, she scrutinized the surroundings. Unfinished houses, no neighbors, no dogs, no other vehicles.

Perfect.

39

Maybe this wasn't the night for the Emma show. Maybe it was. She had to find a spot where she could make that determination. She knew Rollins was tucked into his house for now. Execution was critical. Timing was essential.

Before she turned onto the parkway, she looked left knowing what was in that direction. She then looked right where she saw a mile of trees on both sides of the road. She blew out a breath then glanced in her rearview mirror and smiled. She slipped into reverse and backed the jeep past Twin Trees until pavement met dirt. Kicking up some dust, she continued to back up until she turned the wheel to the right and stopped on a soon to be paved second street in the development. She couldn't see Rollins' house but that was okay. A short walk through the woods would remedy that problem.

She cut the engine and sat for a moment. She wiped her hands over her face, cupped them behind her head and stretched. It had been a long day. The drive from Duck had been a seven hour adventure, highlighted by I-

95 turning into a parking lot for an hour four miles south of Woodbridge. Then, of course, there were the hours at the track, excitement and fear running through her veins from one until five-thirty. She was beat but being tired would not deter her from her plan. Rollins was going to get it, either tonight or some other night. Everything she needed was hiding under a blanket behind the second set of seats, including the gun Russo had given her to use in the robberies. She'd never fired the gun. In fact, she'd never fired any gun, period. She didn't even know what kind it was, three-something is all he had mentioned when handing it over.

She checked her watch. It was approaching eight, daylight saving's time keeping the sun in play for a few more minutes. She opened the car door and stepped onto the dirt then zigzagged around trees until she had a good view of Rollins' front door.

Leaning against a tall pine, she listened to Rick Braun and Richard Elliott kick it up, her trusty CD player and ear phones providing the entertainment.

Three songs in, Rollins and a woman she assumed was his wife walked out the front door and got in his car. Emma turned and hurried back to hers. She waited until Rollins turned left onto the parkway before she gunned the jeep and followed at a distance.

Twenty minutes later, Rollins found a parking spot on King Street in Alexandria. Emma drove past a block full of Victorian buildings before finding her own spot just around a corner. She exited her vehicle and hurried back to King Street just in time to see the twosome enter a restaurant. Calmly, she walked up the brick sidewalk until she reached the door of 219 Restaurant. She was tempted to step inside but decided that was against her best interest. Casually, she peered through a front window. They were being escorted to a table. The place reeked of elegance and, from what she saw on a couple of plates, the food fit the décor.

The Emma show was on.

40

One boom was followed immediately by a second boom louder than the first. The sky lit up like God had flipped a switch and Act I was on stage.

Rollins' body twitched. Kaylan's trembled.

Until that moment, the ride home had been nothing more than a peaceful debate as to which entrée had been the best, her soft shells or his bouillabaisse. Thunder and lightening had suddenly interrupted their hither and thither. Five minutes earlier stars had been winking and the man in the moon had been smiling.

First it was big drops then bigger drops . . . then the clouds got businesslike in a hurry and let loose. Rollins said, "Maybe I should put out an APB for Noah."

"Maybe you should slow down. I'd like to get home in one piece."

He eased off the gas pedal, dropped his speed by ten miles per hour. A mile or so down the parkway he backed his speed down another five, the steering wheel telling him that he was skimming along the surface, hydroplaning.

Ten minutes later, the rain fizzled to nothing more than a mist. A minute later Rollins made the turn onto Twin Trees Lane. Suddenly he slammed on the brakes. "What the hell is that?" he said, pointing, his heart suddenly quivering, not knowing whether to speed up or slow down, his lights bathing the driveway.

"What?"

"In the driveway . . . sitting in the middle of the driveway. What is it?"

Kaylan leaned forward, studied the item for a moment. "Looks like a cooler to me, looks like two of them." She glanced at her husband who was squinting, focusing.

"Yeah, could be, could be."

He shifted into reverse and backed up a few feet.

"What are you doing?" she said, watching him whip out his cell.

"Calling headquarters. We need to get the bomb squad out here."

"You're kidding."

He punched in the number and explained the circumstances, his eyes dancing, his head swiveling, his mind bringing up scenarios he didn't want to think about. He told her to duck down and stay that way. She looked at him as though he was crazy. "It's a couple of coolers. Probably one of the construction guys working on the house next door placed them there for some reason and forgot about them."

"I don't think so," he said as he stepped out of the car, reached to his ankle holster and pulled out his gun. He crouched, duck-walked around the vehicle, using it as a shield if necessary. Street was quiet except for the occasional chirp of a cricket, distant barking of a dog and dripping of raindrops from trees.

Relaxing slightly, he slipped back into the car and told Kaylan it was okay to sit up. For the next twenty minutes they discussed the situation. He explained over and over again that he had many enemies, those he had put away, their families and friends. He never knew when someone would show up and try to dust him. She was convinced that he had been working too hard, paranoia leaking into his brain. But she wasn't sure. He had always stressed being safe rather than sorry.

They heard the vehicles turning off the parkway. Rollins exited his car, stood in the middle of the road with his badge held high as a Crown Vic rounded the corner, followed by a large truck rumbling through standing water.

Skip Lawson pulled up beside him, rolled down his window, said hello. Rollins was relieved Skip was on call. They had worked together often, been friends for years.

Rollins pointed to his driveway and explained the situation. Skip told him to hold tight, they'd check it out.

The bomb truck eased down the road and parked. Hell of a contraption that looked like an old ice cream truck, cab in front, completely separated large box trailing behind on the same frame. But it was imposing with its thirty-inch walls of steel. Two men stepped from the vehicle, Kevlar the uniform of the evening.

Skip backed up and parked behind Rollins' car then slowly made his way down the street on foot. The bomb guys had their headgear tilted upward so that they could talk with Skip. The threesome conversed for a couple of minutes then the driver of the bomb truck opened the door of the cab and a German shepherd leaped from the vehicle. The driver hooked a leash to the dog's collar then held on, the dog pulling hard, raring to go.

Skip remained standing by the truck as the bomb squad guys approached the driveway, the dog in the lead.

Rollins watched, perspiration seeping from every pore on his body. He glanced through the car window at Kaylan who was now on edge, beads of sweat covering her forehead, eyes fixed on their new house.

The dog approached the cooler closest to the street and ran his nose from one end to the other without showing any signs of excitement then tugged his handler to the second cooler, repeating the sniffing action, again showing no reaction other than wagging his tail and looking up at his handler as if to say, "What's next?"

The handler waved Skip forward.

Skip lifted the top of cooler one, took a peek, then stepped to cooler number two and repeated the exercise. From cooler number two, he lifted a sealed envelope, Rollins' name typed in large letters across the front. He turned and waved his hands across each other, sending Rollins the all-clear signal.

Rollins told Kaylan to remain in the car for a few minutes. He quickly stepped from the vehicle and jogged toward the house. Skip met him halfway, handed him the sealed envelope and said, "Someone left you a whole pile of money."

"What?"

"Yep, two coolers packed full."

Rollins' eyes darted down the street at the coolers, his index finger flicking the envelope as he said, "Is it safe to open this?"

"Yeah, it's fine. The dog would have smelled Anthrax, if that's your concern."

Rollins slowly released a breath. "Sorry to make you come out here for nothing."

"We like nothing. It's the alternative that's a bitch."

"Well hell, at least you guys can come in, have a beer or something."

"You know better than that. We're on call."

Skip started to walk away but hesitated. Rollins noticed, said, "What?"

The FBI came out in Skip. "We've been friends for a long time. That's a ton of money. You want to tell me what's going on?"

Rollins shrugged then said, "I have a thought but until I see what's inside this envelope I'm in the dark as much as you." He tore it open, pulled out a single sheet of paper and started reading, shaking his head as the words passed before his eyes. He handed it to Skip and said, "Un-fucking-believable."

Skip quickly read the message then tapped the envelope with the back of his hand before handing it back to Rollins. The tiniest of grins crossed his face when he said, "I do believe that a public relations nightmare just bit you in the ass." He then walked to his car, backed it down the street, waited for the truck then followed it and disappeared around the corner.

Rollins stood there for a moment, looked back at his driveway, shook his head in disbelief then stepped to his car, opened the door and sunk into the seat, his head still moving slowly from side to side.

Kaylan said, "What's in the coolers?"

"Money."

She laughed. "You're kidding, right?"

"Nope, but let's go see for ourselves. Then I'll read you the note that came with it." He folded the note and stuck it in his front pants pocket.

He opened one cooler, she the other. Both stared at the bills, neatly stacked and packed. Kaylan said, "This is pretty unbelievable."

"Yes it is." He tried to lift a corner. "Heavy but I think I can manage to slide them into the garage."

"Okay, I'll get the garage door." She disappeared into the house then reappeared inside the garage as the door motored upward. He managed to slide both coolers into the garage but it was a bit of a struggle, his body glistening with sweat when finished. Both were metal, old.

She plopped down on a cooler and said, "Let's hear it."

"I can't sit."

Instead he pulled the note from his pocket and read while he paced in front of her: "Agent Rollins, just to set the record straight, I am one of the two bank robbers who robbed nineteen banks. Cal Russo was the other but you already know that. I won't go into great detail as to why or how he talked me into robbing a bank but he did. I agreed to one robbery, somewhat as a challenge, but that led to others and, to this day, I can't believe that I went along. He was mad, offended really, that the Academy hadn't awarded him an Oscar for our work on a film that garnered five Oscars. In his mind, if it wasn't for our work the film would have failed miserably. He decided that we'd show the world how damn good we were at makeup. Without question, we did that. The day before the awards show, I buried my father. His death took a part of my soul with him, and if I have any kind of remote excuse for what I did, I guess my depressive state at the time contributed to my decision to give in to Cal.

My father was a wonderful man. He raised me by himself. He also raised me to be a decent human being and I have failed him in that regard. I am so, so sorry for what I did. From each robbery, Cal gave me half of what was stolen. I have never spent one dime of that money. I didn't need it in the first place. I was making other money and I was winning big at the tracks in California. Recently, I used some of my track winnings to buy Mario Bozzella a thoroughbred. Not one dime of the purchase came from a bank robbery. I love Mario. He's a good man. He had no idea what I'd been up to. In the coolers you will find my half of the stolen money. I know that returning this money does not make me less guilty but it's the right thing for me to do."

He tapped a finger on the note. "There's no signature."

"What are you going to do?"

"I've got to call the lab, get them out here immediately, see if they can come up with some fibers, tire prints, trace the origin of the cooler, something that will lead me to her. It's fine and noble that she returned the money but she's still a bank robber and it's my job to bring her in."

"How did she know where we live? Little scary, don't you think? And . . . how did she know we wouldn't be home tonight?"

Pacing again, shaking his head, he said, "I don't know." He thought about Kaylan's questions for a minute then said, "She followed us. That's it. Our address is unlisted. That's the only way she could have . . . ah, damn. Damn. Damn. Damn. She was *at* the track to see the horse run. Had to be. Two bits I walked right by her. Don't know what *she* looks like these days but she evidently knows what *I* look like. She followed me home from the track. Probably hid and waited to see if we'd leave or something but, then again, what the hell do I know? I'm just an FBI agent. Hell, she may have followed us to the restaurant but for damn sure she was at Pimlico and she followed my ass home, that's what she did. Goddamn it."

That's when he finally grabbed a seat on the other cooler, flopped down and shook his head like a dog that had been hosed down.

Kaylan started laughing. He looked at her, irritated at first but then joined in and the two of them got on a roll and didn't stop until five minutes later.

Kaylan said, "She's clever."

"Yeah, I'll give her that. What do you think about what she said in the note?"

"I think she feels guilty and I think she's being very sincere."

"You telling me you feel sorry for her?"

"A little, I think."

"And, right now, you don't feel a *little* sorry for me?"

She smiled, grabbed his hand and said, "Not in the least bit. You'll find a way to catch her, I know that. But what are you going to do with her when you have her in custody?"

He chuckled. "Keep her away from any makeup."

41

The lab crew showed up first thing the next morning and dusted the coolers for fingerprints. Found about a hundred. In addition, a piece of white tape was pulled from the bottom of one cooler. The tape's edges were raggedy, as though someone had ripped it from a roll and used a red marker to indicate the sale price of one dollar. Tape was dirty and so was the cooler. Sand residue told the crew that the cooler had spent a few days at the beach. Rollins chuckled when told, said he had no doubt. But there are beaches in California as well as North Carolina. For that matter, the damn thing could have soaked up the sun in Miami or maybe picked up the sand in Arizona and not the beach. Didn't matter, he knew who delivered the coolers and he knew he wouldn't be able to run down where they had been purchased, neither one of them. It was a dead end not worth visiting.

When he got to the office later, he had his secretary e-mail, via attachment, a copy of the note to agents actively involved in the search, along with a message from him explaining details. The subject line was: Duped.

He was back looking at the map again, the pins still in place. He roamed his office and his mind ticked off some possible leads. Obviously she was at the track on Sunday. Obviously she liked her music and, just as obvious, she liked to tote the music around with her. Obviously, but not so obviously, she would be at the track the next time Shellcracker ran. Obviously, she had expected him to show up for the race based on the story in the paper which she also obviously read. Obviously, she'd continue to bet the horses at the track. Maryland was the obvious spot but maybe that was not so obvious. Perhaps she'd be smart enough to avoid the FBI by playing the ponies via satellite or at an OTB. He stuck that thought aside to visit later then decided he should visit it right now.

Mario answered on the second ring. Rollins told him about the money and the note and went so far as to tell him exactly what she'd written about him. When he asked Mario about her possibly making bets online or at an OTB, Mario told him that a sharp horseplayer needed to see a horse in the flesh. He congratulated Mario on Shellcracker's win and asked when he expected him to run again. Mario told him that if no problems popped up physically, Shellcracker would run a week from Saturday in the Jacobs Handicap at Pimlico. Before hanging up, Mario revisited what Rollins had said about the money being delivered showing special interest of her having been at the track on Sunday. It was another *obvious* to Rollins. Mario was still in love with the lady. He chuckled to himself wondering if Mario loved her because of the person she was or loved her because she bought him a million dollar horse.

His next move was to call the New York office. He needed to get an agent out to Belmont to interview Cappy Ludwig not only about the purchase of the horse---how it all went down---but also to find out if the buyer showed up with earphones attached to a portable CD player.

Ninety minutes later he heard back from New York. The CD unit was in play. The agent giving him the message thought that was cute. Rollins thought it was important.

His secretary buzzed him and told him that the inevitable leak was resulting in an onslaught of calls and e-mails from people throughout the country. Then she added, "Cut on your television."

He grabbed his remote and hit the power button. It was the FBI, shouldn't be a damn leak. If he ever found out who spilled the beans they'd be fired instantly. But leaks were leaks and the source seldom found. His 26" set hanging in the corner of his office came to life on CNN. The return of the money was the topic. He watched for a couple of minutes then switched to Fox. Then ABC followed by NBC and CBS. He wasn't looking like a hero but she was.

By the time he left the office at seven, four thousand e-mails had been received at FBI headquarters, all but one suggesting that the FBI leave Sullivan alone. Returning the money made her a saint now. At least there had been no leak on finding the disguise in the sand, the name Sullivan still attached to the robber. He chuckled when he read the lone non-supportive message. A guy serving twenty in

Attica said Sullivan was a fucking lunatic. Thousands of phone calls had also been received in support of Sullivan.

Skip had warned him that a public relations nightmare had bitten him in the ass. Based on what had taken place, Rollins disagreed. It wasn't a nightmare, it was a monsoon.

Rollins knew what was coming. By tomorrow, every frigging newspaper in the country would run her picture, probably beside a pile of money. Ah, but the press would be running a photo of a Meg Ryan face. And they'd be wrong, as they often were when they jumped before they looked. But that was good. He liked it despite the fact that the agency wasn't going to look so grand. The weekly magazines would be on the horn asking for interviews. A damn zoo, that's what the next few days would bring. The agency's public relations arm would have to handle it.

He had other plans.

42

Emma arrived home at six. She was beat. She'd spent the night at a Holiday Inn Select in Fredericksburg, Virginia just off I-95 in a shopping complex named Central Park. Stuck a Do Not Disturb sign on the door and slept until noon. After checking out, she lunched at a Red Hot & Blue within the complex. She hadn't eaten since spooning clam chowder in her mouth at the track. While blues played in the background she stuffed down a pulled pork sandwich Memphis Style, dipped onion rings in BBQ ranch sauce and enjoyed forkfuls of Grandma's potato salad. A big glass of iced tea helped everything slide down easier. While she was dining, she watched television on one of the monitors provided for customers. Her picture appeared often, along with the Samantha Sullivan name, but the shot didn't look a thing like her. She was taken back by all the kind messages that were coming forth about her returning the money. She hadn't expected that and, in no way, was it a reason for what she did.

Her body was worn out from all the travel and heavy lifting. Sunday had been one very long day. Before she'd taken off for the track, she'd purchased a dolly at Home Depot in Kitty Hawk to help her lift and move the money but she was sore anyway. She popped three Advils then got horizontal on the couch and flipped from one news channel to another. She was still the star and still amazed at how the public perceived her return of the dollars.

43

Within three days Samantha Sullivan had become America's Sweetheart. A real heroine, someone respected for her bravery and repentance. Rollins couldn't believe the public's response to what she had done, wanting to add the word *cunning* to her description, use an alliteration; a *cunning crook*, that's what she was, maybe the best ever.

The number of e-mails and calls had exceeded two million by Friday but he was encouraged that at least one person, other than the guy from Attica, wanted her chased down, caught and prosecuted to the fullest extent of the law. Black guy called from California who had worked with her on a movie, said she ripped him off, stole his identity and used it in the robbery of the bank in Delaware. His damn picture had been all over television. Said he couldn't buy a hamburger without people gawking at him. Security guard cuffed him when he went to make a deposit at his bank the day after the Delaware heist. On one occasion a guy bigger than a house knocked him down, tied his hands behind his back, kicked him in the head and declared he was making a citizen's arrest. Yeah, he wanted to see her in the hands of the FBI, the sooner the better.

Several other Hollywood types called, said they knew her and had worked on a couple of movies together. Rollins followed up with a call to Rick, who immediately interviewed seven callers. Nothing of serious value surfaced.

Over the weekend, the calls and e-mailed slowed to a trickle. America had found another hero when a fifty-six year old woman named June Orcon beat the hell out of pervert trying to molest a young girl at a neighborhood playground in Fairfield, Connecticut. Seems she attacked the guy with an umbrella, stuck the point straight into his crotch and pounded him relentlessly with a pocketbook that contained twenty rolls of quarters she had just obtained from her bank for a trip to an Indian reservation to play the slots. Broke four ribs, knocked out three teeth and created a hole in a god-awful place that required eleven stitches. Ouch.

Emma stayed abreast on a daily basis. Despite all the support, she knew she could end up in a large fed-owned facility where everyone dressed alike.

If apprehended.

Rollins, meanwhile, had every intention of apprehending her. Mario's statement about seeing horses in the flesh led to a decision. At his request, forty-two female agents were assigned to him. At race tracks, females worked as grooms, exercise riders, trainers, assistant trainers. There were female jockeys and female jockey agents. Females were also heavily involved in horse ownership. And then there were those who placed bets. Rollins take was that a female agent just might have a leg up over a male and not be recognized as easily. The dark blue suit would not be the uniform of the day. Casual, and sometimes down and dirty, would rule the fashion scene, jeans and boots at the forefront. But the most important asset, in his mind, was that a female agent could follow the perp into a restroom. That is, if the perp still looked like a female. He was betting that she was one hundred percent back to being whoever she was before she became Samantha Sullivan. Any five eight white female showing up a track with a CD player on her hip could be her. That was the profile.

He assigned six agents to each of seven tracks and three agents to one. He was convinced, because of Mario and Shellcracker, that if she went to the track at all, it would be a track within driving distance of Pimlico. In fact, he figured she was living somewhere in Maryland, possibly holed up in a motel. Pimlico was where the live action was in Maryland but he knew that Shellcracker was stabled at Laurel and worked out on that track along with a lot of other horses that spent some afternoons running for purses in Baltimore. Laurel was also where Mario spent his mornings. Three agents were assigned to Laurel with morning duty only. Belmont Park, Philadelphia Park, Delaware Park, Penn National, Charles Town, and Monmouth Park each had six agents covering. Three agents hung out during training hours and the other three got to watch women watch the races.

He assigned himself the duty of being the seventh wheel at Pimlico.

Quiet takes on many meanings. When Mario got quiet, the guys knew something was troubling him, messing with his mind. He moped around all day Wednesday, didn't bet a single horse, just stared into space as though he expected an invasion from little guys with pointed heads. It was the lady friend again, visiting him, stirring up thoughts. He worried about her well-being, questioned her guilt, but knew damn well that he was wrong. The little pitter-patter he felt when her image flashed before his eyes caused him to toss his feelings against a wall like a strand of spaghetti, see if it stuck, find out if his brain was cooked as much as the muscle hiding behind his rib cage.

His demeanor changed dramatically early Thursday morning, two days before the big race. He walked into a loud exchange between Chuck and the racing secretary in the secretary's office at Pimlico. Seems Chuck wasn't happy with the weight assigned to Shellcracker for Saturday's race, twelve pounds higher than any other entry in the five horse field. In no uncertain terms, Gus Corcoran stated that Shellcracker *would* carry one hundred and twenty-four pounds. The horse had demolished the field in his last start and the weight assignment was justified. Raise hell all you want but the weight was established and that was that. Accept it or you can scratch your horse from the race.

Chuck turned and spotted Mario, shook his head then eased out a smile. He wrapped an arm around Mario's shoulder and edged him out of the office and they headed toward the apron where they could watch one of Saturday's opponents gallop. He told Mario that he'd made an attempt to sweet-talk Gus, tried his best to get the weight lowered but Gus had been racing secretary for over twenty years and he'd heard it all.

The whole episode and the anticipation of Saturday's race brought Mario out of his stupor, quiet slipping into the atmosphere replaced by anticipation.

Handicap races fit the term. In the eyes of a racing secretary, the best horse carries the most weight, the price you pay for being good. Other entrants are assigned weight based on past performance and age, resulting in a race where all horses theoretically cross the wire at the same time, a predictable dead heat. Mario understood the concept but having been witness to handicap races for years, he'd never seen an entire field cross the finish line at the same time, and wondered if it had ever happened in the history of horseracing. He compared the theory to astrology, the same thing happening to every person born in the same month: male, female, young, old, handicapped or not. He read his every day in the *Post*. Today, he was to avoid the color blue, a sky full of clouds already helping him out. Sky was probably clear in California. And hell, what about Australia? Fly from the west coast reading your horoscope on the plane, land in Sydney and find out it's a different day. How does that work? Which horoscope do you follow?

Bottom line was that Shellcracker would carry one hundred twenty-four pounds Saturday afternoon, a handicap Mario hoped he would overcome.

After watching the opponent do his thing, Mario and Chuck visited the track kitchen and ran into Buster. The threesome did extensive damage to some cinnamon buns and several cups of coffee while analyzing the competition for Shellcracker and Cannonball, Buster's horse. Cannonball would face a serious challenge from a horse named Slew Me, shipping in from Churchill Downs. All agreed Shellcracker was a lock although Chuck pointed out to Mario that Shellcracker had never been further than a mile sixteenth but emphasized that he was confident he could go longer and, once proven, that opened up some nice opportunities in the future. He wanted to look around, find a Group 1 at a mile and a quarter and test the water. Mario agreed, visions of grandeur prancing before his eyes.

Other than Wednesday, the past few racing days had been fruitful, the old banking account taking on serious bucks. Mario was back.

Instead of parking in the regular lot at Laurel, Emma pulled her jeep into an area where tour buses parked in the afternoons. She had plenty of company. It was a popular spot for owners who liked to sit in the comfort of their vehicles and watch the morning action without stretching the legs. She'd made the decision Wednesday evening after checking into the Marriott Courtyard near BWI, a short distance from both Laurel and Pimlico. Within minutes after arriving at Laurel, she realized that the location didn't cut it. She liked the close-up version better but being close-up would have to wait for another day, maybe another year, despite the fact that the FBI didn't know what she looked like.

It was now ten and action on the track was beginning to dwindle. She'd been there since six constantly casting her eyes at the spot where Mario and Buster were regulars but hadn't shown. She wondered where they were.

At eleven she was back in the motel room standing under the shower, jets of water spitting from the head as she thought about the rest of the day. Prior to recent developments she'd always gone to the track toting nothing more than the clothes on her back and her CD unit. The day Shellcracker ran changed all that. Now, she owned a tote bag to carry binoculars, snacks, makeup materials, a Yankee baseball hat and a wig. Today, she'd sit in the same seat high up in the grandstand where she'd be inconspicuous. Didn't like it but didn't think she had a choice. Her comfort level at the track was still residing in the lower numbers.

She dressed then checked herself in the mirror. She was finally getting used to seeing Emma rather than Meg. She looked to her hip and stared in the mirror at the CD player. Then she removed it thinking that she might as well stick that in the tote bag, too. Pull it out when she got to the track. That way, she wouldn't have to listen to just one CD. She went to her suitcase and searched through a dozen CDs before deciding Frank would appreciate the company of Billie Holiday, Diana Krall, and Michael Buble.

She arrived at the track thirty-four minutes before post time, paid the two bucks at the grandstand entrance, purchased a *Racing Form* and headed up the escalator. The seat was vacant. She settled in and went to work on the first race. Didn't like a horse, went to the second race and liked the five. She'd wait and bet a hundred on the five to win. Meanwhile she'd take a look around. Out came the binoculars. She pointed them toward the winner's circle and adjusted the focus until the rail went from fuzzy to clear. She panned left and Mario and Buster came into view along with four other guys she was very familiar with. They were huddled around Mario who seemed to be pointing out a horse in the *Form*. She reached into the tote, grabbed the CD player and placed it on the seat beside her then pulled Diana Krall from the jewel box and stuck it in the unit, pushing down just slightly. She adjusted the earphones until comfortable then hit the play button. Diana would stick around for about an hour before giving up her spot to Frank.

The five won the second race by two lengths paying $9.60 to win. Not bad. She didn't bet the third or fourth but dropped a hundred on the nine in the fifth to show. Horse got beat a nose for third.

The binoculars were now focused on Mario---she couldn't help it---but a woman a few feet to his left caught her attention. She had a tight hold on the arm of another woman and was escorting her away from the crowd. The binoculars followed. The two ended up fifty yards up the rail toward the stretch turn, not a soul anywhere near them. The woman who had been grabbed by the arm was running her mouth a mile a minute as though pissed off at the world. Finally, she jerked away and opened a wallet, displaying it in front of the other woman. Suddenly a guy popped into view and grabbed the other woman by the arm. And then all hell broke loose, the guy's right arm ending up behind his back clutched by the other woman. Damn, thought Emma, what the hell was that about? The woman who had been grabbed flashed a wedding ring then pointed to the guy's left hand. Emma could see that she was pointing to a ring on his third finger. Suddenly, the guy's arm was free but he was not happy, his arms flailing, his mouth spilling words although she had no idea what he was saying. That's when the woman flashed a badge and the guy backed off, but was still hot.

The lady with the badge walked away and with her back to the couple, the guy shot her the bird. Emma couldn't help but chuckle a bit. Undercover cop had obviously made a bad decision. The binoculars followed the lady for a few seconds. She looked to be in the five-five, five-six range, with short dark brown hair bob style. She walked with athletic grace, smooth and confident. When the binoculars swung back to the couple, Emma smiled. The woman had a CD player hanging on her hip with earphones receiving the music. She was bopping along to something with a beat. Damn, that could be her down there. The thought hung for just a second before she realized the significance of what had just run through her mind. The binoculars went into the bag. Quickly, she removed her earphones then tapped the off button on her CD player before jamming it into the tote. She slipped into the shoulder strap of the tote then headed for the escalator and rode it two levels down to the ground floor where hundreds of bettors were mingling about. She worked her way through the crowd and out onto the apron. Carefully, she scanned the area to the left then swung her eyes to the right. She didn't see the couple but was determined to find them. They had to be there somewhere. She turned and pushed back through the doors. Bettors were lined up at windows for the next race. Still didn't see them. Damn. Maybe they'd gone to the concession stands on the second floor. She took the escalator to the second floor. When she stepped onto permanent footing, the couple was right in front of her, the last two in line for pizza or a beer, or both. She stepped up behind them and tapped the woman on the shoulder. "Excuse me, but I was looking through my binoculars at the stretch turn trying to find this bum I had bet on when I caught sight of that woman hassling you." She pointed at the guy and quickly added, "And I couldn't believe it when she grabbed your arm and twisted it behind your back. Are you guys okay? I think I can identify her if you want to press charges or something."

The guy's eyes and chin went northward. "Yeah, like we can press charges against the FBI."

Emma's eyes widened. "She was FBI? You're kidding."

Emma shook her head then spoke directly to the woman, "Damn, you must look like an escaped convict or something."

"She didn't say who I looked like but she was arrogant as hell."

The guy, who was a good six two, chuckled. "Quick, too."

"Did she apologize?"

The woman said, "Yeah, but it was weak. Charlie gave her the finger when she walked away."

"I saw that. Good thing she didn't see it, huh?"

Both laughed.

Emma said, "Hey, I hit a good one in the second race. How 'bout I buy you two a couple of beers and get us all a large with pepperoni?"

The guy said, "Why not? Maybe you can give us a horse, too. We haven't cashed a ticket all day."

As the line moved forward, Emma pulled her *Form* from the tote. It was folded revealing entries for the sixth and part of the entries for the seventh. She tapped the two in the seventh. "I think you can drop a few on this first time starter by Valid Expectations. Seen him work several times over at Laurel and liked the way he went. Sire gets early winners."

The guy leaned in and looked at the workout numbers. "You betting him?"

"I may drop a couple hundred down, yeah."

"Couple hundred? We're two dollar bettors."

"You bet every race?"

"Sure, can't have any fun otherwise."

"Can't win any money either." She looked from one to the other and said, "You staying through the last race, the tenth?"

Both nodded.

Emma looked at the board occupying the far wall. "Four minutes before the sixth, you got anything going here?"

She answered, "We were going to bet on the ten."

Emma checked the ten in the *Form*. "Won't hit the board. I'll make you a deal. Combine the bets you were going to make, four dollars for this race and the balance of the card and that'll give you twenty bucks. Bet ten to win and place on the two in the next race. I'll cover your bets if you don't win."

He said, "You sound like you know what you're doing."

Emma smiled and without hesitation said, "I do."

The gal stuck out a hand. "I'm Donna, by the way."

Emma shook her hand, tossed a nod toward her husband and said, "And you're Charlie . . . heard that earlier. Glad to meet you. My name is Maria." All the women currently in Mario's life were named Maria so that's what she went with.

They gathered around a tall table and enjoyed the pizza and beer. When the ten finished eighth in the race, Donna said, "Looks like you know what you're talking about."

Emma said, "I work at it. By the way, your CD player caught my eye." She lifted hers from the tote, stuck it back in. "As you can see, I have one just like it. What's cooking in yours?"

Donna smiled, "Carrie Underwood. We're country fans. We must have called in a thousand votes for her when she was on *American Idol*." Then she added, "The damn FBI lady asked me what I was listening to like my taste in music was important to her for some reason."

Emma said to Charlie, "So you're a big Underwood fan, too, huh?"

Grinning, he said, "Yeah, but it has nothing to do with her voice." Donna punched him in the arm. Emma nodded and smiled.

Donna suggested they make their bets and go trackside for the seventh. Emma concurred, feeling safe being with the couple, but after bets were made, steered them to a spot past the finish line and not too close to Mario and company.

The two-year-old, Super Ex, was 14-1 at post time. Charlie asked why and Emma said it was because most bettors didn't do their homework. He didn't quite understand what she meant but he was overjoyed when the horse won. After Donna and Charlie collected, she insisted that they not bet any other horses for the day. Go home winners. They agreed and said they were going to leave right then so they wouldn't be tempted.

Before they departed, Emma took a long look at Donna; approximately the same age, definitely the same height and body shape. She checked out other ladies in the crowd and came up with at least twenty who fit the same criteria. But Donna was the only one who had been accosted by the FBI. And only Donna had a CD player attached to her hip.

She'd bet a thousand on the horse, not two hundred.

The day had been profitable . . . in more ways than one.

45

Emma was back at Pimlico on Friday, the CD player not making the trip. She wasn't interested in placing any bets. Her sole purpose was to find the FBI agent she'd seen grab Donna on Thursday and get an up close and personal look at her face. There was no question in her mind that the agent would show. Would she have company? It took all of five minutes for Emma to spot her. The same lady was back again, walking around, sniffing, checking out all the women, and in Emma's mind, looking for a CD player.

Emma followed her. Not closely, but close enough. The agent had no idea she was the prey. About an hour into the races, Emma saw two other females join her for a powwow just outside the entrance to the women's restroom on the ground level. Thursday's star was pointing a finger in the direction of a female sitting on a bench checking out a program. The female's head was moving, swaying, in time with the tap dance she was performing on the floor. Earphones were present, connected to an M3 player, not a CD, but conversation within the trio was taking place regardless. Emma found a brave streak and eased by the trio, picking up bits and pieces as she passed. She heard the name William Rollins mentioned and the gal she'd seen Thursday wasn't the one who dropped the name.

"Huh," she said to herself. She slipped on into the ladies room and found an empty stall where she grabbed a seat and flipped the lock. Couldn't come up with a reason Rollins would assign three, maybe more, female agents to search for her and she knew damn well that's exactly what was going on. Puzzling was what it was. She decided to leave, drive on up to Delaware Park, take in the races and see what was popping there, if anything.

When she left the restroom, the trio was nowhere in sight.

An hour and twenty minutes later she drove through the entrance to Delaware Park. She found a parking spot in the last row, a good quarter mile from the entrance. She hoofed it to the clubhouse entrance, plopped down a couple of bucks then hurried to the paddock hoping to see the horses for the next race, but the paddock was empty. She hung her arms over the railing anyway enjoying the peacefulness offered by the surroundings. She knew it wasn't the same inside the building that housed what used to be nothing more than a grandstand for racing. Now, it was glitz and the sound of slot machines. A voice rang out from the sound system. "It is *now* post time."

She hurried to the apron and watched, not the horses but the crowd. A young lady at least ten years younger walked by bobbing her head to a rhythm that fit the rap craze. She knew it was rap because the heavy beat slipped from the earphones plugged into her ears. Emma's eyes followed the connection to the CD player attached at the hip of her jeans. Another female was right behind her moving quickly and another was fast approaching from the front. Emma spotted the badge being flashed, the metal reflecting the sun's rays. Emma murmured, "Damn.' Then she turned and found an exit, walked to the jeep while spitting out four letter words she hadn't used for awhile.

Ten minutes later her XM radio was cranking out some serious big band sounds as she zoomed south on I-95 pondering the FBI female angle, if it was an angle. "Ah, the hell with it," she said out loud. She'd walked right in front of three agents at Pimlico and two at Delaware Park. They probably checked her out visually but without the CD player and earphones, *she* didn't fit the profile.

She laughed. The FBI wasn't the only one using profiling as a tool.

46

Saturday came up clear, eighty-four degrees, light wind out of the west. Main track was fast, turf firm.

The group gathered at its usual spot, buzzing away about Cannonball and Shellcracker. Mario and Buster were showing signs of nerves, both fidgeting, eyes darting, legs moving. Mario had visited the restroom four times already, Buster three.

Rollins had arrived with a very nice-looking woman, about five-five, shoulder length auburn hair---Gimpy called it red---cut in a style that let anyone looking know that taste was part of her persona. She carried herself as though she knew she was worth a look or two, maybe three. The guys were all chatting about her great legs when Rollins stepped forward and introduced Kaylan, his wife, to Mario.

Mario knew exactly why Rollins had shown up but hadn't expected the guy's wife to accompany him. She had seen Mario's picture, not telling William that she thought Mario was quite the stud. Mario got the message when she looked at him. He presented his best smile.

Rollins pulled Mario aside for a moment, leaving Kaylan standing before the group like a trophy. To Mario, he said, "She *will* be here today."

"You figured out what she looks like these days?"

"No. But any woman who fits her size, shape and age will be looked at hard. I've had six agents covering the Maryland tracks on a daily basis, but today, fifty are on the premises, males and females."

Mario flicked a foot along the ground. "I guess I hope you catch her."

"Guess?"

Shrugging, Mario said, "Well, face it, has the FBI ever had stolen money returned before? She's America's favorite thief. Most folks would like to see you leave her alone."

"She been in touch with you?"

Mario didn't like the question. "I would have called you."

"You sure about that?"

A small grin slid across Mario's face. "Not really."

"The horse going to win?"

"I'm confident he will run well."

"Should we bet on him?"

"Only if you'd like to buy that good-looking wife of yours a dinner she'll never forget."

Gimpy interrupted the conversation, "Hey, Mario, sauce man has arrived."

Mario stepped away from Rollins and followed Gimpy's finger point spotting a bunch of Genos and Marias swarming toward the group, a couple of guys in white pushing the old man forward. Papa Geno had convinced

Mario's mom to joint the party. If he could go, so could she. Mario gave her a big hug, happy that she was there. Shellcracker now had a cheering section large enough to threaten the opposition at a Ravens' game.

Gimpy was in rare form. Never before had Mario seen such euphoria from the big guy. Must have been the dozen cups of coffee he'd inhaled earlier. He spread his arms as though he was welcoming everybody into the house of the lord. Then his voice boomed, "Hey, who's going to make the sauce for the Saturday night crowd?"

Junior answered, "Restaurant's closed tonight, private party for all of Mario's track friends. And that includes all you guys with the weird names, Buster's family, everyone at the barn, and the horse if we could slip him in." A big grin stuck an exclamation point on the announcement.

"Damn. What if the horse gets beat?" Gimpy exclaimed, still on a roll.

"Ain't gonna happen," Toteboard said.

Junior pointed at Gimpy. "Doesn't matter anyway, we're having the party regardless of the outcome."

"Yeah," Gimpy yelled, "everyone's gonna get sauced."

Mario shook his head at his friend, Mr. Comedian, who at that moment started passing out Twizzlers to everyone. Seconds later, he spotted his mom chewing on a green one.

From her perch high in the grandstand, Emma had the binoculars hard at work visiting the clan below. She'd also scanned the apron from the top of the stretch to the clubhouse turn. The agent from Thursday was moving about and she was quite sure other agents were on the premises. She'd have to be careful but thousands were at the track for the big race, probably hundreds who fit her height, shape and size. Some would show up with CD players and FBI eyes would be all over them. She was going to remain in her seat until the big race. Then, she was heading down the escalator to the ground level, find a spot along the rail and watch Shellcracker do his thing. She knew she would be taking a chance but her heart convinced her to go for it and her head reluctantly agreed.

Mario didn't make any bets until Cannonball's race. He contemplated an exacta boxing Slew Me with Cannonball. Papa Geno talked him out of it, reminding him again of his rules, stressing that he didn't know a thing about the invader from Kentucky other than what was in the *Form*. End of discussion.

Turned out Geno was right, as usual. Slew Me finished up the track, ninth, beating just one horse. Cannonball won by a nose over a 12-1 shot. Exacta paid $68.

Mario and the little guy joined Buster and his family in the winner's circle for the photo.

Little Geno asked to go to the paddock. Seemed he liked being almost as tall as the jockeys, made him feel older, more mature, one of the guys rather than one of the boys.

Surprisingly, Chuck told the jock not to send Shellcracker, to forget an early lead. He wanted to see if the horse would relax and come on late. The change in tactics worried the hell out of Mario. Shellcracker usually grabbed the lead out of the gate and never looked back. In twelve races, he'd only lost three. With each loss, he never made the lead. Mario questioned Chuck about the strategy as they walked from the enclosed paddock. Chuck told him not to worry. He had told Gomez to let him run if he didn't relax. Still, Mario was concerned, wasn't sure. He'd seen hundreds of horses become rank when held back, the energy level finally taking its toll. He'd planned on betting a grand to win but then settled on five hundred. Shellcracker was 4-5. The rules said he wasn't a bet at all given those odds but the old man said that when you own a horse, you bet with your heart not your head. Mario made the win bet and he and Papa Geno split a hundred dollar exacta box, Shellcracker with the four. The four was the speed in the race and would now have little or no competition up front, a speed horse's dream trip.

Little Geno had bet ten two-dollar exactas in Cannonball's race, taking Cannonball on top of the field. Now, he had ninety-eight dollars. He bet fifty on Shellcracker to win and four ten-dollar exactas with Shellcracker on top of the other four. He held back his remaining eight bucks in case he wanted a snack.

Emma visited four different windows, placing five hundred on Shellcracker to win at each window. At two other windows she placed one hundred dollar exactas, Shellcracker over all. She was confident the horse would win. She was not as confident about making an appearance on the apron at the fence. But she did.

As usual, Shellcracker broke on top. Gomez strangled him and took him back. Shellcracker said okay, didn't become rank and went along with the program, galloping along in third seven lengths behind the expected leader, the four. With three-eighths to go, Gomez asked and Shellcracker responded. It was like a jet chasing a prop. At the eighth pole, Shellcracker passed the horse in second and ran up on the outside of the four, turned his head slightly toward his competition, probably shot him a wink, and then left him four lengths behind at the finish.

Pogo stick action broke out, the little guy holding his tickets high letting everyone know he had the winner and the exacta. Gimpy joined in. Hell of a sight. The Hulk and Mickey Rooney, hand in hand, going nuts. Mario suspected that Gimpy had slurped down more than coffee.

As Shellcracker crossed the finish line, Mario turned and looked at Geno who, using his one good arm, urged him over. The old man grabbed Mario's hand and squeezed tightly while looking him in the eye, not saying a word. Mario felt the message as tears streamed from Geno's eyes.

From fifty yards away, Emma took in the festivities. Casually, she strolled around the outskirts of the group and positioned herself to appear in the winner's circle photo as a fan behind the fence. He'd probably never know it was her.

Rollins' eyes were searching the apron. Through the day, nine women had been seen listening to music through earphones. All were stopped and questioned. One was taken to security and questioned at length. But none proved to be the perp but Rollins' gut told him she was around.

He turned to say something to Kaylan but she wasn't there. Because he was busy directing agents in search of the perp, she'd made the bets on the horse. They had the exacta together on a ten dollar bet and he had given her a fifty to bet on the nose. He didn't know if she had made any bets of her own. She was probably at the windows collecting.

He was wrong.

Emma's black jeans and red top had grabbed Kaylan's attention before the race. The colors were the same as the colors on the silks. She hadn't noticed this woman earlier in the day, hadn't seen her or she would have remembered, she thought. The outfit had attracted her at first but it was what she did after the race that made Kaylan do what she did. The woman had made a real effort to get into the winning picture, actually edged her way forward and stood on her toes. But after the photo was snapped, she immediately headed toward the windows to collect. Curiosity got the best of Kaylan. She followed and it was the following that really got her attention. She thought back about the night she had pointed out to William that one of the robbers was a female. The more she checked out the movement ahead of her, the more she thought that this just might be the same woman.

From her purse, she removed her Nokia cell. All that new technology hadn't come cheap but William had come through on her birthday. She recorded Emma collecting money from different windows. Several times, she tried to sneak around in front of the woman and capture her face but she hesitated, worrying that the woman would see the cell pointed in her direction. What she didn't know was that the woman knew who she was and would have recognized her. Kaylan lost her on the second level when the woman slipped around to a backside window to collect.

Before catching the down escalator, Kaylan reviewed what she had recorded. Lots of rear end shots and movement that was very familiar but no face.

William was standing in the spot she'd left him, circling and looking like he'd lost a dog. She hurried to him and immediately said, "She was here."

"Who was here?" he said, displaying a puzzled look.

Excitingly, she said, "The bank robber. I have her on my phone."

Confused as hell now, he said, "She called you?"

Kaylan shook her head and shot him a glare indicating that he just might be stupid. "No. I recorded her." She held up the phone and flipped open the face. "Take a look." She moved to the side of him where they both could see the small screen then she pushed the play button and a woman's rear came into view.

William said, "We're looking for a woman with a CD recorder. I don't see one."

"Did you ever think about her knowing that you're looking for a woman with a CD recorder?"

"How would she know?"

"Beats me, but you said she was very smart, so she may have figured it out." She placed a finger on the screen, "Check out the colors she's wearing."

"I see black jeans and a red top."

"And they are . . ."

"Uh, I don't know, clue me in."

"The same colors as the jockey's silks . . . Mario Bozzela's colors."

"So . . ."

Kaylan hung her head then stared straight into his eyes. "Who informed you that the bank robber was a female? Me, *right?*"

He nodded.

She said, "Where are the tapes we looked at?"

"I still have them at home."

"Well, get your butt in gear and let's go make some comparisons, your bank tapes and my cell shots. I'm telling you, I'm right, that's her on my cell phone."

Anxious now, William said, "Where did you last see her?"

"Second level of the grandstand."

He immediately sent out the message to all agents on hand to search for a woman wearing a red top and black jeans. Forget the CD player.

Agents searched for an hour but didn't locate the perp.

On the ride home, Kaylan viewed the woman in black and red over and over again, convinced that when they got home, the movements and rear end of the bank robber on tape would match the woman on the cell.

Just as he made the turn onto the parkway he said, "By the way, how much did we win?"

She shook her head. "I forgot to cash the tickets."

47

With his eyes intensely studying Kaylan, William said, "What's with you women?"

The question came at midnight and by this point Kaylan wasn't in the mood. They had been sitting at the kitchen table for five hours viewing tape after tape on a tiny 12" screen comparing the cell shots of the woman at the track to the woman robbing banks. Dinner, at the same table, had consisted of a foot long tuna sub from Subway, one half loaded with her toppings, the other half loaded with his. She balled up the wrapper that had been keeping them company for four and a half hours, took a three-pointer and nailed the trash can. She shook her head. "What the hell kind of question is that?"

"I've been sitting here watching tape after tape with you, listening to your comments, 'See how her ass moves this way and that' and then you tell me that her ass was the first thing you checked out when you noticed the red and black outfit. I've always been under the impression that it was a guy's job to check out a woman's ass."

Kaylan chuckled. "And that's exactly why we do it. We're just checking out the competition."

"I suppose you check out the legs and the boobs and the face, too."

"Don't forget the hair, that's important, clothes, too. And the eyes, you got to watch the eyes. The lady in red and black shot a few looks in your direction."

"Only because she knew who I was and why I was there."

"Oh, so you finally believe me?"

He nodded toward the television screen where the perp was busy robbing a bank in Newark. "What I'm seeing is pretty convincing but I need a whole lot more to get a warrant for her arrest. A judge would laugh in my face knowing that a sharp defense attorney would parade twenty women with an ass like hers in front of a jury."

"You're making too much of her ass. It's about her entire body movement."

He pushed away from the table, stood and said, "You think you could pick her out of a crowd? I'm sure she doesn't wear black and red everyday."

Kaylan bounced his words around for a moment then answered. "Yeah, I think I could but I'd take along my camera phone and make a comparison on the spot, just to be sure."

"I was confident she'd show up for Shellcracker's race but I don't know that she'll show up at Pimlico tomorrow."

"Only one way to find out and besides, I have tickets to cash."

48

Emma typed in her password for Equibase, the thoroughbred site that provided anything and everything for horseplayers. She never traveled without her laptop. The motel provided internet access and that was one of the reasons she was staying there.

It was a few minutes after midnight and she was still awake sitting at the desk reviewing entries for Sunday at Pimlico, her laptop spitting out the info. She'd planned on staying through the weekend using Sunday to do brunch at Gertrude's at The Baltimore Museum of Art where she could spend some time with Renoir, Matisse and a plate full of John Shield's cooking with some live jazz thrown in as a special treat. She knew the museum well having spent many days there while a student at Maryland Institute College of Art. She nodded at the entries deciding that she'd swing by Pimlico, catch the opening race to see a first timer then head to the museum. She wasn't looking to bet. It was all about research for next time.

49

William suggested that they take separate cars. If she showed up, he could end up following her most anywhere. Kaylan's suggestion to him was that a change of clothes would be a good idea. He agreed and packed a small bag, toothbrush and all, then stuck it in the trunk of his Crown Vic to keep company with a load of guns, ammunition, surveillance equipment, and plastic cups that would never reach his lips. Agents named them Bladder Busters. *Never leave home without them.*

The trip to the track was a little like a NASCAR race, the lead changing constantly, but when they pulled into the Pimlico parking lot near the grandstand entrance, Kaylan was in the lead. Luckily they found two empty spots side by side.

Once inside the track, they each purchased a *Form* and decided to separate, keep in touch via cell. William wasn't sure that he'd recognize the correct rear end but was fully willing to check them all out. Kaylan, on the other hand, was confident that she'd spot her instantly, if she showed.

And she did.

Eight minutes before the first race, Kaylan spotted her along the rail with a small notebook and pen in hand taking notes as the horses paraded onto the track. She backed up and kept her distance then called William. They met up seconds later just inside the grandstand doors where she pointed her out as the lady in black jeans and a short sleeved white shirt that looked to be on the dressy side. She said, "Good thing she didn't wear a dress."

"Why's that?"

"A dress may have turned out to be as good as a disguise. She did us a favor wearing the jeans, probably the same ones she had on yesterday."

He looked at his watch. "It sure didn't take long for you to find her."

Kaylan proudly said, "Piece of cake."

William surveyed the surroundings quickly then said, "If she starts this way, we'll just move to the side and bury our heads in past performances."

The perp remained at the rail until the horses crossed the finish line. She made a couple of notations on the pad then stuck the pad and pen into her tote bag, the same one Kaylan had seen her with Saturday.

Then she started walking toward the doors right in front of them.

With Forms in front of their faces, she passed right by without a hitch and kept on walking straight toward the back exit. He looked at Kaylan and said, "I have no idea where I'm heading but I'm sure as hell going to follow her. Keep your cell handy but don't call me. I don't need a situation where the chirping of my cell draws attention to me. I'll call you."

"Be careful."

He nodded and within seconds was close enough to see where she was going. She walked by the lot where his car was parked and turned onto the street to the right. Damn, he thought, this could be a problem. He was pissed at himself for not calling for backup, knowing damn well that was procedure right out of the book. He quickly made his way to the sidewalk, raised the Form to his face then eased it forward just enough to keep an eye on her. She opened the driver's door of a dark blue Jeep Grand Cherokee not more than thirty feet down the street. He couldn't see the plates because she was parked between other vehicles. He hustled to the Vic. Thirty seconds later he was two cars behind her. Both cars turned and he eased close enough to read a North Carolina license plate. He grabbed a pen from the console and scribbled the number across the top of the *Form*. He backed off. He wanted to run the plate immediately but didn't want to risk losing her so he decided to wait for an opportunity. She took a right off Northern Parkway onto I-83 south, toward downtown Baltimore. Her speed picked up. He allowed three cars to slip in front of him. She turned at 28th Street, eastbound. He eased off the pedal then seconds later increased his speed slightly to keep up. At Howard Street she took a left, crossed 29th Street and her right blinker popped on. He slowed, clicked his right blinker as though turning or waiting for a parking spot. She backed into a spot, stepped from the vehicle and walked into the Baltimore Museum of Art.

"Damn," he said, knowing he couldn't follow her inside. He could call the Baltimore office and get some help but she couldn't go anywhere without her car so he might as well sit tight, run the plates and see what developed. He settled on that course of action until he realized that she could have seen him and had exited the museum on the other side and was on her way to the airport. He'd seen too many James Bond films. His gut told him to stay right where he was. He had a license number and that was going to tell him where she lived if the vehicle was indeed hers.

His FBI vehicle was equipped with more technology than NASDAQ listed. He went to work and called up the license number, fully expecting to finally find out the name of the perp, the caveat being that he didn't, at this point, have one piece of solid evidence.

He wrote down the name that came back. Emma Frederico. The Duck, North Carolina address sent his blood pressure on a trip when he thought that she may have rented her own house in the name of Cassie Crawford. If so, he was going to kick himself in the ass until he bled. He thanked God when he found out that the addresses didn't match. When he pulled up a map, the houses were no more than three blocks apart. If she were the perp, that would answer a lot of questions and bring up more. His focus was directed at the computer screen but his peripheral vision was watching her vehicle. He typed her name into the FBI system looking for a hit. Nothing materialized. She was clean. Google was next and Google came through with flying colors. *Damn, he wished he had bought some stock.* Holy shit, the woman was famous. No question about it, an artist recognized by the thoroughbred industry as tops in the field. Her work had been featured in numerous racing publications but that didn't compare to the number of articles in art magazines and newspapers. He scrolled through one after another shaking his head as he read. She obviously made a lot of money. He couldn't envision this woman robbing a bank. Plus, according to the bank in Los Angeles, she was a hell of a handicapper who made a small fortune betting the ponies. Whoa, whoa, he told himself, his thinking running off the rails. The perp *is* the big time handicapper, not this woman. He was on a wild goose chase sitting here in his car outside an art museum in Baltimore where she just happened to have gone to art school. He saw photo after photo of her face. Nice looking lady. Didn't look like a bank robber, but who did? Reminding himself that he'd been fooled many times by upstanding citizens, he checked further into her background, reading a few more articles. One in particular raised questions. Her father and grandfather were involved in the music business. Her father died while in a nursing home in Nags Head, North Carolina. He stared at that piece of information then pulled up a history of Academy Awards' dates. The date her father died was just four days before the Academy Awards show and just a few weeks before the chain of bank robberies began. He recalled that the perp said in her note that she had buried her father the day before the show and he also recalled mention of her making *other* money. He typed in his code and her name and address and seconds later was looking at her tax return for the previous year. Income was enough to max on social security. Year before was about the same. She hadn't done as well the third and fourth years back but neither had a lot of folks, the economy having taken a dive. When he checked the fifth year back, she had made a bundle and done even better six, seven and eight years back. Of course, winnings at the track were nowhere to be found. That was if Emma Frederico happened to be the bank robber?

He ran all that he now knew through his mind and didn't come up with solid evidence. He could see her as a person of interest, though. While he sat there and waited for Emma Frederico, he stared at the last tax return he'd pulled up.

Then he smiled.

She'd signed the tax return as Emma Frederico. He already had Samantha Sullivan's signature, courtesy of paperwork furnished by Marina Community Bank.

He pulled out his cell, tapped the power button and searched phone numbers until he found Dan Thompson's name. If Dan wasn't in the office, he'd try Ken Wallace. The bureau had several agents who were handwriting analysts. At least one would be on duty.

Dan's number took him to voice mail.

Ken answered on the first ring. He explained the situation to Ken. Told him that he had the Community Bank file with him and could be there within an hour. Ken said he'd pull up her signature from the IRS forms until he got the best one to work with. Then he told William that both names ending with the letter A was a plus.

Emma Frederico showed up at her car just as William hung up. She pulled away from the curb and circled around the museum.

He now knew her name, what she looked like and where she lived.

He drove to Washington, DC.

50

After arriving at headquarters, William Rollins went straight to the lab and found Ken Wallace studying a blown up version of Emma Frederico's signature. He handed Ken copies of three Marina Community Bank forms signed by Samantha Sullivan. Ken took a quick look at each, glanced at Emma Frederico's signature then said, "I see a couple of things that indicate that the same hand signed both. Give me a couple of hours and I'll let you know for sure."

William thanked Ken and told him he'd be in his office.

Three minutes later, William was standing in front of the map talking to the pins as though a conversation was about to take place, shaking his head as he spit out the words. "You guys should all be the same color." Then he flopped into his leather chair, grabbed a yellow pad and a pen and started writing. He listed every piece of evidence, significant or insignificant. If the evidence was circumstantial, he scribbled a C to the left then drew a circle around the C. After three pages of notes, he realized that every piece of evidence listed was circumstantial unless the handwriting matched. Otherwise, Emma Frederico was not the bank robber.

He was setting the phone in its cradle after bringing Kaylan up to date when Ken knocked on his open door. Ken didn't keep him in suspense. He said, "No question about it, the handwriting originated with the same person. Samantha Sullivan is Emma Frederico."

William slipped out a smile. "Or Emma Frederico is Samantha Sullivan."

"Works for me."

William stood, walked around the desk, and spoke to the map. "Told you."

Ken chuckled. "Come on down to the lab and I'll show you the science supporting my conclusion."

51

Early Monday morning William was back at his desk watching the minutes tick away in anticipation of a meeting with FBI Director Robert Cooper. He had called Cooper at his home late Sunday afternoon to inform him of the latest developments. Cooper told him to hold off on obtaining warrants until they had a face to face. William was anxious for that discussion to take place. He didn't want her to bolt and take on another identity. The thought that she may have already done so sent a shiver through his body.

The meeting lasted four hours.

When William got back to his office, he realized that his job was tougher than he thought. You take the good with the bad. You go home at night knowing you did your best. You stick the ego in a drawer and lock it up.

Cooper was taking care of the warrants.

An hour later, William was driving and Cooper was riding shotgun as they made their way south on I-95. Cooper had made a call to a retired agent who spent his mornings trying to break eighty at The Currituck Club and his afternoons tempting fish to his dinner table. The agent, guy named Otto Francowski, owned a home five blocks off the beach in Southern Shores. The home was occupied by Otto, his wife Helen, and a bulldog she called Otto Two, because the dog's facial features mirrored her husband's. Otto had agreed to lend a hand and spend the afternoon surfcasting within sight of Emma Frederico's residence. He was to call in as soon as he arrived at the address. That call had been received. The Jeep Grand Cherokee was parked under the house and Otto had spotted the perp through back windows standing at an easel with a brush in her hand. If the perp left the property before they arrived, Otto was to follow and keep them posted.

She painted the afternoon away.

Otto had six bites, two from mosquitoes and four from sea mullet that needed to be dressed for dinner.

At six-thirty, Cooper called Otto's cell and told him they had just pulled into Duck, to sit tight and cover the rear of the house in case she tried to make a run for it. They were going for the straight ahead approach and knock on the front door. Otto said that she was still in the back of the house standing at the easel.

William eased the Vic down the road and pulled to a stop, blocking her driveway. Both were dressed in short sleeve polo shirts and khakis. They hurried up steps to the front door. Cooper pushed the bell and William stood to the side, his back against the shingles, his right arm dropped to his side, a Glock in his hand.

Seconds later, Emma Frederico casually opened the door. She stood there in a smock covered with splotches of paint, a look of dismay crawling up her face as the Director of the FBI introduced himself while displaying an official badge.

William stepped to the door in time to see tears pouring from her eyes. In a calm voice, he said, "Hello Samantha."

She looked at the floor then back at William. "My name's not Samantha."

William then said, "Oh, I'm sorry. You used to be Samantha but now you are Emma Frederico. I know *all* about your various identities but you made one big mistake, Emma. You signed forms at Marina Community Bank as Samantha Sullivan and you signed your name to your federal tax return as Emma Frederico. FBI handwriting experts determined that the signatures were signed by the same hand."

Cooper said, "We have a warrant for your arrest and another to search the premises. You can invite us in and we can do this the easy way or we can throw the cuffs on . . . up to you?"

She glanced at the gun in William's hand then opened the door wider and they stepped through.

William holstered the Glock then pulled a Miranda card from his pocket and read words she didn't pay any attention to. Cooper said, "You're under arrest for nineteen bank robberies. Why don't you and I sit down and talk about those while Agent Rollins searches the premises, including the storage room under the house. He can bust into that or you can furnish him a key." Displaying just the slightest of force, he placed a hand on her arm and directed her forward into a great room where the Atlantic served as a backdrop. He suggested that they sit in the two chairs opposite the sofa. Before she sat, she picked up a set of keys from a table between the chairs and tossed them to William. She wiped her face with the back of a hand, tears still creeping from her eyes. To the room, she said, "I returned the money."

The ball was in Cooper's court.

As William started down the steps off the kitchen, he heard Cooper say, "Robbing a bank is a federal offense. In your case, nineteen counts."

There were three locks on the door, deadbolts. There were only three keys on the key ring. It took William a couple of minutes to work through which key fit which lock but once he had accomplished that and stepped inside, his jaw dropped. A damn fantasyland was what it was. Photos lined the walls. Major league movie stars with bigger noses, smaller noses---didn't know how that one worked---cuts, bruises, scars, bald heads, females who were males, males who were females, eyes that were evil, eyes that were sad, boob jobs that weren't boob jobs. The artistry was masterful. Without question, she was a genius and Cooper had recognized that. Seldom did the Director of the FBI show up for an arrest. He was an administrator not an agent in the field.

William headed back up the steps, motioned with a thumb over a shoulder and told Cooper he needed to see what was in the storage room. Cooper nodded and stood. William replaced him in the chair.

The tears were gone. She looked William in the eye and said, "You know the exact amount stolen from the banks so therefore you also know that I returned every dime of that money. My half of it anyway, and I left it in your driveway. I purchased the horse with money I made at the track."

He surprised her when he smiled and said, "We know that."

"And Mario wasn't involved with the bank robberies."

"We know that, too."

As Cooper stepped back into the room, he said, "Young lady, given your background and your obvious talent, I'm absolutely amazed by the fact that you chose to become a criminal."

She wiped an index finger across her nose, hung her head and said, "So am I."

Cooper paced the room and started talking. "Tell me who else other than the FBI knows that Samantha Sullivan is actually you, Emma Frederico."

The question puzzled her. She had to think about what he was really asking, unable to comprehend what it meant. She shook her head and said, "No one."

Cooper then said, "You're absolutely sure? No aunts, cousins, or boyfriends . . . other than Mario---"

"Mario doesn't know."

William intervened. "Actually, Mario does know that the Meg Ryan face in front of the Samantha Sullivan name was a fake. But he doesn't know the name of the person behind that face or what she really looks like."

Cooper said, "You could spend the rest of your life behind bars."

Her shoulders slumped and tears made another appearance.

Cooper added, "But you don't have to."

Stunned by his remark, she looked up and straight into his eyes. "I don't understand."

"There's enough evidence in this house to make a prosecutor jump for joy. I've talked with the Attorney General of the United States. He's in agreement with me. Agent Rollins and I are here to make you a deal."

"What kind of deal?"

"We'd like for you to go to work for the FBI."

Astonished, she said, "You want me to be an FBI agent?"

"Let me put it to you as succinctly as I can. You can continue with your art. In fact, it's imperative that you do so. Samantha Sullivan is still out there, wanted for nineteen bank robberies and will never be captured. Emma Frederico must be Emma Frederico. You cannot tell anyone of your involvement with the FBI. But when we need you, your time will become our time with no questions asked."

"To do what?"

"The same things you did when you robbed banks . . . makeup. Your talent would be invaluable to the bureau. Instead of fooling the FBI as you have done for the past two years, your talent would be used to fool those who break the law."

She pointed her hand at her chest and said, "I don't believe this."

"And you probably won't believe this, either. You will *not* be paid for your efforts. You will be designated as a freelance operative. We *will* cover all expenses but your time and talent is payback for nineteen bank robberies. It's a twenty year commitment. I'm offering you this deal right now. It's off the table in ten minutes."

"You're telling me that I will have no record of arrest for bank robbery."

"Correct."

"And I will be able to continue my art career."

"You can continue betting the horses, too."

"But when you call on me, I jump through hoops, right?"

Cooper nodded. "Exactly."

"Okay, I'll do it but what about Mario?"

Cooper shot a glance at William then bounced the question back to Emma, "What *about* Mario?"

She hesitated, chewed on her lower lip then shrugged and said, "Nothing really, just thinking."

The Sauce

Extra Virgin Olive Oil

1½ tablespoons butter

¾ cup chopped Vidalia onion

3 whole cloves fresh garlic, peeled but not chopped

⅓ cup chopped fresh spearmint

½ cup chopped fresh Italian basil

⅓ cup white wine

⅓-½ cup red wine (the good stuff, not cooking wine)

¾ tablespoon salt

2 large (32oz) cans crushed tomatoes (Italian plum)

1 large (32oz) can whole plum tomatoes (Italian plum)

⅓ tablespoon black pepper

⅛ teaspoon crushed red pepper

2 tablespoons sugar

1 tablespoon freshly squeezed lemon juice

2 tablespoons fresh chopped parsley

In a large stockpot cover bottom of pot with olive oil, heat over medium-high until it sizzles then add butter. When butter melts, stir and add onions. Saute for couple of minutes then add the garlic. Cook until onion is translucent, about five minutes tops (do not allow onions to brown), stir often. Add white wine, bring to a light boil, add mint and reduce by half. Add red wine and ¾ of basil and reduce. Add crushed red pepper. Reduce heat to medium and add tomatoes. Simmer for thirty minutes, stirring often. Crush whole tomatoes against side of pan during cooking process but do leave some chunks. Add salt, black pepper and sugar. Continue simmering for twenty minutes, stirring often. Taste and add additional salt and pepper if needed. Add remaining basil, lower heat and cook for additional ten minutes. Find and remove the three cloves of garlic. Add parsley and lemon juice. Stir and it's ready for your favorite pasta.

Printed in the United States
120979LV00001B/1-48/P